WINTER COUNTS

WINTER COUNTS

A Novel

DAVID HESKA WANBLI WEIDEN

WHEELER PUBLISHING
A part of Gale, a Cengage Company

LIBRARY OF CONGRESS CIP DATA ON FILE.
CATALOGING IN PUBLICATION FOR THIS BOOK
IS AVAILABLE FROM THE LIBRARY OF CONGRESS

ISBN-13: 978-1-4328-8500-7 (hardcover alk. paper)

Published in 2021 by arrangement with Ecco, an imprint of
HarperCollins Publishers.

Printed in Mexico
Print Number: 01   Print Year: 2021

Dedicated to the Sicangu Lakota people,
and to my sons, David (Tatanka Ohitika)
and Sasha (Tatanka Ta Oyate)

It is not necessary for eagles to be crows.

— *Tatanka Iyotake/Sitting Bull*

1

I leaned back in the seat of my old Ford Pinto, listening to the sounds coming from the Depot, the reservation's only tavern. There was a stream of Indians and white ranchers going inside. I knew Guv Yellow-hawk was there with his buddies, pounding beers and drinking shots. Guv taught gym at the local school — football, basketball, soccer. But, word was, he sometimes got a little too involved with his students, both boys and girls. I was going to let him get good and drunk, then the real party would start. I had brass knuckles and a baseball bat stowed in my trunk, but those wouldn't be necessary. Guv was a fat-ass piece of shit, with a frybread gut as big as a buffalo's ass.

I'd been hired to beat the hell out of Guv by the father of a little girl at the school. Guv had sneaked up on the girl in the bathroom, held her down, and raped her. The girl's parents had confronted the school's principal, but Guv came from one of the most powerful families on the rez, and the school refused to take any action. The principal had even threatened a lawsuit against the parents for making a false accusation. The tribal police couldn't do anything. The feds prosecuted all felony crimes on the rez, and they didn't mess with any crime short of murder. Now the little girl was too scared to go back to her class, and he was free to molest other kids.

I'd waived my fee for this job. Usually I charged a hundred bucks for each tooth I knocked out and each bone I broke, but I decided to kick Guv's ass for free. I'd hated him for years — even as a teenager, he was a mean asshole who'd terrorized other kids, especially iyeskas like me. Of course, Guv had always been accompanied by his gang; I couldn't remember him ever fighting solo. But tonight was his time.

The Stones' "Gimme Shelter" drifted through the door of the bar to the parking lot, leaving little melodic ripples like ghosts in my head. I lit a cigarette and waited for Guv. He'd come out, sooner or later.

An hour later, I spotted him walking out of the bar. He was singing an off-key tune and stumbling. I slipped out of the Pinto and crouched behind his shiny new pickup. He'd parked at the far end of the lot so that no one would ding his expensive ride. That suited me just fine — I could enact some Indian justice away from any of Guv's drinking buddies.

I moved out from the shadows. He wore faded jeans and a T-shirt with a Fighting Sioux mascot. His eyes were foggy and he stank of beer. I could see the birthmark on his forehead that looked like a little tomahawk.

"Hey, Guv."

"The fuck?" He squinted into the darkness, unable to pinpoint who was speaking to him.

"It's Virgil."

"Who?"

"Virgil Wounded Horse."

"Oh. Are you drinking, or what? The bar just closed."

"Yeah, I know. I was waiting for you."

"What for?"

"Grace Little Thunder."

Guv's face darkened. "Ain't seen her."

"That's not what I hear."

"I take care of the wakanheja. Show 'em how to be Lakota. Sometimes the parents don't appreciate it."

"The way of the world, huh?" I moved

11

between Guv and the truck.

"I teach the kids, help their families. Sometimes they want more than I can give."

"Saint Guv."

"Just a guy."

"A guy who likes to cornhole the boys and finger the girls."

"You know how kids are, they want attention. They make shit up, people make a fuss over them."

"The other kids making shit up too? I heard about you and little Joey Dupree."

Guv tried to move past me. "I don't need this bullshit. I ain't seen you out there, helping the oyate. From what I hear, you don't do nothing. You got shit to say, take it up with Principal Smith. I'm getting outta here."

"Don't think so."

"Look, asshole, Grace Little Thunder's family is nothing but trash. Her mom's a drunk, and her dad ain't worked in ten years."

"That girl is only nine years old."

"Eat shit. What business is it of yours —"

I landed a hard body shot to Guv's midsection. The punch would have knocked most men over, but his massive stomach absorbed most of the blow.

"Iyeska motherfucker!" Guv snarled, and

lunged at me.

I saw the move coming, sidestepped it, and smashed him in the jaw.

Guv shook his head like a wet dog. How the fuck was he still standing up? I thought about grabbing the baseball bat, then felt a blinding pain in my side. A blow to the kidney, then another, this one worse than the first. Waves of electricity. Neural impulses. Gotta stay up, don't go down, or it's finished. Reeling, dizzy, I tried to puzzle out a strategy, but my mind was like an iceberg, slowly bobbing in the waters.

"You half-breed bastard!" he roared.

I felt Guv's spittle on my face, and then I was on the ground. Shit. He kicked me in the back, over and over, each blow a jackhammer. I tried to maneuver through the cloud in my brain. Guv panted, out of breath, running out of gas. Grab his feet, I thought.

I snaked out my arm and yanked his legs. He went down with a thud, and I saw my opening. I stood up, grabbed his right arm, and twisted it behind his back until I met some resistance. Then I twisted some more.

"How you like that, you son of a bitch?" I said.

Guv looked up at me and hissed, "Fuck you, halfie."

13

I had to hand it to him, he had some balls. I flashed back to high school when I'd been much smaller, not the big guy I was now. I remembered all the times I'd been held down and beaten by Guv and the other full-bloods, my angry tears, the humiliation still with me.

I wondered if I should let Guv go, show him the mercy I'd never been given. That was the Lakota way, wasn't it? Wacantognaka, one of the seven Lakota values — it meant compassion, generosity, kindness, forgiveness. I remembered the lessons from my teachers back at school. They'd taught that the greatest honor, the greatest bravery, came when a warrior chose to let his enemy go free and touched him with the coup stick. Legend was that even Crazy Horse had shown his courage by counting coup on a Pawnee warrior once, chasing him across the river, but deciding not to kill him, to honor his bravery and grant him his freedom. I knew that the honorable thing to do — the Lakota way — was to set Guv free without any more punishment.

Fuck that.

I twisted his arm until it came loose from the socket with a sickening crunch. Then I stepped back and kicked him in the cheek with all my force, snapping his head back

14

violently. I took my boot heel and smashed it down on his face, teeth snapping like stale potato chips. I kneeled down and grabbed Guv's hair.

"Listen to me, you goddamn scumbag. You ever touch another kid at that school, I'll cut your dick off and shove it down your throat. Hear me, skin?"

He didn't say anything. His left eye was swollen and bloody, and his nose seemingly gone, pounded back into his face. Blood streamed from the black hole of his former nose and mouth.

"How's that for counting coup, asshole?"

I leaned over to see if he was still breathing. A few faint breaths. I saw some teeth lying on the concrete. They looked like little yellow tombstones. I scooped them up and stuck them in my pocket.

2

I opened the door to the shack that the government calls a house. Rap music was pounding, and the smell of frying meat had stunk up the place. My nephew, Nathan, had cooked up some cheap hamburger and was dipping a piece of old bread in the grease. His short black hair stuck straight up, a dark contrast to his light brown skin and hazel eyes. He was wearing his favorite hoodie, a grimy blue sweatshirt with the high school's mascot — the Falcons — on the front. The music was so loud, he didn't even hear me come in until I poked him in the ribs.

He'd been living with me for the last three years, ever since his mom — my sister, Sybil — died in a car accident. His dad was long gone, and there was no way I'd let him go to one of those foster homes or boarding schools. Sybil had been driving to work when someone hit her head-on. I was the

16

one who had to tell Nathan that his mom had gone to the spirit world. The look on his face that day had stayed with me.

Nathan was fourteen now and had finally settled down some. Right after his mom died, he'd started skipping school and breaking car windows with his friends. He'd said he didn't need school because he was going to be a famous Indian rapper — the red Tupac. I told him that was fine, but if I got stuck paying for another smashed window, I'd sell his video game console. Lately he'd changed his tune and was talking about college. Somebody from the local university had talked at his school and lit a fire under his ass. I didn't know if that fire was going to stay lit, but I'd been hiding half of the money I'd earned from my last few jobs in a Red Wing shoebox at the back of the closet. I'd drunk up most of my cash back in the day, but that wouldn't happen again. I'd quit drinking for good. The money I saved would pay for Nathan's college. He'd be the first in our family to go.

"Hey old man," he said. As he lifted his bread out of the grease, some of the hot oil landed on my arm. It felt like the tip of a switchblade.

"Can you turn that shit down?" I pointed to the boom box on the counter.

17

"That ain't shit, skin!" He smirked. "That's some old-school Biggie."

"Yeah, whatever, just turn it off." I grabbed some of the old bread and looked around for more food. "We got any of that cheese left?"

"Nah, but you can have some of this." The pound of fatty hamburger I'd bought last week had cooked down to almost nothing. I scooped some up with the bread, the grease leaving trails on the plate like an oil spill.

"What happened to you?" he asked. From the look on his face, I knew it was bad. I didn't want to look at myself in the mirror.

"I wiped out on the bike."

"Uh, okay." He returned to his bread.

"We got any aspirin?" I could feel the pain in my back and sides starting to come in. Tomorrow would be rough.

"Don't think so," he said. We barely had money for toilet paper sometimes, much less luxuries like painkillers.

"So, what happened at school today?"

"Nothing."

I hadn't expected to get any news. He'd always been quiet, but he'd cut off most real communication in the last year or so. To learn anything, I had to ask his best friend, Jimmy, when he came around. For some reason, Jimmy loved to talk to me, but I couldn't get shit out of Nathan. Maybe he opened up to Jimmy's ina when he went over there. Still, I tried to pry information out of him whenever I could.

"You still reading that *Zuma* book in class?"

"*Zuya*," he said. "No, we're done."

"Oh right, *Zuya.*" The school had assigned a book about Lakota traditions — one of the few books on the topic written by an actual Lakota, not a white man. Nathan had hated it, said it was corny and stupid. But I'd seen him reading it on his bed at night, when he'd usually be playing video games or watching some horror movie for the twentieth time.

"What're you reading now?"

"Some Shakespeare stuff. I can't understand it."

I hadn't been able to understand it either, back in the day, but I knew he needed to keep trying.

"Maybe you can get the movie or something? Help you follow the story?"

"Yeah, maybe."

I gave up and went looking for some Tylenols.

"Hey, I want to ask you," Nathan said. "Can I use the car tomorrow night? Please?"

I could tell he really wanted my old Pinto;

19

usually he'd call it the "rez bomb." Not to mention asking nicely, which was rare. I'd taught him to drive a few years back, but still wouldn't let him ride my battered Kawasaki motorcycle. South Dakota allowed kids to drive at age fourteen, but the tribal cops didn't care much about enforcing the law. Plenty of younger kids drove around the rez.

"You snagging with Jimmy now? Chasin' high school girls?"

He looked down, embarrassed. "Naw, there's supposed to be a party at the center tomorrow. Some dudes I met are gonna be there."

"All right, but you might need to put some gas in the tank. Barely enough to get to town and back."

His face lit up like a slot machine paying out a jackpot.

"And no drinking beers, or I'll kick your ass," I said.

He started to go back to his little bedroom, but stopped and turned to me. "Hey, I forgot. Your friend Tommy came by, said he needs to talk to you. Said you're not answering your phone. Told me to tell you he'll be at the center till late, said you should go there if you can."

Shit, what now?

20

I looked at my phone and saw that Tommy had called three times. I called back, but there was no answer. Not surprising. Cell phone service on the rez was hit-and-miss. I was tempted to let this wait, but I needed a smoke pretty bad, so I decided to run to town. Maybe someone would have an Excedrin they could spot me.

I took the motorcycle to save the gas in the Pinto for Nathan. As I rode, my mind kept drifting to my sister, Sybil. She'd had a hard life. Her scumbag husband had left her when Nathan was born and taken off for California. She'd worked for the tribe as an office assistant, barely bringing home enough money to buy food, but she'd made beaded necklaces and earrings to sell for extra cash. She'd even taken some classes to finish her high school degree. I hadn't helped out as much as I should have, but I had my own problems. After a particularly bad night, I used to go over and hang out with Sybil and Nathan. She'd tell me I needed to eat, then make some hamburger soup and brew some coffee. I'd play with the baby while she studied and did her reading for school. On those nights, it was easy to imagine that I had a real family. I thought about a conversation we'd had, right before she died.

*Brother, you remember when we were kids,
and we used to draw winter counts, like they
did in the old days?*

Yeah, I guess so.

Winter counts were the calendar system
used by the Lakota, but they weren't like
modern ones. I'd loved the little pictures in
the calendars, each image showing the most
significant event from the past year. Sybil
and I used to make our own with paper and
crayons when we were kids.

*Do you remember what symbol we used for
the year Mom died?*

Why do you ask?

Because it's important to remember.

It's no big deal.

Yes, it is! I feel like I'm forgetting Mom.

*You're just getting older. It's hard to remem-
ber stuff from back then.*

*I used to be able to remember everything.
Now it seems like it's all going away, getting
fuzzy in my head. You know, I had a dream
last week that I left the rez and never came
back.*

Yeah, where'd you go? Paris, France?

*I don't know, smart-ass, can't remember . . .
But this dream, it was so real. An eagle flew
in the house and started to talk, and I knew
what it was saying, even though its beak didn't
move. The eagle told me to get ready, that I*

had to leave soon, I was going on a journey. I asked how long I'd be gone, but it wouldn't tell me, just looked at me with these strange eyes. I asked if Nathan was coming with me, but it flew away.

Hey, you know that weird shit will mess up your head.

I'd laughed then and tried to cheer her up, but she'd just looked away.

I parked my bike by the entrance and stuck the keys in my pocket. The community center was a squat gray bunker, with cheap vinyl windows that were clouded up like an old man's cataracts. The center served as the informal gathering spot for the rez. There was a pool table for the teens, and tables and chairs for the elders. During the day there were usually at least a dozen teenagers hanging around, gossiping and flirting with each other. The elders would be complaining about the youngsters and talking about the old days.

I headed to the basketball court, where I saw about twenty teens and ten adults. I made my way through the people, who were gathered in clusters and talking. Two of the younger kids were trying to freestyle rap, but their attempts sounded pretty lame, even to my rock-and-roll ears. I kept an eye out for anyone I might have had a conflict with in the past, anybody who might still hold a grudge. Didn't need more problems tonight.

I spotted Tommy, who sometimes went by the nickname "Ik-Tommy," after the trickster spider in Lakota children's tales. He and I had been friends since high school, but had been out of contact while he did a two-year stint at the state prison in Sioux Falls for aggravated assault. Four years ago in Rapid City, a group of three college boys spotted Tommy drinking a beer in a park and thought they'd have some fun with a drunk Indian, but he wasn't drunk and wouldn't put up with any shit. He was a joker, but you didn't want to mess with him. The college boys started pushing him around, but Tommy grabbed a can of Axe body spray from one of the guys' pockets and smashed the kid in the face with it. Even though he pleaded self-defense, the prosecutor argued that the can of body spray was a dangerous weapon and Tommy got two years at the state max. In prison, he'd hooked up with some radical Native prisoners and started reading books by Vine Deloria and other Indian writers. He'd gotten out a year ago, and had been trying to convince me to join some activist groups, but I wanted no part of that.

"Yo, homes!" he said, walking over to me. His long black hair hung down over his skinny frame and his denim jacket, which had so many rips and tears that I doubted it gave any protection against the chill. His shoes were old skateboarding slip-on sneakers, with a black-and-white checkered canvas top. However, there was a hole in the left one, his big toe protruding through the gap.

"Hey Tommy."

"Got some forties if you wanna go out back." He smelled like he'd already downed a forty, maybe even an eighty.

"No, I'm good." I grabbed an old plastic chair and sat down. I felt in my pockets for my cigarettes by habit. Tommy didn't smoke, so there was no point in hitting him up.

"I tell you about this book I read? *For Indigenous Eyes Only?* Shit been blowing my mind. Turns out we all been colonized like a motherfucker. Before the white people came, we didn't have no laws, yeah? Didn't need 'em. Didn't need no jobs either, because we hunted our own food! Am I right?"

"Dude, you haven't had a job in years," I said, scanning the crowd for someone who might let me bum a smoke.

"That's not the point! Jobs are for suckers. I'm saying we don't see the world the same way as the, uh, colonizers. They're all about getting stuff, buying stuff. What happens when a white kid has a birthday party?" He looked at me, eyebrows raised.

"They eat cake?"

"No, dude! They get presents! Shitloads of presents!"

"We give our kids birthday presents."

"Because we're colonized. Exactly what I'm saying. What do Natives do at a naming ceremony?"

"Give the kid a Lakota name?"

"Yeah, but that's not what I mean. The giveaway! The giveaway, man, before the spirit name is announced. That's what I'm talking about. Indian kids give away presents to everyone there, they don't get stuff for themselves. That's the Native way."

"Not every Indian gets a spirit name," I said. "I never got one."

"Well, it's time! Time for you to walk that red road. You should come with me to the next AIM meeting, meet some peeps."

"I'll think about it." I saw that people were starting to leave the gym.

"Or maybe you should come with me to the Sun Dance this summer. Get right with

26

yourself. You down with that? Hoka!"

"You know how I feel about that bullshit. Dancing around a tree ain't gonna do me no good."

Tommy looked at me with a rueful expression. "Homeboy, someday you're gonna hear the Creator. For real."

I'd had enough of this. Time to take off, dig up some change and buy a pack of cigs. "Nathan said you had something to tell me. What's up?"

"Yeah, so I ran into Ben Short Bear the other day. He wants to talk to you, right away. Says he been looking for you."

"What does he want?"

"Don't know. Said it's important — sounds like he might have a job for you or something."

Strange. Ben Short Bear was a tribal councilman and usually kept as far away from me as possible. Not to mention, the last time I'd spoken to him was when he kicked me out of his office, right after his daughter Marie broke up with me. She'd said that I was an asshole and she deserved better.

I didn't disagree.

As I left the community center, I saw a man helping a little boy with his shirt, and my

27

father's face flashed into my head. My memories of him had faded over time, but certain things always brought him back. I remembered him teaching me how to tie my shoes when I was very small. How to throw a baseball, how to use a hammer and screwdriver, how to read a map. I remembered how I'd felt safe at night, knowing he was sleeping near me.

I remembered the bad year too. Nobody told me at the time he had cancer, but I knew he was sick. Later I learned he had pancreatic cancer. I guess that's the worst kind, the kind that can spread in just a few months. He lost a lot of weight rapidly, so much that he didn't even look like the same person. I remembered him throwing up a lot, and because I didn't know how serious it was, I wondered if he'd been drinking. When I was older, my mom told me that the local doctors were so bad, they didn't diagnose his illness until it was too late. Years later I looked up pancreatic cancer on the internet, and it sounded like there wasn't much that could have been done. But my mother always held a grudge against the doctors.

In his last few months, he was too tired to get out of bed and in terrible pain. Pain so bad, it was hard to be around him. I felt weak and worthless because there wasn't anything I could do to help. I was scared too, scared to think about the possibility of him dying, and scared to talk about it with anyone.

Finally I gathered up my courage and asked the medicine man what I could do to help my father. The holy man was respected by our people, and I knew he'd have the answer. He told me I should go into the woods and pray. He said I should spend a full day and night up there, but I could stay longer if I needed to. He told me I shouldn't eat or drink anything while I was praying. He said an animal might come and send me a message, maybe one of healing, and if I got a message, then I could end my prayers early and come home. He told me I should try not to sleep, but to listen to the birds and the animals and to keep praying.

I felt like a hero even though I hadn't started the prayers yet. I imagined what my mom and sister would say when I got home from the prayers and they realized I'd saved him. I ran back home to start preparing for my vigil. I was pretty scared about going out there alone, but it would be worth it when I got back. I told my mom I'd be camping with my best friend. She was so distraught and worried about my dad's

29

condition that she didn't ask about my plans.

I can't remember much about the first day. What I remember is being massively bored, even though I tried to focus on my prayers. It was hard to be alone with no one to talk to, no TV to watch, no music to listen to. The hunger and thirst were overwhelming, and it was tough to concentrate on anything but my stomach. I daydreamed about hamburgers, french fries, frybread, ice cream. I tried to stay awake but fell asleep at some point and woke up at dawn the next day. I spent most of the second day curled up into a ball, holding my stomach and trying not to cry.

By the third day, I no longer thought about food. I prayed and wondered about my father, what I could do to heal him. In the evening, I slipped into some sort of dreamlike state, even though I was awake. I fell asleep at some point, and my dreams were really strange. I dreamed that a deer came by my camp, but the animal had two faces. I was so scared, I turned away from the creature. Later I dreamed that a white hawk flew in from the north and started speaking to me about my father and his life. It seemed like the bird was telling me I shouldn't worry, that I should go home.

When I woke up from the dream, I decided I'd been gone long enough, and I went back. I knew I should visit the medicine man as soon as I could — after eating some food — and ask him about my dreams. He'd be able to tell me what they meant and how I could save my dad. But when I got back to my house, I could tell something was wrong. There were strange cars parked in our yard, and our dogs were missing. When I walked inside, my mom told me that my dad had passed away while I was gone. She hugged me and told me it was okay. But it wasn't. I'd been away when he died and hadn't even had a chance to say goodbye.

I stared at my hands while I fought back tears. I tried to say something to my mother, but no words would come. I'd thought that I'd be able to invoke the spirits to save my father, but all I'd done was miss a chance to comfort him when he made his journey.

I knew then that the Native traditions — the ceremonies, prayers, teachings — were horseshit. I believed I'd be the savior of the family, but all I'd done was make a fool of myself. I vowed that I'd never be tricked again by these empty rituals. From that moment forward, I'd rely upon myself only.

My sister handed me some burning sage,

a sad look on her face. I took it and stomped on it. Long after the flame had gone out, I pounded that sage with my feet. My mother watched as I pulverized it. I kept at it until the plant vanished, only a green stain on the floor and a bittersweet aroma hanging in the air.

3

The next day, I watched a college basketball game on the TV above the bar while I waited for Ben Short Bear. I'd heard he was planning to run for tribal president, which didn't surprise me. Ben was ambitious, which explained why he'd never liked me when I was dating his daughter. Although he'd never said anything, I knew he wanted Marie to end up with some doctor or lawyer, or at least somebody with a real job.

"Hello, Virgil."

I drained the last of my Coke and turned around. He looked like he'd just come from a council meeting, wearing a dark-brown blazer and a silver bolo tie in the shape of an eagle. I saw he'd grown a little mustache the color of a dog's asshole.

"Councilman."

He frowned and sat down next to me. "Ben. No need to be formal here." He signaled for a beer and placed a twenty

33

down on the bar. "Thanks for meeting me."

"Tommy said you had a job."

He scowled and took a drink of his beer. "You hear about that high school kid who died a few weeks ago, Paul Ghost Horse?"

"Yeah, I think so."

"Well, the story going around is that he was another suicide. Sad, right? But that's not it. I happen to know he overdosed. On heroin."

He raised his eyebrows, waiting for me to say something.

"Okay. So what does this have to do with a job for me?" I slid an ice cube from the soda glass into my mouth.

"You know Rick Crow?"

I knew him. He was a real piece of shit — a mean drunk, a thief, and a liar. He always had some hustle working. Not to mention he'd been the leader of the kids who had tormented me when I was in school. He'd been the king of the bullies, the one who always went after the weaker kids. I'd been the weakest one back then. But not anymore.

"I need you to find him and set him straight. Bastard is the one bringing that crap around here. Strong stuff from Mexico."

"Are you sure?" I said. "Haven't heard

34

anything about that. Weed, yeah. But not heroin."

Something didn't make sense. Rick Crow was a booze bootlegger, not a smack dealer. He'd buy cases of Bud Light down in Nebraska and then sell them by the bottle to the local drunks. Every so often, he'd drive down to Denver and pick up some pot, then unload that. But he never fooled around with anything stronger, as far as I knew.

"It's just starting up," Ben said. "That's why we need to shut this down right away."

"Why don't you go to tribal police?"

"You know why. Even if they catch him, tribal court can't hand out any sentence over a year. No point."

This was true. "Why not go to the feds?"

He sneered. "They won't take any case short of murder. Besides, there's no hard evidence linking him to the drugs."

"Then how do you know he's bringing it in?"

"I've got my sources." He finished his beer and waved his arm for another.

"Even if this is true," I said, "why do you care? Plenty of other drugs floating around here if you want to start some sort of crackdown. You can buy weed on every corner."

He frowned. "You know, some of us give a damn about this place. And that dead kid. Big difference between pot and heroin. Not to mention, my constituents won't be happy if hard drugs keep spreading here."

The upcoming tribal election. Now I understood why Ben wanted to clean out the smack dealers. But I still didn't get one thing.

"If you want credit for getting rid of those guys, why hire me? If I make him stop, no one knows you were responsible."

Ben signaled again for a drink, without success. "I just want that stuff gone, don't care who does it." Then he held up his hand and snapped his fingers. "I'll be honest. More kids start overdosing, I'm out of a job. But the main thing is keeping our people safe."

The bartender was nowhere to be seen, so Ben reached across the bar down into the well, lifted a couple of beer bottles, and set one in front of me. It was some fancy brew, St. Pauli Girl, the type of beer that cost six bucks a pop. I left it unopened.

"I don't drink anymore."

He ignored me. "There's five thousand dollars in it for you if you can find him and get him to stop smuggling that shit here," he said. "Do what you have to do. Any means necessary."

Five grand. More money than I made in a year.

"I hear he's down in Denver now, that's where he gets it," he said. "Don't know exactly where in Denver, that's your deal. I'll advance you a thousand for expenses if you leave right away."

I studied the St. Pauli Girl label. There was a drawing of some blond wasicu girl holding six foaming beer steins. She was smiling, but there was something cruel in her eyes. She reminded me of the teachers that used to smack the hell out of me when I was little because I didn't act right.

"No thanks," I said. "Not my type of job."

Ben looked like a dog that's heard a strange noise. He even turned his head a little to the side like some damn poodle.

"What, you want more money? That what this is about?"

"It's not the money. This has a bad smell."

"That asshole is selling heroin here, killed a kid. Don't you want to shut that down?"

"Not my problem."

"Same old Virgil," he said. "Doesn't give a shit about anyone but himself. You change your mind, let me know. But it's got to be soon."

I gave the St. Pauli Girl a final glare and walked off.

Heroin. It still didn't make sense to me. I'd thrashed around in bed all night thinking about it, but I still couldn't figure out the deal. There were plenty of pills around the rez, strong opioids that popped up years ago, no shortage of those. Weed was always easy to get, and there was meth available too, but usually just bathtub crank, small quantities. The local cooks would get some smurfs to buy boxes of Sudafed at all the drugstores in a hundred-mile radius, then pay them off in product.

But I hadn't heard anything about smack. And Rick Crow was a low-level hustler — he wasn't the type to mess around with serious narcotics. He was too lazy to get any big deals together. Still, I'd heard he spent a lot of time in Denver, so I supposed it was possible. Maybe Ben's information about Rick was accurate, but it seemed doubtful. How would Ben know anything about heroin? He moved in a different world than the hustlers and scammers around here.

I needed to find out more, and then I could decide whether I should take the job — if the offer was still on the table. Yesterday, something had seemed off to me about Ben's proposal. My gut said to decline this deal, but it had been wrong before. And I couldn't deny that five thousand dollars was tempting. Normally I pocketed only a few hundred from a job. I decided to take a look inside Rick's trailer, see what was in there. Get more information, find out what he was really doing.

I took my bike straight out on the highway, focused only on the road and my machine. I took a left, then another, going past the Little White River near Crow Dog's camp. The vast sky opened in front of me as I traveled through the rolling grasslands and small canyons, the grace of the land lifting my spirits. Then I circled into town, back among the people, and I passed by the little houses, usually no more than six hundred square feet inside, but crawling with families and children. Some of the homes were in disarray, trash and old cars strewn across the yards. Others were neatly maintained, with little plots of grass and small lawn decorations. A few were boarded up, condemned because some asshole had cooked meth inside. I saw little kids playing in the streets, their parents sitting on plastic chairs keeping a watchful eye, teenagers striding in groups, a handful of elders slowly walking on the side of the road.

I rode past the big tipi-shaped building of the tribal college, then down Main Street with its small collection of businesses: the dollar store, the pawnshop, the off-sale liquor stand. The little motel where they used to sell Indian tacos. All the churches established by missionaries long ago to convert the heathens. The car repair shop where my uncle had spent most of his life before dying of diabetes. The snack shop where my mother had eaten her last meal.

I pulled up by Rick's trailer, the gravel crunching under my tires. Ben had said Rick was in Denver, but I'd be careful anyway. No telling who might be poking around out there. As I walked over, I tried to slow my breathing, which sounded too loud in my head.

The trailer looked abandoned. There were no cars around, but that didn't mean it was empty. It was one of the corrugated metal types of trailer homes, with ridged gray sides like an old battleship. The front door was closed. Faded beige curtains covered the tiny windows so I couldn't make out what was inside.

I wasn't sure, but I thought I heard some rattling coming from within. I took my handgun out — a Glock 19 with a standard magazine — and crouched behind a bush. If anyone came out, I'd have a clear shot if they tried to mess with me. Who could be in there? Maybe kids looking for drugs?

Another noise from inside. I wished I'd left my bike down the road and out of sight, but it was too late for that now. The seconds ticked by slowly as I waited for someone to come out. Then a sound like something falling came from inside the trailer.

I was done with this shit. I pulled my gun up and slowly moved to the door. I waited for five seconds, then made my move. I stood back and kicked the flimsy door. It made a crumpling sound as it gave way, and I nearly fell on my face as it opened.

"Who's there? Come out now!"

My eyes adjusted to the light, and I saw a window was open, the wind blowing in. Trash was scattered all over, and there was a large hole in the corner of the floor. The wooden floor had rotted out, leaving the pink insulation exposed. It looked like dirty cotton candy. Feeling foolish, I slowly moved to the little bathroom and stuck my head in. No one in there, just a filthy toilet and more rubbish. One room left.

The bedroom door was ajar, and I pushed it open with my foot but stood back in case anyone took a shot. I waited a few seconds, trying to stay as still as possible.

No gunfire, so I slowly moved inside the doorway. There was no one there either, just a small bed, a dresser, and more trash. I relaxed a little.

I poked my foot in one of the piles on the floor. It looked like mostly food wrappers and empty beer cans. I didn't see anything that looked like heroin. I started going through the drawers. Nothing, just an old phone directory, matches, ballpoint pens, and a few razor blades.

Then I saw it. Son of a bitch.

A package of balloons, the little ones used to wrap up heroin and other drugs. Sure, they were just balloons, but I didn't think Rick Crow was having too many kids' parties in this shithole. I felt anger rising up through my spine like a red wave.

But a bunch of balloons didn't prove anything. Ben had said there was no solid evidence linking Rick to heroin, and I hadn't seen any clear sign that junk was being sold here. I could use the money, but something about this job still seemed wrong. It was hard to believe that a two-bit hustler like Rick had the connections for serious drugs. Maybe someone had given Ben bad information — someone who wanted to set Rick up. There was no shortage of people who'd be happy to see Rick gone, and I was one of them. But I still needed to be sure that this job was legit.

I sifted through the garbage with my foot, looking for anything else that might give me more information. I picked up a notebook on a counter and leafed through it. There was a little writing on the first page. Some random numbers and a name: Martin Angel. The name wasn't familiar to me, but I could look it up later. I poked around a bit more, looking for some clues. Nothing. On a whim, I picked up the filthy little twin mattress to see if there was anything underneath.

A box of .38 Super ammo.

But no gun.

There were only three restaurants on the rez. A sandwich shop, with perpetually soggy cold cuts and wilted vegetables, the grill at the Depot bar, and JR's Pizza, a shack selling something that vaguely resembled Italian food. I had a few bucks left — after buying some smokes — and wanted to treat Nathan, so I took him to the pizza place, which was his favorite. There was a flyer tacked outside the restaurant with a picture of a smiling young woman: MISSING, DONNA FLYING HAWK, HAVE YOU SEEN

43

ME? A grungy rez dog sat on the sidewalk outside the place, eating what looked like a dead bird.

The place was tiny, with a small counter and a couple of broken-down tables and chairs. A handwritten sign taped to the drink cooler proclaimed WALL OF SHAME. It listed the people who'd passed bad checks and the amounts they owed: Yolanda White, $9.27; Stephanie Turning Heart, $19.48; Owen Bear Runner, $47.77. The one thing I liked about JR's is that they had Shasta Cola, the low-rent Coke alternative I'd grown up drinking. My mother brought home six-packs when I was a kid, and I still loved them. They had a deep sugar punch that was like a horse kick to the head. We grabbed two cans and sat down.

"What do you want, a large pepperoni?" I asked him.

He grinned. "Sure, if you can afford it."

"Yeah, I got you covered."

"What's the occasion?"

"Nothing. Wanted some food. You have a good time last night?"

"It was okay. Just hung out with Jimmy. Probably go over to his place tomorrow."

I knew he wouldn't tell me about his social life. He'd become more secretive as he entered his teenage years, but I'd figured

44

out how to get him talking. He and Jimmy had become obsessed with UFOs, life on other planets, and why humans hadn't been contacted by these space aliens yet. They would talk on their cell phones for hours, arguing about theories that explained why there'd been no contact from extraterrestrial beings and whether it was a good idea to send out a message from humans to the stars, directed at alien civilizations. Given the living conditions on the rez, it wasn't hard to figure out why the boys were so fascinated with worlds far away from here.

"What's the latest on the Martians?" I asked.

He squinted at me, checking to see if I was making fun of him. "Well, Jimmy still argues for the distance argument, but I been telling him that a Bracewell probe shreds the theory. Remember I told you about that?"

I didn't remember, but I nodded.

He went on. "It just makes sense, but he won't give it up. Yeah, the closest intelligent society may be millions of light-years away, but they must have sent a probe out! Why wouldn't they want to find other worlds? Worlds with intelligent life? Not to mention, their civilizations developed millions of years before ours, so there gotta be like thousands, maybe millions of probes out there, but we haven't seen one! Why not?" He looked at me expectantly.

"Uh, because they ran out of fuel?"

He rolled his eyes, then took a drink of his soda. "Jeez, no. The probes are obviously running on nuclear fusion. They *can't* run out of fuel."

"Okay, so why haven't any alien ships found us yet?"

"Probes, not ships! Ships contain living creatures, which can't survive thousands of years while traveling. Probes are AI, like robots; they can travel for millions of years because they're machines."

"All right, so why haven't any alien probes discovered Earth?"

"Because obviously there are no probes! They would have found us by now. It's only logical. If there were any alien probes, they would have detected our radio and TV transmissions, duh! So, process of elimination, the only possible answer is the simulation theory." He looked at me with a triumphant smile.

I was enjoying this. "What's the simulation theory?"

"It says that our world is just a computer simulation created by advanced beings to study us, and we don't even know that we're in it."

"Like the *Matrix* movie?"

"Yes, exactly! Except that the rebels in the movie were able to escape from the matrix. We can't do that. Not yet, anyway."

"So who controls this matrix? Are we like the people in that movie, just batteries for their civilization? What do they want from us?"

He finished his Shasta and grabbed another one out of the cooler. "Well, that's the part I haven't figured out yet. I been thinking, if someone could learn how to alter the simulation, then maybe they could reprogram it, go back in time, maybe do something."

"You mean like change something that already happened?"

"Yeah, I guess." He looked away from me.

I could tell what he was thinking. Although he'd hidden them, he had pencil drawings of his mom buried in his drawers at home. Pictures of his mother dancing at a pow-wow, drawings of her holding him as a baby, pictures of her graduating from school. Drawings of what she would have looked like if she'd lived. Some elaborate drawings, some just simple pictographs like those used in our winter-counts calendar. He'd never

47

shown me the pictures, but I'd seen them.

Our pizza arrived, and Nathan started eating like it was his last meal. I took a bite. Cardboard covered with tomato soup and commodity cheese. Disgusting. I'd had real pizza before. I let him go at it while I sipped my Shasta.

After we finished, it was quiet. He started messing around with his phone, and I decided to give it a shot. I knew Nathan had fooled around with pot a few times, but I'd never given him grief for it. Maybe he knew something about the other stuff.

"Hey, you hear anything about heroin around here?"

He looked up from his phone. "No. Why do you ask?"

"Somebody said Rick Crow might be starting to bring it in. You ever talk to him?"

"I know who he is, that's all."

"C'mon, don't bullshit me. I know he sells peji, beers. You see any harder crap going around?"

"I've heard some of the kids talk about pills, I guess, but I never heard nothing about heroin," he said. "Maybe monkey water, I don't know. I think they do more of that stuff over at Pine Ridge."

"Okay, but let me know if you hear anything." I finished the last of my Shasta.

48

"Hey, can you check out a name on your phone for me?"

My cell phone was an old-fashioned flip model, without any fancy features. We both got cheap mobile phones at the Walmart just over the border in Nebraska, but his model had text messages and the internet.

"Yeah, what is it?"

"Martin Angel," I said, spelling it for him. "Maybe in Colorado."

He pulled his phone out of his pocket while I made my way to the men's room. I got the key from the counter and went inside. There was an ancient gas-station vending machine mounted on the wall, advertising three different products for the bargain price of only seventy-five cents each. Genuine Horny Goat Weed, which promised to enhance desire and improve performance; the Quickie Marriage License, apparently a phony certificate for those in a hurry to consecrate their sacred pizza-shop union; and scented, neon-colored condoms. The circle of life.

When I returned, Nathan handed his phone to me and I looked down at the screen. MARTIN ANGEL, WELLNESS RELIEF CENTER, 1280 S. FEDERAL, DENVER.

Wellness Relief Center? What was it, a massage parlor? Then I scrolled down

further. COLORADO'S BEST CANNABIS DIS-
PENSARY.

4

The next day, I decided I'd give one last shot to learning more about Rick Crow's activities, whatever they were. It was no surprise that Rick Crow had a marijuana connection down in Denver. But that didn't necessarily mean he was involved with heroin. On the other hand, I needed the money, and I liked the thought of putting the hurt on Rick. I just had to make sure that I wasn't stepping in someone else's mess. If anyone knew what the deal might be, it was Jerome Iron Shell. Jerome was a medicine man and knew everyone and everything in town. He ran a sweat most Saturdays at his house, so I could talk to him there.

When I pulled up, he didn't seem surprised to see me. His long gray hair hung down over a bright-blue Pendleton-style jacket, the kind you buy at powwows for forty bucks and a wink.

51

"Need any help?" I asked him.

"Sure. Give me a hand with these stones."

I grabbed the pitchfork and wedged it under one of the grandfather stones in the pit. Jerome and I took turns moving the grandfathers to the fire box.

"You want to take a sweat?" he said. I was surprised he'd asked — he knew that I didn't do ceremonies. But maybe if I did sweat, he'd be willing to give me some information. Or maybe I'd hear something from one of the others there. And hell, it couldn't hurt.

"Yeah, okay. But I got to head home right after." I grabbed another stone with the pitchfork. "Hey, ask you a question?"

He nodded.

"You hear anything about Rick Crow selling heroin?"

"Heroin?" He shook his head. "No, that's not his deal. He smokes some peji, sells a little. Why? You gonna go after him?"

"No, just asking. Listen, keep this quiet, okay?"

I noticed Jerome's grandson Rocky and about fifteen other people standing outside the lodge. Jerome pointed at the crowd, and Rocky placed three buckets of water inside the lodge. Jerome nodded, and everyone took off their shoes and the men took off their shirts. Some were wearing gym shorts, others just towels. The people wearing eyeglasses stuck them in their shoes outside the tent. I briefly wondered if I was wearing clean boxers, then stripped off my jeans and shirt and crawled into the lodge with the others. I sat down next to the drummers. It had been a long time since I'd sat in a sweat lodge, and I wondered if I'd remember what to do in there.

After a few minutes, the drums started pounding and someone began to sing. After they finished, Jerome started to pray in Lakota. I listened to his words, not understanding most of it, though I could grasp the basic meaning. Then Jerome poured a bucket of water over the rocks. I heard a hissing sound like a large, angry snake as a huge cloud of steam filled the lodge. Then he closed the door, enveloping us in darkness. I tried to get comfortable, but my legs kept bumping into someone else's. It was hard to breathe, and I could feel sweat already pouring down my chest. The heat was excruciating, beyond words, and I lost track of time. My lungs felt like they were burning from the inside, and I tried to keep my mind off the extreme temperature by listening to the sound of my own breathing and the drums, which had started again.

I tried to focus on the beat of the drums, but became distracted by someone sobbing on my left. It sounded like one of the women, but it was hard to tell. The crying and wailing went on for what seemed like hours, and it began to rise and lower in pitch, so it became less like sobbing and more like a chant of some sort. Then it sounded like the sobbing was somebody speaking or whispering very softly. It seemed important that I understand what was being said, and I tried to quiet every thought so that I was utterly still.

At some point I must have fallen asleep despite the heat, because I dreamed that my sister, Sybil, was next to me. She whispered things I didn't understand at first, and I felt sad and told her to go away. But she kept telling me, over and over, to remember the birds. And to hurry. Remember the birds. And the lost bird. What does that mean? I asked, but she wouldn't say any more.

We must have gone through four rounds in there, but I couldn't remember. The sweat ended when Jerome shouted "Mita-kuye oyasin!" and I crawled out into the light. As I drank cool water, I thought about my dream and what it meant. Then it came to me.

The year our mom died, Sybil and I had

drawn a picture of dead birds on our winter-counts calendar to represent her death. That winter, not only had our mother passed away, but it had been so cold on the reservation that many birds froze to death as well. To us, that time had always been the year our mother and the birds left us.

By the time I got home from the sweat, it was late. The lights were on, so I knew Nathan was there, probably asleep or playing video games. He'd been alone all day, but he knew how to take care of himself. I was exhausted and hungry. No fresh food left in the fridge, but I found an old frost-covered Tombstone Pizza in the bowels of the freezer. I heated it up in our ancient microwave, which required five extra minutes to cook anything.

I settled back with my soggy pizza and contemplated the Rick Crow situation. I still couldn't figure out why Ben would offer me five large to take care of Rick instead of just going to the feds. I understood why he wouldn't go to the rez police. By federal law, tribal police couldn't prosecute any felony crimes that happened on the rez. Jerome had told me that this law was because of the murder way back in the 1880s of Chief Spotted Tail. The killer had been banished, but not jailed. He said the wasi-cus were so upset by the Native way of justice that they passed a law taking away our right to punish our own people. So tribal courts could only charge misde-meanor crimes — little stuff, like shoplifting or disorderly conduct. The tribal police had to refer all felonies to the federal investiga-tors. But the feds usually declined to prose-cute most of them. They'd follow through on some, usually high-profile cases or violent crimes. But standard sex assault cases, thefts, assault and battery — these crimes were usually ignored. And the bad men knew this. It was open season for rap-ing any Native woman, so long as the rape occurred on Indian land.

When the legal system broke down like this, people came to me. For a few hundred bucks they'd get some measure of revenge. My contribution to the justice system.

But heroin was different. This wasn't a wife-beating or car theft, crimes that the feds never gave a shit about. Busting a heroin ring would get major press and prob-ably make some federal prosecutor's career. Ben had to know that, so why wouldn't he take his intel to the FBI? Maybe he was be-ing straight with me, and there wasn't enough hard evidence linking Rick to the dope.

I'd had enough for the night, so I went to go check on Nathan. I could see that his lights were on, so I'd turn everything off and cover him with a blanket. I opened the door and saw that he was passed out on his bed, all of his clothes still on, one arm hanging down at his side.

"Dude, why don't you get into your shorts and get under the covers?"

He didn't respond.

"Nathan, let's go to bed, I'm tired."

Still no response.

"Nathan?"

I looked at him closely. His face and lips were gray, almost blue. I saw an empty balloon, a lighter, and some crumpled, burned foil on the floor. There was an acrid vinegar odor in the air.

Oh no.

"Nathan, wake up! Get up!"

I tried to sit him up, but he was too heavy and fell back onto the bed. I pulled his eyelids up. His pupils were tiny and dark, like miniature black holes, and his skin felt cold and clammy. I slapped his face, hard.

"Nathan, open your eyes! Wake up!"

No response, but I saw his chin move, just a little. I ran to the living room for my cell phone. The IHS hospital was fifty miles from here, and the tribal police station about twenty. The tribal cops were my only hope.

My hands shaking, I dialed the number.

"Police."

"This is Virgil Wounded Horse. My nephew — he's overdosing! He won't wake up, you need to send —"

"What is your address?"

"Please hurry, he's unconscious —"

"I need your address, sir." He sounded pissed off, like I was stopping him from going home after a long shift.

"Eighty-three and Spidergrass Road — we're the only house out here."

"Just stay on the phone with me, okay? Is he breathing?"

"I think so, yeah, but not much —"

"Stay on the phone, stay on the phone, all right?"

"Just hurry."

"How old is he?"

"Uh, I don't — he's fourteen! He's only fourteen."

I flashed back to Nathan as a little kid, playing with some toy cars I'd given him. What difference did it make how old he was, if he was overdosing!

"How long has he been down?"

58

"I don't know, I just found him. Do you have a car free?"

The dispatcher sounded angry again. "We're on the way. You said it was an overdose?"

"Heroin, I think. There was a balloon and some foil on the floor."

"Do you know how much of the drug he took?"

"How the fuck should I know? I didn't know he was doing that shit!"

"Just trying to help. How much does he weigh?"

"I don't — maybe one forty?"

"We'll be there soon, stay with me, okay? Can you stay on the line? Sir?"

I let the phone drop to the floor. Black clouds entered the room, taking up all the oxygen, all of the air. I couldn't breathe, so I let the darkness envelop my lungs, my skin, my body.

"Sir? Sir?" I heard the voice on the phone from far away. "Are you still there?"

I picked up the phone. "Yeah, I'm here," I said. "How close are they?"

"Do you know how to do CPR?" he asked.

"Uh, kind of. Mouth-to-mouth resuscitation?"

"Not exactly. I need you to start chest compressions right away. You remember that

59

movie, *Saturday Night Fever*?"

"Movie? What're you talking about?"

"I need you to put both hands on his chest — right on top of his heart — and press down hard; do a hundred compressions a minute. Think of the disco beat from that song 'Stayin' Alive.' The song from the movie. *Use that beat on his chest.* Put the phone down and do it now! Keep doing it until they get there."

I pulled up Nathan's sweatshirt. His skin wasn't brown anymore — it was a strange shade of gray, and weirdly cold and damp. I clasped my hands together, like I was praying, and put them right over his heart. I'd always hated disco music, but my mother had played that old Bee Gees album constantly when I was a kid. I couldn't remember the lyrics, but the beat of the song came back to me instantly. I pushed down on Nathan's chest steadily, like I was dancing at a 49 party. Was I pressing too hard? Did I need to push harder? I focused on the beat of the music as I forced his heart to pump blood through his veins. *Stayin' alive, stayin' alive . . .*

As I pushed, I tried to remember the Indian prayers my mother used to say to me. I'd heard them so many times as a kid, it seemed urgent that I remember just one line, but nothing would come. How was it that I could remember some shitty disco song from years ago but couldn't remember my mother's own words? The weight of my failures — all of them — felt like a shroud wrapped around me.

As my nephew lay dying in the little house, I sent my words up to the Creator.

Please don't let this child die. I will do anything, just spare him.

Spare him.

5

The noise of the breathing machines and
the sharp smell of the cleaning fluids used
by the hospital were giving me a headache.
I stared over at Nathan, still unconscious
and hooked to a respirator. His chest moved
up and down slowly; the breathing ap-
paratus on his face was like a cruel imita-
tion of the masks worn by heyoka clowns at
ceremony. I barely recognized him, with his
pale skin and swollen eyes. What had happened to the boy I'd been eating pizza with
just days before?

The night before, Nathan had flatlined but
had somehow come back. One of his lungs
had collapsed, and I'd been told he'd need
help breathing for a while. The doctor
wasn't sure yet if he'd sustained any brain
damage because of the lack of oxygen. He's
going to make it, he's going to live, I kept
telling myself to tamp down my dread. The

Creator, or someone, had answered my prayers.

The doc told me that Nathan had possibly taken heroin mixed with fentanyl, a deadly combination. She'd told me she'd seen a lot of these overdoses lately, and that the kids probably hadn't even known they were taking a mix of the two drugs. The doc said fentanyl was fifty times more powerful than heroin and much more likely to cause a person to OD. I didn't understand why these ratfuck dealers would sell a drug that could kill their customers, but she said that these lethal drugs were actually a selling point. The doc even said the nickname on the street for heroin cut with fentanyl was Pawnee.

Jesus Christ. The Pawnee tribe were the bitter enemies of the Lakota people. We battled them for a hundred years, especially after many of the Pawnee aligned themselves with the white men in the 1800s. It was too much to take that the poison killing our kids bore their name.

At that moment, I flashed to a vision of Rick Crow in my mind. My hatred was so strong that I felt stomach acid begin to churn upward, burning my gut and throat. Then my phone buzzed, startling me. Not many people had my number, and that's how I liked it.

"Virgil?"

"Yeah?"

"It's Marie."

I paused for a second. I hadn't spoken to Marie Short Bear for a long time. Not since she'd packed up her stuff and moved out of my place.

"Virgil, you there?"

"Yeah, I'm here."

"I heard Nathan was sick."

Sick. That was one way to put it. "He overdosed last night."

"I know. I ran into Ty Bad Hand at Turtle Creek this morning, and he told me."

"Who's that?"

"He works for tribal police. How's Nathan doing?"

I thought about how to answer this. "They say he's going to live, but they're not sure if he has, uh, brain damage. He's unconscious — hooked up to a machine to help him breathe. They say he'll be out for a few days."

"I'm so sorry. Is there anything I can do?"

I realized I was starving, but I didn't want to ask Marie for anything. I'd caused her enough trouble.

"No, I'm good. Right now, I just need to wait and let him heal."

"Of course," she said. "I'll burn some sage tonight."

"Uh, thanks."

"This is so sad; you know I always loved Nathan. He's a good kid."

I felt my heart tearing, and my voice broke. "Yeah, he is. He's had some problems, but —"

"You hang in there, all right? The Creator is going to look after him. He's going to make it, I can feel it. Stay strong and have a brave heart, kiksuyapi."

My throat was locking up, so I stayed silent.

"You still there?" she said.

"Yeah, I'm here. Just thinking."

"Nathan's in high school now, right?"

"Yeah. Todd County."

"Does he like it there?"

"I think so," I said. "He's doing okay with his grades, not great."

"Is he playing any sports? Or clubs?"

"No. Not really his thing. He fools around with video games, listens to a lot of music."

"Hey," she said, "I don't want to pry, it's not my business, but is he hanging out with any, you know, bad influences?"

I stopped for a second while I considered this. "Not really. He did some stupid stuff a while back. His best friend is this kid, Jimmy

65

Two Elk. They play their games, run around."

"You know what he needs?"

"What?"

"A yuwipi. Heal him, get his spirit right. I could get Jerome Iron Shell or Pete Ictinike to run the ceremony after he gets out of the hospital."

Oh no, not this again. The last thing Nathan needed was some goddam ritual like a yuwipi. I'd never been to one, but I'd heard about it. The medicine man comes to the sick person's house, and his family tape up all of the windows and doors so it's pitch-black inside. The medicine man gets tied up tightly with a quilt, and then the spirits supposedly come to the room and heal the sick person. No thanks. Right now what Nathan needed was bed rest and oxygen so his lung could heal. And his brain.

"You working with Jerome now? Training to be a medicine woman?" I asked her, try-ing to change the subject. Back when we were together, Marie had been convinced that she'd had a vision, that the spirits had come to her and asked her to become a medicine woman. Marie had told her vision to Jerome, but he told her she wasn't ready.

"Not really," she said. "He taught me a few things, but said it would be better to

66

wait until my moon cycle ends."

"Oh." I didn't know what to say.

"Don't know if you heard, but I went back to college for a year. Black Hills State. Needed to take biochem and some labs — Sinte doesn't offer those. It was weird to be back, but I needed those classes. Required for med school."

"Medical school? Didn't know you were still thinking about that."

"Yeah, I finally caved in and took the MCATs. My mom and dad convinced me. And I'm getting pretty tired of my job. Been there too long."

Marie's parents had been pushing for her to become a doctor for years, decades even. As I recalled, they wanted her to be like her sister, who had some fancy job in finance out in California.

"Hey, that's great," I said. "Being a doctor. Healing the sick and all. So, which, uh, med school will you go to?"

"Not sure. It's pretty tough to get accepted these days. You got to have solid grades and board scores. My numbers are good, but you never know. It's all right if I don't get in. Just sent off my application to USD."

"In Vermillion?"

"For the first two years of school, then

67

you go to Rapid City for rotations."

"What are those?"

"You learn specialties, like pediatrics, internal medicine."

"Sounds serious. You really going to do this?"

"Too early to say. I'm a long way from being admitted. Word is that USD looks down on tribal colleges. I also sent an app to the med school in New Mexico."

"Good luck. Really."

"Thanks." I heard her take a breath. "So, what do you think about a yuwipi for Nathan? I could set it up, no problem."

I paused for a moment while I thought about how to respond nicely. "You know how I feel about all that. It's fine for some folks, but I got my own way of doing things."

"Virgil, it's time. Stop this tough guy routine. No more Indian vigilante posing. Nathan needs you — you're his only family. What happens if you take on someone tougher than you?"

No conversations for a long, long time, and already she felt entitled again to tell me what to do. "No one's gonna take me down. And shit, if I don't do anything to help people, the assholes win. The gangs and drug dealers. That's how I'll help Nathan."

She sighed. "The way to stop drugs and

gangs is to teach children the Lakota way. Our values and traditions."

"Right. How am I supposed to stop Rick Crow from bringing heroin to the rez with some Indian ceremony?"

There was utter silence, then she said, "Rick Crow? Are you sure?"

I closed my eyes for a moment. After Marie and I had split, I'd heard a rumor that she'd taken up with Rick Crow for a while, but hadn't believed it until now. Shit.

"Think so. I found heroin stuff at his trailer. And people told me he's the one bringing the drugs here." No need to tell Marie it was her father who'd ratted Rick out. "I hear he's in Denver now, getting more dope. As soon as Nathan is up, I'm going down to Colorado to put an end to this."

I guess I'd made my decision.

She cleared her throat. I braced myself for more lecturing about the evils of violence.

"If you go after Rick Crow, I'm coming with you."

6

Hours passed while I waited for Nathan to wake up. I'd tried to stop my mind from going to dark places, but images of my nephew as brain-damaged crowded into my head. I was proud of him, his intelligence and his curiosity and his fierce defense of music I hated; it was breaking my heart and spirit to imagine that these parts of him might be gone for good. Then I started to obsess over things Nathan had done that might have tipped me off to hard drug use. Had he been acting strangely? Maybe I should have searched his backpack and phone. I gave up trying to stop this parade of images and just sat with my fear and guilt.

The window in the hospital room was murky, like it hadn't been washed in years, but I could still glimpse the russet hills and rolling prairie of the reservation outside in the dying light. Back in the time before Columbus, there were only Indians here, no skyscrapers, no automobiles, no streets. Of course, we didn't use the words *Indian* or *Native American* then; we were just people. We didn't know we were supposedly drunks or lazy or savages. I wondered what it was like to live without that weight on your shoulders, the weight of the murdered ancestors, the stolen land, the abused children, the burden every Native person carries.

We were told in movies and books that Indians had a sacred relationship with the land, that we worshipped and nurtured it. But staring at Nathan, I didn't feel any mystical bond with the rez. I hated our shitty unpaved roads and our falling-down houses and the snarling packs of dogs that roamed freely in the streets and alleys. But most of all, I hated that kids like Nathan — good kids, decent kids — got involved with drugs and crime and gangs, because there was nothing for them to do here. No after-school jobs, no clubs, no tennis lessons. Every month in the *Lakota Times* newspaper there was an obituary for another teen suicide, another family in the Burned Thigh Nation who'd had their heart taken away from them. In the old days, the eyapaha was the town crier, the person who would meet incoming warriors after a battle, ask them what happened so they wouldn't have to speak of their own glories, then tell the people the news. Now the eyapaha, our local newspaper, announced losses and harms too often, victories and triumphs too rarely.

Why didn't I leave? People here always talked about going to Rapid City or Sioux Falls or Denver, getting a job and making a clean break. Putting aside Native ways and assimilating, adapting to suburban life. But I thought about the sound of the drummers at a powwow, the smell of wild sage, the way little Native kids looked dressed up in their first regalia, the flash of the sun coming up over the hills. I wondered if I could ever really leave the reservation, because the rez was in my mind, a virtual rez, one that I was seemingly stuck with. Then I fell into a half-sleep, immersed in fugue dreams and transient thoughts, images of Indian children dancing in my head.

In the morning, I thought I saw Nathan begin to stir; his head moved a bit, and his eyelids fluttered and quivered. I quickly roused myself and moved closer to the side of the bed, watching, hoping that he would fully open his eyes. His eyelids continued to open and shut. This was a good sign, right? Then he moved his head to the side and looked straight at me.

"Nathan, you awake? Dude, how you doing?" I felt relief wash over me like a flood of rainwater. I wanted to hug him, but worried that maybe I'd knock out the IV line attached to his arm.

"Nathan, can you hear me?"

His eyes were open, but he didn't say anything. He looked puzzled, like he'd been taken away to some strange land where he didn't speak the language. I felt a stab of fear — I needed him to speak, needed to know that he was still Nathan. Then the nurse came in.

"He's awake," I told her, "he just opened his eyes."

At that point, I was shepherded out of intensive care. While I waited, I put a dollar in the machine for some weak coffee, which I gratefully drank. I tried to sort out my feelings while I watched the others in the waiting room. A Native couple sat next to me, their faces pinched and anxious. My body began to unwind, and I realized how much tension I'd been carrying while Nathan was in his coma. Had it been a coma? That seemed more serious than I wanted to acknowledge. He was alive and awake — that was all that mattered.

After an hour in the waiting room, my

anxiety returned. Why hadn't they updated me? Was it bad? My body begin to tense up again, and I asked the lady sitting at the front desk if there was any news on Nathan Wounded Horse. She said that someone would talk to me shortly. Then she said I was lucky, because the emergency department at the hospital had been closed for six months and had just been opened again. Apparently the federal government had made large cuts to the Indian Health Service budget, so the emergency room had been closed to save money. But, she'd said, the government had recently contracted with some private company to run the hospital, rolling her eyes to let me know what she thought of her new bosses.

Three cups of coffee later, a different doctor — white guy — found me in the waiting room. He didn't look like a doctor, you know, crisp and professional and competent. Instead, he looked rumpled and tired, like someone who'd been on a ten-day bender. I wondered why this guy was on a reservation. Maybe he'd lost his license somewhere else, and this was the only place where they'd take him.

"Well, it was definitely heroin, but we don't know if there was any fentanyl present, because the tox screen doesn't catch that. We've extubated him and moved him out of the ICU. We had him on a mild sedative, which may seem strange given that opioids are a major depressant, but it's important we manage the patient's airway after an episode like this. We used to use lorazepam, but it turns out that you get a much longer ICU course with that."

I had no idea what he was saying. "Uh, does it look like he's going to be all right? You know, was his brain injured?"

"It's too early to say. His corneal reflex was fine, and the EEGs and SEPs look okay. We'll probably keep him for another day or two and monitor him. I'd like to keep him longer, but we only have thirty-five beds here, so he could even be released as early as tomorrow. He'll be weak and dizzy for a few days, so just let him stay in bed. He'll have the worst headache of all time after the naloxone leaves his system. If the headache gets worse, bring him back."

I tried to take all this in. "What happens next? Do I get him in some drug treatment program here? Counseling?"

The doctor smiled at me, but the smile didn't reach his eyes. "I wish we had something, but we don't receive any funding for behavioral health at this facility. I believe there's a program in Rapid City."

"IHS doesn't have any drug programs here? You gotta be kidding." I looked at him, but he averted his eyes.

"I'll remind you that your care here is paid for, courtesy of the US government. No charge to you. If I were you, I'd be grateful he survived and that you didn't have to pay for it. Now, please excuse me." He turned and walked away.

I felt the urge to punch him in the back of the head. Jesus, the Americans stole the land from us, and all we got in return was shitty health care and crappy canned goods. I wanted to tell the nasty doc that we'd be happy to take our land back and give up the health care and commodities. But there was no point. I had to focus on Nathan and not piss off anyone here.

There was one thing I could do. I took my cell phone out to the courtyard, where I'd get some reception. I dialed the numbers and waited.

"Ben?"

"Yeah, who's this?"

"Virgil Wounded Horse."

A pause. "How's Nathan? Marie told me what happened."

"He's going to make it." This was the first time I'd said this out loud. I hadn't wanted to speak the words out of some weird fear of cursing Nathan. But as I spoke, I felt angry. Angry that Nathan had done this to himself, angry that he'd put me in this position. Angry that Natives like Rick Crow would sell dope to kids on the rez, starting the whole cycle over again.

"That's good," he said. "Glad to hear it. We don't need any more overdoses. Not on my watch."

I waited for him to say something else, more sympathetic words, but I realized that this was the extent of Ben's compassion.

"I'm ready to go to Denver," I said. "What we talked about. Rick Crow."

"Are you sure — with Nathan in recovery?"

I hadn't thought this through. "I'll look after him. Soon as he's on his feet, I'm good to go."

"Okay." Ben cleared his throat on the other end of the line. "Best to take care of this away from the rez. Less complicated. How long do you need before you'd leave?"

"I could maybe take off by the end of the week."

"All right," he said, "you need money to get down there?"

"No, I got enough." I'd tap into the college savings, what little there was.

"Need some extra help? I got a couple of

guys I can possibly set you up with down there."

"No."

"You positive? Rick runs with a pretty bad crowd. You got to promise me you'll handle this. Fix this problem — for the people."

For so long, I'd been unsure about what it meant to be Indian. I'd believed it meant going to powwows, speaking the language, wearing Leonard Peltier T-shirts. Maybe it did mean all of that stuff. But I knew one thing now. Rick Crow might look Indian, but he was no Native. He was a cancer, and it was time to cut out the tumor.

"I don't care about his crowd. When I find him, I'll jam every bag of drugs I can find up his ass. I'll burn off every one of his goddamn fingers. Motherfucker will suffer. That's a promise."

7

Nathan was sleeping again, his chest moving slowly up and down. He'd be released from the hospital in the next few days, so I didn't have much time to decide what I was going to do about his care. Ben had said Rick was in Denver now, buying more dope, so there was no time to wait. Not to mention, I was burning to find that fucker and show him the front side of my fist and the back side of a baseball bat.

The problem was Nathan. I couldn't leave if he was still sick, and I sure as shit didn't want to take off until I was positive he wouldn't mess with drugs again. I needed to find out where he'd gotten the stuff and why he'd made the colossally stupid decision to take it. When he was ready, I'd talk to him and find out more.

The only answer was to have him stay at my auntie's place. She was eighty years old and lived in a two-room house about twenty miles from town. If he stayed there, he'd be away from his friends and any trouble. He could take a few weeks off from school while he recuperated. There wasn't much space there, but Nathan could help her gather firewood when he got his strength back. The place had no central heating, just a wood stove in the middle of the main room, but he'd be fine. Having Nathan stay there was the best — maybe the only — option I had.

I felt bad about leaving, but what did I know about taking care of sick kids? My auntie was better at this; she'd raised three children and knew all about this stuff. I stared at the dregs of my coffee. Truth was, I was scared about screwing up with Nathan. Even though I'd had my own struggles with booze, I didn't know anything about addiction recovery. What I was good at was knocking the shit out of assholes.

"This a bad time?"

I looked up into the eyes of Marie Short Bear, standing in the doorway of the hospital room. Her black hair was longer than when I'd last seen her, falling past her shoulders and down her back. She had on a white strappy blouse that showed off her shoulders and long slender frame, and a dark skirt that appeared to be decorated with ledger art. Her face looked sad and beautiful, her brown eyes flashing with glints of copper.

"I like your skirt."

She looked embarrassed. "It's Bethany Yellowtail. My mother gave it to me."

"Looks good."

"Can I come in?"

"Let's go out to the waiting room," I said. "He's still sleeping."

Marie peered over at Nathan. "Poor guy."

We moved to the dingy waiting room, which was thankfully empty. I tried not to stare at Marie as she pulled out a chair. It had been a long time since I'd seen her, and memories surged into my brain like a flash flood. Thoughts of our time together, images of Marie as a schoolgirl.

She'd been a weird kid in grade school. And I do mean weird. She wore plastic wolf ears and a wolf tail in class for the entire fourth grade, and would howl periodically throughout the day, which infuriated her teachers. She claimed she was half wolf and couldn't stop wailing and yowling. Thankfully, she grew out of the wolf stage, but the damage had been done. All throughout elementary school, kids would bark behind her back, and they called her "Dogbreath." I was too small to help her when the teasing started, and in any case, I was more concerned with my own social status. At the rez school, the pecking order was as clearly defined as that of some fancy prep school back east. Marie was at the bottom then, and I wasn't far away.

In high school, Marie had tried to fit in with the super-Natives, the tradish kids who decreed who was sufficiently indigenous and who wasn't. Those girls froze her out, which wounded Marie deeply. I guess they resented that her mom was Osage, not Lakota, or her family's money, or maybe they just didn't like her. She became friends with a Navajo girl, Velma, who'd somehow ended up in South Dakota. Velma was a big girl with a roaring laugh and a don't-fuck-with-me personality. They'd drive down to Denver to shop at the thrift stores, hit the punk record shop, and go to all-ages concerts. They pasted loads of stickers on their school lockers: Wax Trax Records, Misfits, Black Flag. None of this endeared them to the popular kids, but Velma and Marie claimed they didn't give a shit what the other kids thought.

But I knew that Marie did care. She joined every environmental and indigenous club at school, becoming president of most of them by sheer willpower. She formed teams for the hand games and Lakota language competitions in Rapid City, holding monthly

Indian taco sales to pay for the travel. She graduated near the top of the class and was accepted to Dartmouth College, where her sister had gone, but she'd refused to go to school out of state, instead insisting on attending our local tribal college, Sinte Gleska University, where she could study Lakota language and culture, her qualifications as a super-Indian then beyond question. Her parents had fought her on that, long and hard, but Marie prevailed, graduating in just three years. Her father got her a job working for the tribe in the family services office, where she helped kids and elders. She'd started at the bottom, but as usual worked harder than everyone and got promoted to the commodity food program, where she had to take orders from people she didn't like or respect.

In a sad twist of fate, her boss was one of the girls who'd been nasty to her in high school, Delia Kills in Water. A full-blood Lakota, Delia had been a cheerleader in high school, the popular girl who knew everybody but talked behind everyone's back. They'd hated each other then, and the passage of time hadn't smoothed things over. If anything, their rivalry had gotten worse. Last I'd heard, Marie was still working there.

I pushed aside my memories and suddenly became aware of my own physical condition. I hadn't showered in at least two days, hadn't brushed my teeth, and was wearing clothes that probably smelled like a locker room.

"Listen, I haven't had a chance to clean up —"

"Don't worry about it. I didn't know if you'd eaten anything, so I brought this." She pulled a sub sandwich out of her bag. Black Forest ham and cheese. Until that moment, I hadn't realized how hungry I was, and I gratefully took it. I looked over to see if she had food for herself.

"Please, go ahead," she said. "I already ate."

I started eating, unable to wait.

"I came because I wanted to talk to you. In person." She put her hand on my shoulder for a moment. I realized how long it had been since she'd touched me. I put the rest of the hoagie away and used a napkin to clean myself up as best I could.

"Thanks for coming," I said. "And for the lunch."

"You're welcome." She smiled, which was nice. There hadn't been many smiles during our last few months together. "So, have you had a chance to think about my offer?"

"You mean, you coming along to Denver?"

She nodded.

"Sorry, not going to happen. I'll handle this on my own."

The smile went away. "What makes you think you'll be able to find Rick there? Do you know anything about his deals, or where he stays?"

"I found some info at his trailer. I'll get him, don't worry about that."

Her face darkened. "For Christ's sake, Virgil, Denver isn't the rez. It's a big city with millions of people. It's not like you can just hang out at the corner store and eventually run into him."

"I suppose you know where he is?" I tried to keep my voice low.

"As a matter of fact, I do. I have a pretty good idea, and if he's not there, then I know where he's likely to go."

"Can you call him? On his cell phone, find out where he is?"

"No," she said, "he uses those disposable phones, the ones you buy and throw away. Don't know his number anymore."

I was afraid to ask this question, but I had no choice. "How is it you know so much about him?"

Marie turned away and looked out the window. The harsh glare of the fluorescent lights illuminated her skin as she stared out at the rolling hills of the reservation.

"After I left you, I was pretty angry. Angry at you for being such an asshole. Angry at myself for not being able to help you. You were messed up, and there was nothing I could do. I saw you were hurting, but you wouldn't talk to me. You wouldn't say a word for days. I'm not like you. I need people, I need somebody to tell my stuff to. So I met Rick at the Depot one night. After you and I broke up. He talked to me, listened to me. I knew his reputation, but I just needed somebody. It's my life, I don't have to defend my choices."

Now my anger was back and in full bloom. "So I'm an asshole and a hired thug and won't talk, but you take up with a drug dealer? The way I see it, you're just as bad as him if you were with him."

She looked defeated, and I instantly regretted my words. "Yeah, he's not a good guy," she said. "I left as soon as I found that out. Someday I'll tell you about it. That's why I want to help. I know where he stays in Denver, and I'm pretty sure I know who he gets the drugs from. It's a street gang, the Aztec Kingz." She looked off into the distance. "You have to believe me, if I'd known he was bringing heroin here, I would have told you. Someone. I never heard anything about that, I promise you."

I considered what she'd said. "Why don't you just give me the address, tell me what you know, and I'll go down there on my own?"

"No. If you want the details, you have to let me come with you. I can use my vacation days." Her face was an angry, steely mask, and she looked me straight in the eyes. "Look, I've got some things to say to him. This is something I need to do."

Having Marie come with me to Denver was out of the question. Rick Crow was a bad dude, and it sounded like he'd hooked up with some even worse people in Colorado. It would be completely wrong to bring her into this.

I looked at Marie, her long black hair, the swell of her blouse, and her dark-brown eyes.

"Okay, we leave in three days."

8

When I got back to the hospital room, the nurse told me that Nathan had been sitting up and talking a bit. A wave of relief shot through my body. When he saw me walk in, his face trembled and he started to cry a little.

"I'm sorry, Uncle." His lips contorted as he tried to contain his emotions. "I messed up."

We'd never been the hugging type, but I moved to the side of his bed and held him. Now he really started to weep, and stuck his head on my shoulder. His breath stuttered and jerked.

"It's okay, buddy, it's all right," I said, and we stayed like that for a while. Finally I moved back and took a look at him. His eyes were sunken and dark, and his skin was ashy. But he was alive.

"How you feeling?"

"Not so good. I feel weird, like I'm a

zombie or something. Like I'm watching stuff happen, but nothing's real. And my head really hurts."

"You want some water?"

"No, I'm okay. They gave me a little. Said I can have food later, but I'm not hungry."

He still had an IV hooked up to his arm, but the other machines were gone. "They told me you're probably gonna get out soon."

"Really?"

"Yeah, you're going to stay with Auntie Audrey for a bit," I said. "She'll look after you."

"What? Out in the country?"

"It'll be fine. You can rest up, get your strength back. She used to work at the hospital, you know, she's good at that."

"How long will I be there?" He slumped back into the bed.

"Depends how you're feeling. I got to go out of town, but I'll call and check in. You need anything, you can call Tommy."

"Where're you going?"

"Denver."

He didn't say anything. It was time to ask the hard question.

"Nathan, I know you're still sick, but I got to know something. So, what happened?"

He looked puzzled. "Uh, I guess I over-dosed."

"No, I mean, why did you take that stuff? The drugs."

He sat up and focused his attention on the IV line in his arm, as if the answer to my question was there. "I guess I screwed up."

"Come on, you can tell me. The truth, okay? Have you done this stuff before?"

"No. This was the first time, I promise." He looked away and stared at the wall.

"All right. So why'd you do it?"

"Well, school has sucked so bad this year —"

"Sucked? What's going on?"

Now he turned to me with a resentful expression. "You don't know what it's like there. Most of the kids are freakin' shitty; they make fun of me sometimes. You know, 'cause my mom is dead or I'm not Indian enough or whatever. I barely have any friends. I just been like, really stressed out, feeling like crap all the time."

Yeah, I did know what it was like at the school, and I remembered pretty well what it was like to be harassed and bullied. But my heart cracked when I realized he'd been going through it too. Alone.

"Why didn't you come talk to me? You

90

know, let me help out."

A pause. "Uh, you're not exactly a person people talk to. Like, have a heart-to-heart or whatever. I mean, I need someone's ass kicked, you're the guy."

This hurt.

"You don't want to talk with me, that's cool," I said. "But you got issues, you can go to a school counselor or someone."

He smirked, looked at me like I was the stupidest person alive. "Yeah, okay."

I decided to try a different tack. "Don't you hang out with Jimmy, talk to him? He's your bud, right?"

"Ah, not so much anymore. He's, like, starting to get all sporty, playing b-ball, hangin' with those dudes. I'm more into rap, hip-hop, cool stuff."

I knew when I'd hit a dead end. "All right. But you got to tell me one thing." I looked him in the eyes. "Where'd you get the drugs?"

He paused. "At school. By the football field."

"What do you mean, the football field? From who?"

"I don't know, some dudes hanging out there."

"Rick Crow?"

"No. Some other guys, like four of them. I

seen 'em once or twice before, don't know their names. We were talking about music and stuff, you know, chillin'. So they said I could try it, didn't ask me for no money. Said it was no big deal, like smoking a joint or whatever. I guess I just wanted to do something different. I didn't think none of this was gonna happen."

I wondered if he was bullshitting me. There was no way that drugs were being given away, and I knew he didn't have money to buy them. There was more to this story.

"You being straight with me? Whole thing sounds shady."

Now he was staring at me like I'd been the one who'd caused him to overdose. "I'm telling you the truth! You know, I got the right to make friends. Live my life. I made a mistake, all right?"

"I'm just trying to find out who these guys are, okay? You're sure it wasn't Rick Crow?"

He relaxed a little. "I'm positive. That dude's creepy. It was these other guys, they're not from around here. Can't remember their names, only thing I remember is the main one was called Loco. Short guy, had a scar on his face."

Loco. Sounded about right.

■ ■ ■ ■

There was one more thing I had to do before I left for Denver. I drove out on the main road, the dust of the rez rising up around me, until I got to the unmarked street I knew so well. I headed down the dirt road and parked outside the gate, then walked through the weeds and grasses, keeping an eye out for rattlers, and went over to the second-to-last row, where all of the Wounded Horses and Peneauxs were buried.

There they were. My mother's and my sister's graves, right next to each other, my father's two rows away. The cemetery was unattended, so there were no manicured lawns or landscapes. It was just an empty lot where some Indians were buried. I came to the cemetery every few months, depending on the weather. I used to bring Nathan, but it made him upset, so I stopped. I wanted to come more often, but there were times I couldn't handle the sadness.

I stopped by my mother's grave first, and bent over to clear off the small granite marker. After my father's death, my mother struggled to raise Sybil and me, working several jobs to pay the bills and keep us in school clothes. She'd tried to sell Avon cosmetics by going door-to-door, but the local rez ladies mocked her and nicknamed her "Avon-calling." But one of her friends bought a big order, so she got a nice commission, which we spent on our first real vacation to Rapid City. There, we explored tourist attractions like Flintstone City and ate out in a real restaurant for the first time. My mother had to spit out the food, which embarrassed us. She had a very strong sense of taste and could tell when food had spoiled before anyone else, just by taking a small bite. She could even taste the flavors left over in pots and pans, telling us that a cook had made chicken noodle soup in a pot before using it for spaghetti the next day. Once she told me that she could even taste the weather on the day that the food was cooked, but I didn't believe her. What does a thunderstorm taste like? I'd asked, but she'd only laughed.

A few years after that, she died, and Sybil and I were left all alone. Aunt Audrey took us in, but we mainly raised ourselves, becoming our own little unit. Sybil and me against the world. No one to defend us against the petty brutalities of the local assholes. I vowed I'd get my revenge someday. And I did. Every beating I laid down felt like a victory, the payback of the bullied and the persecuted.

As I looked down on my mother's grave-stone, I remembered what she told me just before she died. "Akita mani yo," she said. *See everything as you go.* I think she meant that I needed to be aware of the world as it really existed, not the way I wanted it to be. Indian awareness.

I walked over to my sister's grave. Sybil had been like a mother to me in some ways. Even though I was older than her by a few years, she'd taken care of me when I needed it. She'd supported me when my drinking had gotten out of hand, fed me when I was hungry, nursed me when I was beat up and wounded. I tried to tell Nathan as many stories as I could about his mom so he didn't forget her, but he'd always get quiet when I started, so I eventually gave up.

"Sister, I got to tell you something. It's Nathan. He's sick, he nearly died."

I had to stop for a bit.

"I tried to keep him away from the bad guys around here. I tried to tell him the right stuff, have him do good in school. I really tried . . ."

The wind blew on my face. "I'm sorry. But I promise you, I'll get the people who gave him that stuff."

I took one last look at her grave and turned away. I knew the medicine man would've wanted me to burn some sage before I left, but instead I picked a few black-eyed Susans and set them next to the headstones. It was time to go.

When Sybil died, everyone said that the grief would get better over time, but that hadn't happened. What I'd discovered was that sadness is like an abandoned car left out in a field for good — it changes a little over the years, but doesn't ever disappear. You may forget about it for a while, but it's still there, rusting away, until you notice it again.

9

Black shadowy clouds gathered on the horizon as I loaded up the car. The TV had said a bad storm was coming, probably heavy rain and thunderstorms. We'd agreed to take Marie's much nicer and more reliable car to Denver. I was grateful for this, as I'd been worried about the dependability of my old banger.

But first I had to take Nathan to his auntie's house. I'd packed a load of groceries, all of the junk foods I knew he liked to eat, his schoolbooks and cell phone, and forty dollars I'd taken from my stash. He'd been complaining all morning, lobbying to be left alone at our house while I was gone.

"You know I'm old enough to take care of myself," he said. "And what about not going to school? It's stupid to be all the way out there."

I kept my eyes on the road as I drove out to Audrey's house. "You can miss some school while you rest up."

"What am I supposed to do there? She doesn't even have TV or internet."

"Maybe catch up on your schoolwork, get ahead if you can."

"How am I supposed to know what we're working on if I'm not there!"

I swerved around a large tree in the road. "You can call your teachers or have Jimmy give you the assignments."

"Do I have to go? Please, will you turn around and take me back home? Please?"

Part of me wanted to let him stay home alone. At fourteen, I'd been almost completely independent. But Nathan was still recovering from a drug overdose. The best thing for him was to take some time off — maybe he'd think about things and get his head straight.

"Dude, I know you want to stay at home. But I need to let Auntie Audrey look after you for now. That's the way it has to be. And help her out, all right? Remember, she's pretty old, she needs help gathering firewood."

A big sigh. "When will you be back?"

"I don't know, maybe a week."

"Okay, I'll do it."

We were quiet for a long time as I drove. After a while, I turned the car radio to the local rez station, which was playing country music.

"Can I ask a question?" Nathan said. "Like, something kind of weird?"

I nodded.

"Well, I've always wondered about this thing, but never really asked. Maybe I didn't want to know."

I wondered where he was going with this.

"You remember when Mom died, you know, in the car accident?"

How could I forget? I nodded again.

"I guess . . . Was she, like, drunk when she crashed?"

I glanced over at him. He looked worried, scared even. I flashed back to that terrible day, the phone call I'd gotten from the tribal police, the drive to pick up Nathan from school, the wreckage of her vehicle at the tow yard, the handwritten Post-it note from Nathan miraculously still stuck on the ruined car's dashboard, proclaiming i love you, mom.

"No, bud. She wasn't drunk, not at all. She was driving to work when the other driver crossed over into her lane. He might have been, but she wasn't."

He looked somber. I wondered if he'd been carrying this weight around since her death.

"I guess I got one more question."

"Yeah?"

"If something happens to you, where do I go?"

It took me a second to understand what he was saying. "Nothing's going to happen to me."

"Leksi, I'm not stupid. I know what you do. Everybody knows, okay? So, if you get, uh, killed, what do I do? I won't have no one, except Auntie Audrey, and she's like ninety years old, she could pass on at any time. What happens to me then?"

"I guess you'd go to Audrey, and if something happened to her, you'd . . ."

My voice trailed off, and I stared at the road, the pine trees and the long grasses rushing past us.

After dropping Nathan off and saying my goodbyes, I drove over to Marie's place. She looked great, wearing jeans, a navy-blue V-neck shirt, and beaded earrings that looked like purple tulips. She had only one suitcase, so there was plenty of room in the hatchback of her car. I'd taken my beat-up gym bag, which was stuffed with a few pairs of jeans, some T-shirts, underwear, socks, and a toothbrush. At the bottom of the bag I'd stashed my gun and plenty of ammo, a knife, and some brass knuckles I'd inherited after a fight many years ago. Made sense to come prepared.

"Hold on a sec," she said, and went back into her house. She came out with a large bowl filled with something I couldn't see.

"What's that?" I asked.

"Dog food," she said, putting the bowl down by the side of the street. "A few dogs come by every so often. I'm worried they won't have anything to eat while I'm gone."

"Oh." I suspected that other animals would get to the food first, but I kept quiet.

Because of the weather, we decided to take the shortest route to Denver, even though it meant plenty of driving down two-lane highways. We'd take Route 18 through our rez and into the Pine Ridge reservation, then swing down into Nebraska and eventually get onto the big highway into Denver. I was glad to skip the longer drive through the Badlands — those strange rocks and formations gave me the creeps.

As we started off, I felt some guilt at leaving Nathan behind at his auntie's house, but also a sense of freedom as we drove away from all the daily rez dramas and problems. And excitement, I had to admit, at being with Marie for the first time in years.

"How's Nathan doing?" she said.

"All right. He's still weak, but it looks like he'll be okay. I dropped him off at Audrey's place. He didn't want to go, said he could stay by himself. I told him, no way."

"You made the right decision," she said. "Too soon for him to be alone. Not to mention, be good for him to spend some time with an elder."

I pushed down a twinge of worry. "He'll keep out of trouble there. I think."

"So, I've been praying on this, and I had an idea," she said. "Maybe he could help out at the center. You know, volunteer, spend some time with the elders or the kids at day care. The community, right? Stay away from the gangs and drugs."

"Not a bad idea," I said. "Problem is getting him motivated. You got any ideas on that, let me know."

"Well, best way to get kids motivated is to teach them about their culture."

Not this again. "He needs to focus on his school stuff," I said. "He graduates from high school, he can go on to college if he wants. Get a real job, a career. But he's got to do the work."

"You're being a little hard on him, don't you think? You weren't exactly a model student."

This was true. I knew when it was time to shut up, so I asked her to put on some music. She hit a few buttons, and the gloomy sound of some punk band filled the car, something I didn't recognize.

"Who's this?" I asked.

"Siouxsie and the Banshees. Their third album. Still the best."

It was a little slow for me, but I'd heard worse. Even though Marie was long past her Goth phase, she'd retained the music of her high school years, to my dismay. When we were together, she'd made me listen to a variety of strange bands and singers — Joy Division, Bauhaus, PJ Harvey, among others. I didn't mind the stuff with strong guitars, but the electronic bands left me cold. When the song ended, I asked if she could put on something with more of a beat. She hit another button, and a twangy country tune started playing.

"When'd you start listening to this?" I asked. "Doesn't sound like your usual stuff."

"Lucinda Williams? I don't know, a few years ago, heard it on the radio. You like it?"

"Not too bad. Got any metal in there?"

A smile and shake of the head.

"Maybe we can trade off songs, you know, alternate music during the ride?" I asked.

"We'll see."

I settled in for a long drive.

Twenty songs later, we passed through the desolation of Whiteclay, Nebraska, just over the state line from South Dakota and the Pine Ridge reservation. Pine Ridge was dry, so a handful of liquor stores had popped up in Whiteclay decades ago. The town — population twelve — existed solely to support the beer barns that sold booze to the citizens of Pine Ridge right across the border. Of course every visiting newspaper reporter and TV camera crew had to take shots of the Indians passed out in town by the stores. The bums with the dirty clothes and the vomit smeared across their faces. Poverty porn. The camera crews never ventured one hundred miles east, where liquor was sold openly on the Rosebud rez. Sure, we had alcoholics — I'd been one of them for a while — but there was far less sensationalism to be filmed or written about on our rez. Instead, every TV anchorperson like Diane Sawyer had to focus on Pine Ridge and the supposedly sad Indians there. There was plenty of sadness on our rez as well, but why not cover the good things that were happening at Rosebud and Pine Ridge? All the rez artists and musicians, the skateboard parks, the new businesses, and the groups revitalizing Lakota language and culture?

I watched the desolate Nebraska landscape pass by, and soon I dozed while Marie drove. After a while, I woke up and looked around.

"Where are we?"

"Just outside Alliance. Still Nebraska. You need to stop?"

It had been a long time since I'd eaten or taken a bathroom break. "Yeah, if there's a gas station I could go for some beef jerky."

She turned the music off abruptly. "You ever seen this? I forgot about it till now."

"What?"

"Look over there."

The sign by the parking lot declared CAR-HENGE and below that, in smaller letters, ENTRANCE. We pulled into the empty parking lot.

"What's all this?" I said, getting out of the car.

"Look behind you."

I blinked a few times. I couldn't believe what I was seeing. About twenty old cars were buried in the ground, front bumper down, standing straight up like monoliths. They were arranged in a large circle, and I realized that they were obviously some sort of bizarre homage to Stonehenge. Not only were the cars buried on their edges, the artist had placed some autos on top of the others as a kind of cap or connector, just like at the real Stonehenge monument. There were a few cars buried on their sides in the center of the circle, serving as the focus of the installation.

"Crazy, huh?" Marie said, looking up at the vehicles, which were all painted a uniform gray. Graffiti scarred some of the cars' bodies. I saw ARCHY SUCKS, I LOVE MEHITABEL, DADDY LONGLEGZ, and in the corner, WANAGI TACAKU. We walked around the circle.

"I'll say. Who did this?"

"I don't know. Some guy with too much time on his hands. I read a little about him last time I was here."

My first impulse was to mock the crazy man who'd created this weird folk art and make cynical comments about the ways of the wasicus. After all, what sort of cracked person spends their free time building giant sculptures at an abandoned farmstead in Nebraska? It must have taken years to create this odd mélange of old autos in the middle of nowhere.

We stood there for a while in the shadow of the statues, and walked around the circle together. As we strolled between the buried vehicles, I began to appreciate the scale of what the artist had attempted. These were full-size American automobiles, buried, welded together, and painted gray, bottom to top. The artist clearly had a vision, a dream of what he wanted to express. A cynical statement about American consumerism? I didn't think so. For some reason, I had the feeling that the creator of this monument was guided by some deeper philosophy. There were no fees for admission, no chain-link fences keeping out gawkers. It seemed to me that the artist had been driven by a goal to convey some deeply held conviction, expressed through the medium of 1970s automobiles.

I wandered off by myself to the edge of the circle. It was quiet at the site, no one there except for Marie and me. I positioned myself at one end of the circle so that I could see the entire thing. In the silence, I began to appreciate the weird majesty of the buried cars. I thought about what it must have felt like, four thousand years ago, to stand before the real monoliths in England and feel connected, truly connected, to the earth, the stars, and the spirits.

I stared at the cars so long that my head began to spin, and it felt like I was drifting off into space, floating in the heavens. Time seemed to stop, and the Lakota phrase mitakuye oyasin — we are all related — came to me, and in that moment I understood what those words meant. I inhabited them, as images, thoughts, and memories arose amidst the old vehicles.

I saw my mother, gone but still with me, my father, who'd died too soon, and my sister, who I'd loved like my own life. Grandparents, aunts, uncles, friends. They appeared before me, all of my relations, my ancestors, Native and white, who'd loved and struggled, hunted and gathered, worked and played; they'd stood on this continent, looking up at these stars and these planets. It was daylight, but I could see the stars now, all of them, surrounding me, lighting the air, their brilliance shining and radiating off the monoliths. And then it was dark, a black-hole sky. But I looked down and saw that the stars — every one of them — were now in my hands, lighting up my veins, my muscles, my bones.

I stood there, alone with my ancestors, and listened to them. Finally I turned away. As I walked back to my life, the words my mother used to say finally came to me.

Wakan Tanka nici un. May the Creator guide you.

10

Marie and I were both quiet after our visit to Carhenge. We rode in silence for a while, then she turned her music back on, the mournful sound of Johnny Cash's version of the song "Hurt" filling the car's cabin. In a few hours, we'd hit the big highway, Interstate 76, which would take us straight down to Denver.

After a few songs, she turned down the stereo and glanced over at me. "So, I've been waiting to talk about this. Seems like now's a good time."

I came out of my trance instantly. "Yeah?"

"Well, I want to know more about the plan."

"The plan?"

"When we find Rick. What are you going to do —"

"I'm going to kick his ass and make him stop selling drugs on the rez."

"Come on, you can't be serious," she said.

"Are you going to kick all their asses? I told you, he's with the Aztec Kingz. Don't know how many of them there are, but you can't take them all on. Not by yourself."

"I'll figure that out when we get there. Not worried about them — they sound like a bunch of kids."

She stared straight ahead. "You don't understand. This is a real gang, not like the wannabes we have on the rez." She paused for a second and looked outside the window. "I remember Rick didn't like going to their place, he wouldn't tell me why. He said they were scary guys."

I'd taken care of plenty of scary people. I wasn't worried about some Denver gangbangers. But my beef was with Rick Crow, not them. "Like I said, I'll handle Rick. Don't know anything about the gang, but I'll teach him a lesson. Catch him alone if I need to. He won't sell dope on the rez anymore, not when I'm done with him."

Marie looked over at me. "Is this revenge for what happened to Nathan, or something else? Maybe this is payback. For how Rick treated you in school."

I thought about what she'd said. I'd been telling myself I wanted to find Rick because of Nathan's overdose. But maybe that wasn't the whole story. It was true, Rick had tormented me in school. He'd been the ringleader of all the bullies who had made life a living hell for me and the other sad sacks at the bottom of the ladder. Maybe it *was* about vengeance. And what was wrong with that? I wasn't the goddamn savior of the Lakota people, but I could make Rick Crow pay for what he'd done to me and the other half-breeds.

Marie continued, "The goal here is to make sure there are no more hard drugs on the rez. That's the purpose, right? You can save the vengeance for another time."

I didn't understand why she was trying to convince me not to kick the shit out of Rick. "One way or the other, I need to stop that asshole," I said. "Got to be honest, I don't see why you're so concerned about him."

She was quiet again, and I watched the road rushing by us through the window. Finally, she spoke. "All right, I'll tell you the story. But just let me say it, okay? No judgment."

I nodded.

"So, I was with Rick for about three months."

My gut tightened.

"It's not like we were serious or anything. I just wanted to have some fun, I don't know, maybe I was rebelling against my parents a little. They always pounded it into us — we had to be smarter than everyone, do well in school, not drink, be good daughters. I guess I wanted to do my own thing for once. And I was still angry at you."

I had to ask. "Did your parents know you were with him?"

"No," she said. "Not at first. But I got into a fight with my mom and told her. To shock her. Let her know I was my own person, and she couldn't tell me what to do."

"What did she say?"

"She didn't know who he was. But she told my dad, and he was furious; he said I needed to stay away from Rick. He threatened to disown me, everything."

Her parents obviously didn't like Marie's choice of boyfriends. I couldn't say I blamed them in Rick's case.

"Like I said, Rick and I weren't together long. I don't think you'd even say we were dating. Mainly we just had drinks at the Depot. But I heard him talk on the phone a lot. You know, I didn't mean to eavesdrop, but I couldn't help listening. So, here's the thing." She stopped for a second. "I knew he was bringing marijuana to the rez. I knew it, okay! And I didn't say anything. I thought, it's just pot, what's the harm?"

She held the steering wheel so tightly I

thought she might break it.

"But it was wrong. I knew it in my heart. The whole point of the Red Road is to get our people away from that stuff: weed, booze, whatever. I should have done something, said something, but I didn't. Didn't do a freaking thing. Who knows how many kids messed up their lives with Rick's weed? Because of me."

"Hey," I said, "pot is not exactly a dangerous drug —"

"That's not the point! People can get addicted to it, and it's illegal in our state. I should have told Rick what he was doing was wrong. But I won't screw up again. This time, I'll get him to do the right thing."

Now I understood why Marie had insisted on coming with me to Denver. She believed that you could reason with thugs, get them to change their ways with words. I knew better.

"I've known Rick a long time," I said quietly, "and I know he'll do what's best for him, no matter who gets hurt, unless someone stops him. By force."

"Make you a deal." She took her hands off the steering wheel to emphasize her words, and I wondered if we were going to crash.

"Yeah?"

"I'll tell you where Rick stays in Denver, but I talk to him first. Alone. Before any violence, okay? Let me see if I can get him to stop bringing that stuff to the rez. I think I can convince him."

"Uh-huh. And how will you do that?"

"There's something Rick really doesn't want people to know, something that'd hurt his reputation if it got out. Don't ask me what it is. I know he'll listen to me." Her face started to tremble a little. "This whole thing is my fault. The heroin, I mean. He started selling pot and then moved on to harder drugs. Shit."

"None of this is your fault, it's on him," I said. "He made his choices. And he needs to pay the price."

"Look, I know you don't like Rick, but there might be some good left in him, okay?"

The image of Nathan with his blue-gray face flew into my mind, and I struggled to keep my temper. "If he's such a good guy, why is he bringing that crap to our people?"

"I don't know," she said. "But if I talk to him, he'll —"

"What makes you think he'll change his ways? Your threat to expose him? He's a punk; he's always cared more about hustling cash than anything else. And what about

114

your safety? I'm not leaving you on your own with him."

"I can take care of myself."

The blood was rushing in my veins. "I'm not letting you alone with that asshole."

"That's the deal," she said coolly. "You agree that I get to talk with him first, then I'll tell you where to find him. If our conversation doesn't work, you try your way."

I pondered my options. There was no chance that I'd let her out of my sight if she met with Rick Crow. But there was no need to tell her that now.

"All right, it's a deal."

The skyline of Denver appeared before us, the Rocky Mountains visible to the west, the skyscrapers presenting a synthetic counterpoint to the jagged peaks in the distance. I'd spent some time in Denver years ago but heard it had massively changed, as young people fled the high costs of living on both coasts in search of something less artificial and more real. And the legal marijuana in Colorado served as a beacon for a different sort of pioneer.

We drove down Colfax Avenue near Broadway, which I remembered as a pleasantly seedy boulevard with an abundance of street people, punk rockers, and vagrants. I was surprised to find that the seediness had been replaced with boutiques, bicycle shops, restaurants with strange names, and beer breweries. Where was the White Spot? I'd nursed many late-night cups of coffee there years ago.

After a few miles, we saw what looked like a budget motel, the Getaway Motor Lodge. The name suited me, as did the prices. The clerk asked whether we wanted a smoking or nonsmoking room. I realized we hadn't discussed the sleeping situation — one room or two. I started to ask Marie what she wanted to do, but she said, "Two rooms, nonsmoking." I guess that was settled.

After I brought my bag inside, I called Tommy back at the rez. He answered right away.

"Yo Virg, where you at?"

"Just got into Denver, we drove through Pine Ridge and Nebraska. Made good time, just stopped once. Hey, you ever seen that Carhenge thing? In Alliance?"

"Yeah, saw that mofo a while back. Some crazy-ass shit. Them cars freaked my head out, I was trippin' for sure. What you think?"

I paused. "We didn't stay long," I said. "It was pretty weird."

"Aight," he said. "So, I hear Marie came along?"

116

"She kind of insisted."

He chuckled. "You two gonna light the campfire again? Damn straight."

"Nothing is gonna happen with us. I'm here to find that asshole Rick Crow."

"I know she moved her shit out of the tipi — Indian divorce — but there ain't no rule that she can't move back in, know what I'm saying?"

"That ended a long time ago," I said. "She's probably going off to medical school in a few months anyway. Look, I'm calling about something else. I need you to go out and check on Nathan at my auntie's place. Make sure he's not doing nothing wrong, see if he needs anything. You do that for me?"

"I'm your boy! Head out there tomorrow, check him out. All my relations, right?"

"Call me if you see anything strange. Thanks, man, I owe you."

"Toksa, homes."

The next morning, Marie and I grabbed some coffee in the motel's lobby and discussed our plan for the day, then she took a break to call her dad. I wondered how much Ben was telling her, whether he was keeping silent about the fact that he was the one who'd hired me. In any case, before we made any contact with Rick Crow, I needed to get as much intel as I could. I decided to check out Martin Angel and the Wellness Relief Center, see what I could find out there. I asked Marie if Rick had ever mentioned it, but she said no. Still, I needed to visit the place, ask some questions.

Marie and I drove down Colfax Avenue to Federal Boulevard, watching the neighborhood change from little shops and breweries to taquerias, Mexican grocery stores, and, surprisingly, Vietnamese restaurants. I figured out from the signs that pho was a Vietnamese soup and apparently very popular here, as there were at least twenty cafés selling it in a six-block area. Pho Noodle House, Pho 77, Pho Chim U'ng. We also saw an increasing number of cannabis dispensaries, judging from the logos and names on the signs: Frosted Leaf, High Altitude, Green Solution. Finally we found the shop we were looking for, tucked back into a little strip mall. Wellness Relief Center. I could certainly use some relief and wouldn't mind some wellness, but I doubted they sold the type I was looking for.

Before we could enter the store, we had to show our IDs at a little window at the front of the shop. Once the clerks verified that we were over twenty-one, they ushered us into

118

the main area of the store. I'd never been in one of these dispensaries before, but of course I'd heard about them. There were three sizable display cases with a variety of marijuana strains in glass jars. On the wall were shelves with a large number of candy bars, cakes, and drinks, all infused, apparently, with cannabis. In a much smaller case, there were a number of waxes and oils in tiny jars.

It was surprising. I'd expected a small dingy space that replicated a seedy drug dealer's apartment; I didn't anticipate this bright and well-designed store. And the smell. The skunky but sweet aroma was overwhelming, like being trapped in a marijuana rain forest. I looked more closely at the containers with the marijuana buds and flowers. Each of them was labeled with a name: Bubba Kush, God Bud, Spyder Bite, Bone Games, Ghost OG, Medicine Man, Juanita la Lagrimosa.

A white guy with long brown dreadlocks wearing a Philadelphia Eagles T-shirt was standing behind the counter.

"Can I help you?" he said.

"No, just looking."

He motioned to the glass cases. "The indicas are over there, the hybrids in the middle, and the sativas right here. Concentrates are back there; some killer shatter just came in, full nug run, no trim. You should check it out."

"Are you the owner?" I asked.

"No, I'm the doctor."

"Doctor?"

"Yes, Dr. Maximilian Pratt, doctor of entheogenics."

Was he kidding? I looked over at Marie to gauge her reaction.

"What's that? Entheo — what?" she asked, her eyebrows arched.

"It's the science of psychedelic therapy and spiritual development," he said haughtily.

Marie and I glanced at each other. I decided to go first. "What's psychedelic therapy?"

"I help people suffering from depression, emotional PTSD, or spiritual ennui by administering microdoses of cannabis, LSD, and MDMA. Once they ingest the medicine, we work on their loop thinking, toxic patterns, and repetitive scenetics."

Marie said, "What are, uh, scenetics?"

"You know, scene transference and visualization. Changing our patterns to embrace our wholeness. You interested in trying it? I've got a sliding scale, three hundred to five hundred for the entire session, or you

120

can pay by the hour. Seventy-five dollars. Get rid of your spiritual toxins and purify yourself."

"We'll pass," I said. "Where'd you learn this stuff?"

"Well," he said, warming up, "I heard about this school in Boulder, the Shamanistic Institute, which offers education in psychedelic medicine, psychosocial therapy, and Native American healing. It's very prestigious, so I signed up. So rewarding to be a healer. It's my life's purpose, you know, to help those less spiritually evolved than myself." He looked at us more closely. "Hey, you guys look Native American. Yeah? You must know all about this stuff! Like peyote and healing circles."

"Actually, no," Marie said, "we have different traditions."

That was diplomatic. But it was time to end this happy horseshit.

"Thanks for all that," I said. "Very interesting. Anyway, does Martin Angel work here?"

"Yes, he's our grower. One of the finest around. A genius, really. Pioneered several CBD strains. Now he's creating a new RSO hemp oil for cancer patients — cures asthma and arthritis, too. Probably change the world."

121

"Know where we can find him?" I asked.

"I'm afraid that's confidential."

"Does he have a phone number I can call? Email, anything?"

"We don't give out that information, sorry." He turned away from us.

"One more question," I said, rapping my knuckles on the counter. "You ever see a guy in here called Rick Crow? About six feet tall, long black hair? Indian guy?"

"I believe you mean *Native American*. And no, I've not seen that gentleman here. But all our patient contacts are private, of course. We are a therapeutic facility and take medical confidentiality very seriously."

"All right," I said, taking one last look at the doctor and his medicines. "Good luck with the healing."

Our visit to the Wellness Relief Center had yielded no concrete information about Rick Crow, so our next move was to confront him on his own turf. Turf that Marie claimed to know about.

"All right," I said, "let's hear it. Where's this place that Rick hangs out? I'll keep my promise; you can talk to him first if it looks safe."

She put on her seat belt, then looked at her phone.

"I'll be fine. All right, what I know is that the gang runs a bar in Denver called Los Primos. If he's here, he'll be at that bar."

Los Primos. Time to do some homework.

I used Marie's smart phone and found out that the bar was located on the north side of Denver, in a neighborhood called Swansea/ Elyria. The name sounded fancy, but a little internet searching revealed that the neighborhood was one of Denver's poorest, almost completely Latino, but was starting to change as wealthier people in search of cheap and quirky housing began driving out the original inhabitants. The newspaper article I found said that the earliest residents were openly hostile to the gentrifiers, but that there was little they could do against the tide of the neighborhood settlers. Sounded familiar.

We drove down Interstate 70 to the area. A giant dog-food factory stood imposingly next to the highway viaduct while railroad tracks ran right by some of the tiny houses. It was hard to see why this neighborhood was becoming overrun by urban colonizers. After a few wrong turns, we found the bar, which was attached to a little market and a liquor store. About twenty vehicles were parked outside, mainly small pickup trucks and older-model American cars. Just to be safe, I parked a few blocks away. I hadn't told Marie, but I'd stuck my folding karambit Spyder knife in my back pocket and stowed my Glock in the hatchback of her car. The Spyder had a small curved blade that could be used to gut an enemy in close-quarters combat. I didn't think I'd need it, but it couldn't hurt to bring it along.

"Okay," I said, "let's see if he's there. You go in first, stick your head in. I'll stay by the windows where I can watch. You know what you're gonna say to him?"

"Yeah," she said. "I'll tell him what's happening back home with the drugs, especially the kids. I've got a few other things I'll say if I need to. Just stay out of sight, okay?"

"All right, but I'm coming in if he makes a move."

"I can handle myself, big guy. Remember back in school? I punched Theresa Bad Milk once."

"What? I never heard about that."

"She was making fun of some kid. You know, the one who couldn't stop playing with himself in class. Can't remember his name."

"Potato Juice! Shit, I forgot about him. Didn't you put canned salmon in her gas

124

tank, too? I remember people talking about that."

"She deserved it."

I positioned myself outside in front of the bar. There were a few grimy windows, but I could see inside. About ten people were sitting at the counter, maybe more to the side. I peered in, trying to see if Rick was one of them, but all I could see were the backs of the customers, a variety of leather jackets and checkered flannel shirts.

Marie went in while I pretended to make a call on my phone. All of a sudden I wished I'd brought the gun rather than leaving it in the car. Too late now. I spotted her in the bar, walking around the front counter, and then she went out of my field of vision. I moved over a bit, trying to get a different angle, but couldn't see her. A few minutes passed. I wondered if she'd found Rick, and what she might be saying to him.

I waited a few more minutes, then walked over to a different window and looked inside. No Marie, no Rick. I'd promised that I'd let her talk to Rick without interfering, but I needed to keep an eye on them. I decided I'd give it a thirty count, then go in.

I hit twenty-nine, and readied myself to

go inside and confront Rick and the gang. Just as I put my hand on the door, it opened.

"He's not there," Marie said. She looked frustrated.

"You sure?"

"Yeah. Checked the whole place, front to back. Even stuck my head in the men's bathroom. Bad idea." She shook her head.

"All right, let's get out of here."

"Wait," she said. "Let's go back in, see if anyone knows where he is."

"You think that's smart?"

"Come on, tough guy. Can't hurt to have a drink."

I stood there at the front door for a moment, then pushed it open.

My eyes adjusted to the darkness inside the bar, and I looked around. A solitary pool table, a battered Formica bar, and a dozen men — all Latino — staring at me.

The bartender sauntered over to us. He looked to be about forty — slender with a small goatee on his face. He wore a backward baseball cap with sunglasses on top, and I noticed the tattoo on his arm, in stylized cursive letters: SUR 13. On the other arm was a crude drawing of an Aztec warrior holding a woman. The Aztec Kingz. We were in the right place.

"Help you?" he said, not smiling.

"Bud Light for her, a Coke for me."

Without being too obvious, I sneaked a glance around the bar. A few people were still watching us, but the attention our arrival had brought was dying down. We sipped our drinks and tried to look like we fit in. I stared at a college football game playing above the bar. Marie took out her phone.

After a few minutes, a man wearing a faded orange Denver Broncos shirt turned to us. Well, turned to Marie. In his inebriated state, I don't think he even noticed me. The stench of hard liquor radiated from him.

"You from Globeville?" he said to her.

I could see her effort to mask her distaste. "No, we're not from around here."

"Commerce City? I got a cousin over there, lives by the oil refinery. Stinks like shit. Not him, the refinery. Well, he stinks like shit, too."

"We're from South Dakota. Just visiting," she said.

"You a chola? You got pretty hair," he said. "But the eyebrows ain't right. You look like a tough girl. Chido." He motioned to the bartender for another drink. "You want to do a shot? You ever had a Mexican Killer?

Tequila and peach schnapps. Kick your ass."

"No, thank you," Marie said.

"Su pérdida. Los niños y los borrachos siempre dicen la verdad."

This guy definitely spent a lot of time in this bar, so I reached over and tapped him on the shoulder. "Hey, we're looking for a friend of ours. Tall guy, long black hair, Indian dude. You know, Native American. Comes around here every so often. Name of Rick Crow. You see him lately?"

The drunk guy was losing interest in us. "No, ain't seen nobody like that."

There didn't seem to be any point in hanging around Los Primos. The bartender hadn't shown any sign of friendliness, and the other customers looked equally disagreeable. I signaled to Marie with a little motion of my head. We finished our drinks and left.

We started walking back to the car. I was disappointed we hadn't gained even a shred of info as to where Rick might be. Marie had been pretty confident we could find him at the bar, and I didn't know our next move.

All of a sudden, I heard footsteps coming behind us. Fast. I looked around and saw a man about a block away running toward us.

"Stop!" the guy yelled. I checked to see if there was someone else he might be chasing. No, he was after us, and from the speed he was going, it didn't look like he wished us well. I turned around to see what the possibilities were in the event of a confrontation, which seemed imminent. We were in an industrial area with no cover available. I calculated whether we could make it to the car — and my gun — before the guy caught up. Not enough time. There was only one option.

"Get behind that dumpster!" I barked at Marie. "Hurry!"

"I will not," she said, "it's filthy over there —"

"Hide behind it now, or I'll throw you in!"

She scurried over to the large trash container. I ducked around the side of the building in the alley.

"Hey!" the man yelled, looking down the alley for me. I grabbed him from behind, trying to pin his arms. He broke my hold and faced me. I feinted a jab with my left hand. He went for it, opening up his side. I used the opening to land a hard blow to his face. He made some garbled sounds as he bent over and tried to shake off my punch.

I used that split second to assess him. Latino guy, a little older, big dude, short hair. Dressed in black jeans and flannel shirt. Standard gang wear. Couldn't see any weapons, but that didn't mean anything. I had to get him down before anyone else joined in to help.

I moved behind so I could force him down. Suddenly the world went gray as he hit me with a hard uppercut to my jaw. Hadn't seen that coming. I reeled backward and tried to stay up, attempting to clear my head.

"Asshole!" Marie screamed at the guy, and I tried to place where she was. My vision was blurry and hazy, but I saw her start to pound the guy on his back.

This was bad. The guy turned his attention to her, and that bought me another moment. There was only one thing to do. The knife.

I pulled it out of my pocket and tried to open it. Because of its design, the Spyder was a bitch to get open, especially when you were half-unconscious. I saw the guy struggle with Marie and tried to keep my focus on unlocking the weapon.

Finally. I got the thing open, its curved blade shimmering like a deadly talon. It was super sharp, with a serrated hawkbill edge that would carve up flesh, tendons, muscles. If the guy wouldn't back off, I'd do what I had to.

I thrust the knife forward, only to look up

and see a handgun pointed straight at my chest.

11

"Drop the knife. Now."

The gun remained pointed at me. I dropped the knife. He kicked it away.

"Get on the ground! Facedown. Put your hands behind your head."

I complied.

"Do you have any other weapons?" he asked.

It was beginning to dawn on me. "Are you a police officer?"

"Do you have any concealed weapons?" he asked again.

"No, just the knife. Look, I didn't know you were —"

"Just be quiet and keep your hands on your head." Then he turned to Marie, who was now standing back by the trash dumpster, her hands up in front of her. "Do you have any weapons?"

"No. Look, we're just —"

"Get down on your knees," he said to her.

"Put your hands on your head and keep them there." He put the gun back in his pocket and patted my legs, torso, and arms. Then he moved to Marie and did a quick pat-down on her. He seemed to relax a bit after he determined that we didn't have any guns on us.

"Both of you can sit up, but keep your hands where I can see them."

"Are you going to put handcuffs on us?" Marie said.

"No. Just want to ask a few questions." He turned his attention to me. "Why'd you hit me? Did somebody send you?"

"You're a police officer, right?" I said. He didn't say anything. "Look, we didn't know you're a cop, we thought someone from the bar was coming after us. If you'd identified yourself, we —"

"What are you doing here?" he asked. "Why are you asking for Rick Crow?"

"You know him?" I said.

Before he could respond, Marie said, "We're from the Rosebud Indian Reservation. In South Dakota. We're looking for Rick because he might be bringing drugs to our community. We just want to speak to him, find out what's happening."

I looked over at Marie, trying to signal her that we should be cautious and not say

133

too much until we knew more about what was going on. But, to my surprise, the guy pulled out a scrap of paper from his pocket and a pen and started writing.

"We need to talk," he said, "about Rick Crow. But not here. Meet me there in two hours."

I looked down at the paper. "Taco Mex, Colfax and Joliet," it read.

Taco Mex turned out to be a little Mexican restaurant in a different part of the city, about an hour away from where we were. We had some time, so we looked at the menu. Tacos, no surprise there, but with fillings I hadn't heard of. Buche, tripas, lengua, cabeza. Pork stomach, intestine, beef tongue, cow head. Anticuchos de corazón. Skewered beef heart.

My own heart had been skewered enough, so I tried some cow-head tacos. Greasy, but tender. I offered Marie a bite, but she declined with a grimace.

I glanced over at her. She was eating her rice and bean tacos after carefully removing all of the chili peppers and placing them on a napkin. That didn't surprise me; she'd always had some strange eating habits, even though she loved to cook. She wouldn't eat pork, because she claimed that pigs were as

134

intelligent as humans, if not more so. She detested brussels sprouts, said they smelled like feet, but was crazy about roasted carrots. I remembered there'd been a period in elementary when she would only eat chocolate pudding and cold french fries, which she would mix together in a large bowl and eat with a wooden spoon. The other kids had teased her relentlessly about that, but she was used to it by then.

The mocking and bullying she'd endured had toughened Marie, and she became the kid who stood up for others. I guess her time as a pariah had made her sensitive to the plight of the tormented. I fell in love with her, as much as an eleven-year-old can, when she defended me one day.

I'd been walking home from school when the mean kids pressed their advantage — the fate I'd feared most then. A gang of cruel girls decided to taunt me mercilessly, calling me iyeska, insulting my family and our poverty, which was extreme even for the rez. I remember looking down at the ground during this jeremiad, trying to disappear into an anthill, when Marie wandered by. She immediately saw what was going on and dove into action. She teased one of the bullies about a birthmark on her face, another one's ugly shoes, and a third's outdated hairstyle. The mean girls were absolutely overwhelmed and quickly fled.

You'd think I would have been grateful to Marie and at least expressed my thanks, but instead I projected my anger and humiliation onto her and left without saying a word. After that, I avoided her, just as I tried to elude my own shame and sorrow.

Of course I saw Marie around in high school — she was the smart girl with the weird clothes, half Osage, the one putting up posters for PETA and the World Wildlife Fund. I, on the other hand, focused more on drinking beer, lifting weights, and listening to heavy metal music, even paying forty bucks for a Slayer tattoo on my shoulder. Marie's father was elected to the tribal council during this time, which put even more pressure on her. Reservation politics, then and now, are a cesspool of nepotism and favoritism, and grudges and feuds run deep. Marie tried to stay out of the fray, but she would be drawn in to disputes and clashes, even though none of it was her doing.

I lost track of her after high school, although I'd see her in passing at the grocery store or gas station. As for me, I wandered through years of crappy jobs in Mission, Valentine, and Rapid City. Because of drinking and general fucking up, I was fired from jobs in construction, roofing, auto repair, and dishwashing. I had some girlfriends, but nothing serious. One girl said she loved me, but then she ran off with a dude from Pine Ridge.

My career as a hired thug began when Lonnie, one of my high school buddies, told me about his sister, Angela. She'd been living with her boyfriend in Norris and was five months pregnant. The boyfriend had gotten blackout drunk and got it into his head that the father of the baby was another man. So he beat the crap out of her, trying to end the pregnancy. He succeeded. She miscarried the next day but kept quiet about it. Lonnie found out and called the tribal police. They referred the case to the feds, who didn't even bother to interview Angela in person. Instead, they just did a phone call and declined to prosecute, calling it a standard spousal abuse case, not worth their time. Two months later Angela killed herself and her cat, leaving nothing living in the tiny house. She'd wrapped the dead cat up in a little star quilt that had been intended for their baby.

Lonnie told me this story a few months after it happened. He was a pretty stoic guy but broke down during our conversation. I

137

felt something twist inside myself like a razor blade, and I told Lonnie that I'd take care of the boyfriend, whose name was Rulon. I tracked him down in Two Strike, already shacked up with another woman. After I finished with him, he wasn't able to make a fist or turn a doorknob again, and I hoped the asshole would think about Angela and their baby every time he had to ask for help. Lonnie tried to give me some money for what I'd done, but I wouldn't take it.

Word got around after a while, and others began to approach me, asking to help them get some justice. Sometimes they called it revenge, but I suppose that depended on your point of view. At first I only took a few jobs, ones where I was really angry over the circumstances, like the case where a guy forced his young niece to perform sex acts on him. But over time I became less picky, and I took almost any job. I didn't think too much about it — after all, if the cops wouldn't do anything, what was wrong with a private enforcer taking action?

Yeah, I liked the fighting. Ambushing some asshole, pounding the crap out of him, teaching him a lesson — I never felt so alive as when I was administering some righteousness. When I started fighting, I'd lose myself, enter a zone where I stopped thinking. Often I'd forget who it was I was pounding and begin to imagine I was back in junior high school. It was like being in a dream, except that the fighting began to feel like my real life, and everything else felt hollow, fake. One time I was hired to beat a guy who'd broken his girlfriend's arm, so I broke his, then made him lick the filthy public toilet at the convenience store until he vomited and passed out. I knew I had a problem, but there was no support group for hired vigilantes.

Marie never liked the way I made my money, and it became an issue in our relationship over time. She and I had met again some years after high school, and we had our first adult conversation at the Derby, an Indian bar in Valentine, Nebraska. Natives knew to stay out of the other three taverns in town, unless you were looking for a fight with a group of drunken white dudes.

I'd been drinking some Bud Lights, waiting for the pool table to open up, and she'd sat down next to me. I looked at her in surprise and we started a conversation, a conversation that continued for the next few years, until I said the one thing that Marie couldn't forgive. The words I wanted to take back more than anything.

"Let's move over here."

Startled, I looked up from my tacos and my memories and saw the guy I'd nearly knifed just two hours earlier, and who might have shot me. The cop dressed like a gang member.

We moved to a table outside on the patio, away from the other customers.

"Thanks for driving out here." He grabbed a Jarritos coconut soda from the counter and sat down. "All right, tell me what you know about Rick Crow. You two from the same area as him?"

"We are," I said. "So what's going on? He under investigation?"

"Let me ask the questions," he said. "You said something about drugs on the reservation. Tell me the details."

Marie and I looked at each other. She shook her head a little.

"Can we ask who you are, who you work for?" she said.

"Yeah, sure. I'm Dennis, DPD," he said. "We're investigating some individuals in the area." He reached into his pocket and pulled out a card. I couldn't make out the fine print, but I think the word *police* was on there.

"Uh, don't you have to show us your badge?" Marie asked.

He smiled. "No badge, just this. All right,

140

let's hear about the drugs."

I glanced over at Marie. She gave a little shrug with her eyebrows.

"Well, some guys brought heroin to the reservation last week," I said. "They gave some to my nephew. He took it and overdosed, nearly died. I heard Rick might be part of that."

Now he looked more interested. "What type of heroin was it?"

"What do you mean?"

"Black tar, white powder, brown powder."

"Don't know."

"Do you know when they started selling? On the reservation?"

"Not sure. Nathan — my nephew — said they gave it to him for free, he didn't pay for it. Maybe that's just BS, though; he's only a kid."

"You say they gave it to him?"

I nodded.

He took a drink of his coconut soda. "How old is your nephew?"

"Fourteen."

"So the transaction, it occurred on reservation land, you're sure?"

"Yeah," I said. "At the high school. That's what Nathan told me."

He took out a small notepad from his pocket and started writing. "I'll need to speak to your nephew, get a statement."

"Sorry," I said, "but why does he need to talk to you? I just told you everything."

"Part of an ongoing investigation. Would he be available to speak to me on the phone?"

"No. He wouldn't." I got up and threw my trash away.

"Look," he said. "I've been tracking these mutts for a while. I know they're starting to move their product to reservations, but couldn't confirm it. Until now. Been dealing with a boatload of jurisdictional bullshit, too. DEA, FBI, they all claim authority. Your nephew gives me a statement, I can start moving against these guys, get there first. Understand?"

I grabbed a Mexican soda — tamarind flavor — and opened it up. "Would anyone see his statement — I mean, would his name be protected?"

Dennis shook his head. "No one will see it except for law enforcement."

"Hold on," Marie said. "We've been working with you. But you need to tell us what's happening on the rez. With the drugs. Give us some background, maybe we can help you more."

He was quiet for a moment. "Let me see your IDs."

We handed him our driver's licenses, and he walked off to his car.

"You think I should give him Nathan's info?" I asked Marie, quietly. "Don't know if that's smart."

She shrugged. "Let's hear what he has to say. I want to know more about Rick, what he's supposedly doing."

Supposedly. From the cop's interest in him, it looked like Rick was in pretty deep. But it made sense to get as much information as possible.

The cop came back to the table and returned our IDs to us. "Okay, everything checks out." He paused. "I can't tell you anything that's part of the investigation, but I can give you the big picture — what's already out there. Let me get some water first." He got up from the table and returned with a plastic cup. "Okay, bear with me, I got to go back a little bit. You hear this, you'll understand why we'll need your nephew to cooperate."

I nodded.

"How much do you know about opioids?"

"You mean heroin?" I said.

"Well, heroin is just part of it. Opioids — pain pills — are the biggest drug problem we've ever had. And created by the big pharma companies, pretty much."

143

"Of course," Marie said. "Overprescription. Not exactly a new thing."

He took a gulp of his water. "Sort of. Few decades ago, the drug companies started selling pain pills — like OxyContin — and created a massive marketing program. Bad back? Here's a scrip for oxys. Chronic pain? Take more oxys. Now you got a generation hooked on pills. Then the damn pill mills popped up — so you got even more addicts out in the boonies."

Marie said, "Yeah, but the government shut down those clinics. That's what I —"

"Not exactly," he said. "Feds wised up and slapped the drug companies with massive fines, so they reformulated the pills. Can't be crushed up and abused as easily. The pills are still around, but tougher to get and way more expensive. So what do the addicts do? Start taking heroin — same drug, different form."

Marie looked at Dennis intently, like she wanted to argue with him. I wondered if Dennis smoked and if I could get a cig.

"You got an increasing demand for the stuff," he continued. "But the supply hadn't kept up. So some Mexican cartels start to focus on heroin instead of weed. But it's not the white powder dope — it's black tar, looks and feels like a Tootsie Roll. Easier to make and smuggle. Here's the kicker: it's ten times more potent than powder. We're seeing black tar that's seventy-five percent pure. China White heroin back in the day was maybe five percent."

"Holy shit," I muttered. Marie kept quiet.

"It gets worse. One of the cartels developed a new distribution system — a better method to get the drugs to the customers. They started using a decentralized structure. More efficient, more profitable."

"What do you mean, decentralized?" I asked.

"They sell to the customers themselves — cut out the middleman. They set up dozens of small cells with drivers and a phone operator. Customer calls the mobile phone and gives his location, operator calls a driver who meets the customer in the parking lot of a burger joint. Buyer hands over his cash and gets a dope balloon. Just like ordering a pizza. In the old days, you had to go to the drug dealers, now they come to you. What's more, they run specials, like every tenth balloon free, and they hand out samples like crazy, trying to create new customers."

I remembered what Nathan had told me about getting the heroin for free. I'd doubted him, because I couldn't believe someone would give away drugs.

Dennis drank the rest of his water and crumpled the plastic cup. "They're like the Domino's Pizza of dope. And they're careful. They drive regular cars, nothing fancy, and switch drivers a lot. So you got a perfect storm: pill addicts looking for a fix, superpotent heroin, new distribution scheme. Now all the cartels are getting in on the action. They're starting to compete with each other and looking for new markets. You can guess what their next target is."

"But why reservations?" said Marie. "It's not like we have a large population. Seems like they'd go somewhere with more people."

"Rest of the market is saturated, at least out west. And it makes sense to expand to the reservations — lack of police presence. What are there, like fifty tribal police out where you guys are?"

"Not even that many," I said.

"Problem is, the cartel doesn't have people on the reservations," he said. "They'll stand out if they try to sell there themselves. So they're starting to recruit local Native Americans for their cells — using gangs here in Denver who have connections out there."

"Rick Crow," I said.

"I can't say anything about that. What I will say is, if we catch the reservation guys,

146

the salespeople, we might get 'em to roll on the bosses. At least slow them down. These skells are like rats — they find a way to get in and shit all over everything."

I went inside and got some water while I thought about what Dennis had said.

"All right, that's the background," Dennis said when I returned. "Let me ask again: You're sure the transaction with your nephew went down on school grounds?"

"Yeah, he said they gave him the stuff by the football field," I said. "Why does that matter?"

"Federal law states that selling narcotics within one thousand feet of a school brings a massive punishment. These guys are too smart to do that here. But if we caught 'em selling at the school on your reservation, might be able to force them to testify in exchange for a plea."

I saw where this was going and didn't like it.

"I'll need to talk to your nephew," he said. "We'll get him to set up a buy, put a wire on him. He'll get more stuff from these guys. At his school."

Dennis tried to sell me on the plan. He said that being a confidential informant — or CI, as he put it — was safe, that they never send CIs into dangerous situations, and that they're observed and protected during the buy. He said the wire was very small, not as large as it looks on TV, and they could even use a cell phone if necessary. Then he tried to tell me that using Nathan was the best way to get at these guys, since he already knew the dealers. They'd trust him for another sale before they figured out to sell the drugs away from the school.

He said it was crucial to shut down these heroin pushers, that we'd be saving the lives of innocent people. He made it sound like the future of the rez, if not the nation itself, depended on my decision to wire Nathan up. Another positive, he said, was that getting rid of the drugs on the rez would prevent him from being tempted to use again.

"So what do you think?" Dennis said. "I can have my people out there by next week. We can talk to — Nathan, right? — get him set up, have this thing wrapped up pronto. It's a win-win. We stop these guys from selling heroin on your turf. And no more kids using this shit, including your nephew."

I pondered the offer. Contemplated it. For maybe a millisecond or two.

Fuck that.

"I can't see letting him do this," I said to

Dennis. "Don't want him involved."

There was no way I'd let Nathan buy more drugs. I'd almost lost him once, and he needed to stay as far away from these assholes as possible. Not to mention that he'd be labeled a rat if word ever got out. Nobody liked a snitch, but Indians especially hated the feds, who'd never shown much interest in arresting criminals on the rez. Easier just to keep him out of the whole thing and handle it myself.

"Take my card," Dennis said. "Think it over. Talk with your boy. You know, I didn't mention that we can sometimes pay CIs. Cash money. But I'll need to hear from you fairly soon. That's how this works. If you want to do the right thing."

The right thing. I'd lost sight of that a long time ago.

12

We left the Mexican restaurant, a litter of empty soda bottles on our table. By now, it was getting dark, and the lights of the bars and restaurants flickered as we drove west on Colfax Avenue back to the motel. I saw a drunken man stumbling down the sidewalk wearing a T-shirt that proclaimed EMPTY SEATS IN CHURCH, MORE ROOM IN HEAVEN FOR ME!

"What do you think?" Marie said. She'd been pretty quiet during Dennis's tirade.

"He's crazy if he thinks I'd let Nathan wear a wire. No fucking way. Too dangerous."

"But he said Nathan would be safe, they'd be watching him the whole time."

I looked over at her. "You're not suggesting I agree to this?"

"Well, he said this was the best way to stop the cartels — get at the bosses or whatever. They're the bad guys. Maybe Rick could stay out of it."

Again she was trying to protect Rick Crow. Jealousy blossomed in my gut like a bout of food poisoning. I said calmly, "Why is it so important to keep Rick out of it? If he's working with them, he should go to jail too."

"I'm just saying the important thing is to keep the drugs off the rez. Look, you know I'd never want Nathan to be in danger. But what happens if no one stops those guys? Maybe they keep selling, and he gets some of that stuff again."

I glanced over at her and saw that her arms were folded across her chest, so that the top of her shirt puffed out. "Yeah, but I'm sure the cops can find somebody else to wire up. Doesn't have to be him."

"Maybe," she said. "But it sounds like it's not that easy to arrange these, uh, stings, or whatever they're called. If it were, they'd have already shut them down."

"Don't know about that. I just know Nathan has been through enough. They can find another rat."

"Rat? How is someone a rat if they're doing a good thing? In my world, that person is a hero. You think Crazy Horse would be afraid to go after bad guys?"

"I don't know what Crazy Horse would

151

do," I said. "Just know I'll fight my own battles."

It was funny that Marie — the sometimes-pacifist — was invoking Crazy Horse, the Lakota who vowed to fight the white men until his last breath.

"Nathan won't wear a wire. He's no snitch. That's my decision — and it's final."

We rode in silence back to the motel.

The next morning, Marie was still mad at me. Maybe I'd been too stubborn, not willing to consider her views, but it was impossible for me to be neutral when it came to Nathan's safety. Yes, he was my nephew, not my son, but Indians never made that distinction. Nieces, nephews, cousins — these were all viewed as family by Natives, not as lesser kin that could be ignored. Of course this sometimes led to some titanic battles between family members. I knew quite a few tiospaye on the rez where warring relations had refused to speak to each other for decades.

I waited for Marie to finish a phone call to her father. When she was done, we both needed caffeine, so we drove on Colfax Avenue until we found a place called La Capulina, which looked like a coffeehouse but might have been a bicycle repair shop, given that there were about fifteen bikes parked outside, the old-fashioned kind that didn't have gears or brakes. Most of them had wicker baskets on the handlebars. These bicycles were cute, but would last about ten minutes on the pitted and scarred roads of the rez.

Inside, the coffeehouse resembled an abandoned factory, with bare metal walls and jagged fixtures, but strangely, a variety of objects were haphazardly scattered around the room: antique wheelchairs, battered birdcages, hand-stitched pillows, and dozens of old cameras — Polaroids, Honeywells, many I didn't recognize. Behind the counter was a man in his mid-twenties with a full brown beard and long waxed mustache. He was dressed in old-fashioned mining garb, as if he'd just stepped out of a quarry in 1850s Appalachia, minus the dirt and grime. He said something to me, but it was hard to hear over the music playing in the background, which sounded like a car's transmission seizing up. I moved closer to the counter, where it was marginally quieter.

"I said, what can I start for you?"

"Two large coffees, one black and one cream," I replied.

"Today we're brewing La Mestiza. These are washed beans from Guatemala, the terroir is Southern Huila, and the varietal is Caturra. If you'd like to read the cupping notes, I have them right here. It's a light and clean body with the aroma of caramel popcorn and brown sugar. And I'm sorry, we don't serve any milks with our coffee. We want you to experience the flavor and bouquet of the coffee, not of some hormone-infested animal product."

"Uh, okay, fine."

We waited about ten minutes for him to make the coffee, which involved grinding some coffee beans and setting up an oddly shaped funnel over a jug and then pouring one molecule at a time of boiling water into the funnel. The whole thing reminded me of chemistry class, nothing like the Indian brewing process of tossing some grounds into a coffeepot over a fire. I have to say, the coffee was pretty good, maybe even exceptional, nothing like the java they served at Big Bat's in Pine Ridge. This was no small compliment, as Big Bat's coffee was widely considered to be the best in a hundred miles. Of course, the fancy coffee had better be good, given that each cup cost roughly the price of a pound of Folger's.

We took our coffees to the patio, being careful not to spill a single expensive drop.

"Hey," Marie said, "I'm sorry if I gave you

a hard time about Nathan. I just want the best — for him and the rez. But it's your decision."

I was relieved that Marie'd had a change of heart. Yesterday I'd wondered if she'd be so willing to send a young kid into a drug buy if it was her own child. But maybe that was unkind.

"Thanks," I said. "You know I want those assholes behind bars, too."

"I have an idea," she said. "Let's do something fun tonight, take a little break. I don't know, go out to dinner or whatever. I have a few dollars."

This morning was getting better.

"That sounds good. Where do you want to go? Get some steaks?"

She smiled. "I don't know, maybe something kind of touristy? What is Denver known for?"

"I don't know," I said, "it's changed a lot since I was here last."

"Let me ask someone." She turned to the small table next to ours. There were three white women and two strollers parked there. "So sorry to disturb you, but we're not from here. Could we ask you a question?"

The woman sitting closest to our table looked us over. She was wearing an expensive-looking camping jacket. I felt out of place in my old denim jacket and boots.

"Sure, what's up?" she said.

"We want to do something fun in Denver," Marie said, "go someplace special or see something unique to Colorado. Maybe a local restaurant? Any ideas?"

The women conferred. I tried to listen in, but it was hard to make out what they were saying because of their accents. They looked to be about thirty or forty years old, but their voices were high and nasal, like twelve-year-old girls with a cold. They sounded like a gaggle of ducks quacking. The first woman turned back to us while the other two continued their discussion.

"Do you mind me asking, where are you from?" she said in a friendly way.

"Not at all," said Marie. "We're from South Dakota, just visiting for a few days."

"Are you, ah, Native Americans?"

"Yes, we're Sioux, from the Rosebud Reservation."

I observed that Marie had code-switched, referring to our people as Sioux so as not to confuse the women. The French word *sioux* meant "little snakes," and was rarely used by Lakota people. The other two women turned back to us, having completed their discussion of Denver restaurants.

"We have the perfect spot for you! It's

been here forever, it's kitschy and fun. Everybody goes there at least once; it's like a restaurant and theme park. The food is meh, but you will have a great time, we promise! It's called Casa Bonita."

As promised, Casa Bonita was a weird blend of amusement park and Mexican food joint. The place was huge, with a giant pink bell tower standing in the middle of a parking lot. Inside, we were amazed to discover a thirty-foot-high waterfall and pool, cliff divers, strolling mariachi bands, puppet shows, and even a pirate cave. The hostess took pity on us and seated us away from the families with shrieking children. We were led up a series of stairs to a table near the top of the waterfall. The table was surrounded by fake palm trees and tiki torches, giving us some privacy and a close view of the divers. They appeared to be college kids, dressed up as bandits, pirates, and, yup, Indians. The divers would shout out the lines of their skits, which all seemed to revolve around good guys being chased by villains, before diving into the pool below. I was relieved to see that the bad guy was not a faux Indian but a person dressed up in a gorilla suit. After the divers made their jumps, the kids below us screamed their appreciation, and it was easy to get in the spirit of the place.

Our food came, and it was pretty far from the street tacos I'd had at Taco Mex. This was gringo fare masquerading as Mexican food, like a white man wearing a sombrero. Bland tacos, tasteless enchiladas, and mild refried beans. Three Coronas for Marie, a Coke for me. I'll admit that the desserts were pretty good. At first I thought they'd brought us frybread, which surprised me, but the waiter told me these were sopapillas, or "little pillows" in English. Sweet fried dough, topped with powdered sugar and dipped in honey. They were lighter than Indian frybread, and, it pained me to admit, much better.

After our plates were cleared, we strolled around the place. We visited the run-down arcade, where we played Skee-Ball and ancient video games. Then we wandered through Black Bart's Pirate Cave, a sort of haunted house with battered skeletons, treasure chests, and weathered old skulls, trying not to step in the random pools of liquid left by overenthusiastic children.

"What do you think of this place?" I asked.

"I love it." Her eyes gleamed like the polished gems we'd held in the gift shop. "If I had a child, I'd take her here every week."

I wondered what it would be like to have

a child with Marie. Her smarts, my tough-ness. A little son. Maybe a daughter? I looked over at Marie and wondered if she was thinking the same thing I was. The music drifted through the fake palm trees, and it was easy to imagine that we were really in Mexico at some beach resort.

I turned to Marie. She moved closer, wait-ing for me. I started to embrace her, but I hesitated. I'd dreamed of this, but in an instant I also remembered the pain and depression I'd felt when she left me. The heartbreak had been so overwhelming, I wasn't sure I'd ever recover. For months, I visited that grief every evening. I'd buy a twelve-pack of beer and play some gloomy songs. It was strange because, after a while, I'd started to look forward to those late-night sadness sessions — just my music, my beer, and my grief. It had become a part of my life, my new routine. The nightlands.

I'd finally gotten past that sorrow — and the booze — and carved out a good space for Nathan and myself. Things weren't perfect, but I was content with the life we had. What would happen if I started things up again with Marie? I didn't want the complications and the problems, not when I'd finally gotten some steadiness back in my life. It had been tough to get over Ma-

159

rie, but I'd made it through.

But then I smelled Marie's perfume. Not just her perfume, but the scent of Marie herself.

It hit me right in the chest, and it seemed that I sensed it with every cell in my body. It was overwhelming, the aroma of her, and I felt desire travel throughout my body. My resolve slipping, I tried to tell myself this was a mistake, that I should leave things as they stood. But, that scent.

I dove off the cliff.

13

The next morning, I awoke in Marie's room next to her, my body positioned at the far side of the mattress, taking up as little space as possible. In the quiet of the morning, I reflected on the previous night. Maybe we'd made a mistake, moved too soon. She began to stir. Her eyes opened, and she looked at me in surprise. "Oh shit," she said, and ran into the bathroom.

What the fuck? I'd assumed she'd wake up with some affection and warmth, maybe even desire. Had I done something wrong? We'd kissed at the restaurant, awkwardly at first, then with confidence as we began to remember each other. I'd driven back — way too fast — to the motel, where we continued where we'd left off. The lovemaking had felt effortless. We already knew each other, and there was none of the discovery process necessary with a new partner.

I wondered if I should hightail it back to

my room, avoid any further weirdness. But before I had a chance to make a decision, the door opened and she came out. She'd rearranged her hair and was wearing one of the scratchy white motel bathrobes.

"Hey," she said, "sorry I dashed out of here like that. I needed a moment to catch up. You know, process a little. Also, my hair looked like the Wicked Witch."

"I get it," I said, relief flowing through my body. "It just happened, not like we planned it or anything."

She sat on the bed and took my hand. "I don't know, maybe we can take it one step at a time; what do you think?"

It sounded good. In fact, that had been my guiding philosophy most of my life. But the awkwardness of the situation hit me. Did she want me to stay here in her room, maybe go for round two, or should I clear out and give her some space? I realized I was completely naked, and my clothes were scattered across the room.

"Lord, my head hurts. You want some Tylenol?" she asked as she started rummaging through her bag. Suddenly shy, I covered myself with a sheet and began to recover my clothes, although I couldn't find my underwear. I resigned myself to that loss and slipped on my pants.

"How about some coffee?" I said as I pondered whether to kiss her again or escape with no contact. Christ, we'd been together for a long time, why was this so complicated?

Marie made the decision by leaning down and giving me a quick kiss on the cheek. "That would be great, thanks. I'm getting in the shower. Just set it on the table if I'm not out yet. Thought I'd do a little shopping today before we get started, maybe pick up something for my mom. I'll take the car, you mind?"

I'd been thinking that we'd go to the café together, but it looked like I was on my own. I didn't mind that she wanted to go shopping by herself, and I understood why. Her mother had instilled a love of expensive goods in her and was willing to finance her spending, but Marie struggled with this, feeling that materialism was inconsistent with Lakota values. In the past, I'd told her to buy what she liked and not worry about it. But I knew she'd likely beat herself up and end up returning some of the things she'd purchase today.

"And listen, I'll make some calls while I'm out," she said. "I've got a few people I want to ask about Rick."

I spent the morning trying to watch TV in

my room, but was too distracted to focus on anything but *Scooby-Doo.* Marie returned, hours later, with some sandwiches and several large shopping bags. While we ate, she told me that she'd gotten a lead, someone in Denver who might have knowledge about Rick Crow.

After eating, Marie and I left the motel. We drove about half an hour to a run-down neighborhood that had numerous pawn shops, dollar-a-scoop Chinese restaurants, and more cannabis dispensaries. I wondered if there was a correlation between the poverty of an area and the abundance of marijuana stores. We pulled into the parking lot of a large building with a well-tended garden in front. The sign read DENVER INDIAN CENTER.

Inside, a young Native woman was at the front desk. We passed through the lobby, where a dozen pamphlets were on display: *Signing Up for the Children's Health Program; Native Americans Uniting to Fight Alzheimer's; Veterans' Benefits and Natives; Heart Healthy Practices Start with You!* I considered taking one of the booklets to learn how to protect my heart, but realized it was probably too late for that.

"Can I help you?" asked the receptionist.

"We're looking for Reuben," Marie said.

"He's leading the elders talking circle, but they're almost done. Go ahead and go on in; they're down the hall in the Thunderbird Room."

We quietly opened the door and walked in. About ten elder Natives were sitting in a circle. We sat down in chairs near the back of the room to listen. A senior with long silver hair tied in a ponytail was holding an eagle feather and speaking. He glanced at us as we walked in.

"— the white man sticks their old ones in nursing homes, assisted living, whatever you want to call them — I call 'em warehouses, 'cause that's what they are, a place to stick the old folks until they die. You know Indians don't hide away our elders, we keep them with the little takojas so they can learn from us. Pass it on to the little ones, that's what the Creator wants. Well, that's all for me today. I want Reuben to know I appreciate what he's doing, high time someone stuck up for us."

He handed the eagle feather to the man at the front of the circle, presumably Reuben. An older Native man, he looked about seventy years old, in good shape, with long gray braids and an easy smile. He was dressed in faded jeans and a dark-blue T-shirt.

"Okay, good seeing you all today, and don't forget about the potluck next week. Get your tickets from Iya at the front desk." People began filing out of the room.

We waited until everyone was gone, and then Marie approached the man while I stayed back a little. "Hi, are you Reuben?" she asked.

He nodded in a friendly way.

"I'm Marie, and this is Virgil. We're wondering if you had a few minutes?"

"Sure, let me get my stuff together." He put some papers and a notebook in an old tote bag. "What's up?"

I decided to jump in. "We're looking for someone, heard he might be in town. Do you know Rick Crow?"

The smile left his face immediately. "Yes. I'm his father."

It took me a second to take this in.

"What's going on?" he said. The expression on his face revealed far more than his words — he looked weary and sad. I let Marie take the lead.

"We're from Rosebud. Sammie Wolf Song said to look you up," she said, smiling politely. "Anyway, we know Rick, someone said he was in Denver. Have you heard from him?"

"No, we haven't been in touch. A long

time. Sorry I can't help you." He gave us a strained smile and started gathering up more papers and putting them in his bag.

"Well, we don't want to take up any more of your time," Marie said. "Thank you." She began moving toward the door, but I stayed put. "Is there anything you can tell us?" I asked. "Maybe an old address or phone number?"

Reuben shook his head. "Wish there was. I really don't know what he's doing these days. Last time he called, he was asking for money. I wouldn't give him any, he got mad." He looked off into the distance. "I still think I did the right thing."

I decided to gamble. "Sir, he might be mixed up with some bad people. Real bad. Be best if we find him before the police do." This was not strictly true. "Sorry for this news, but any info you have could help. Be in his interest to fix things without the cops."

He paused. "Tell me who you are again."

"Virgil Wounded Horse. This is Marie Short Bear."

"You're tribal police?"

"No, sir," I said. "Marie works for the tribe — family services. Me, I'm a . . . handyman."

Marie jumped in. "I know this is strange, us showing up here, but I'm a friend of

167

Rick's." She glanced over at me. "We used to, uh, date."

He was quiet for a long moment, then motioned for us to sit down. "Have some coffee."

We poured ourselves some black sludgy brew from an ancient pot on the counter. He poured himself a cup and picked up a little plastic container of nondairy creamer. We waited while he struggled to open the creamer, his hands trembling a little.

"I think he mentioned you once. Marie. He calls me every so often, usually when he needs something."

He took a drink of the coffee. I drank some too and nearly spit it out, it was so bitter.

"His name isn't Rick, you know. It's Waowakiye, it means 'helper.' It was given to him by a medicine man when he was five. When he was twelve, he made us start calling him Rick and stop using his Native name."

I nodded.

"We raised him in the traditional way, took him to Sun Dances, taught him our customs. He did well. You might be surprised, but he was very quiet when he was little. He loved to sit outside and watch the birds and the sky. He'd sit for hours, watch the

168

squirrels, the butterflies, the clouds. But we had to move to Rapid City because I lost my job, and that's where he went to school first. One day in second grade, he came home crying because some kids bullied him and made fun of him for being Indian. He told us he wanted us to cut his long hair, but we said no. My Lord, how he screamed! We finally gave in. I've always been ashamed of that. I just wanted him to stop crying."

He stopped talking and added another nondairy creamer to his coffee. Again we waited while he tried to open the little plastic package. I wondered if I should offer to help.

"Things got worse. He made some friends, and there was one kid that invited him to his house for a sleepover. When he got there, the boy's mother made Rick go home. She wouldn't let him stay at their house because he wasn't white. He was so humiliated, he cried and told us that he didn't want to be Indian anymore. He said he wouldn't speak Lakota, wouldn't go to powwows, wouldn't do anything Indian. I knew we had to leave the city, so I quit my job and we moved back to Rosebud. But I wasn't making much money, and Rick's mother started fighting with me."

He took a spoon and started stirring his

coffee, even though it was nearly empty.

"We argued, sometimes in front of Rick. We put him in the rez school, but something had changed. The sweet boy I loved — he was like a different kid. He got into fights, trouble. Lots of trouble. I prayed about this and tried to help him. I know this was my fault, because I didn't show him the right way to be a man."

Marie shook her head. "No, none of that was your fault."

He wouldn't look at us. His attention was focused on his coffee cup, as if it contained the answers that had evaded him. "I was doing my best, but couldn't get enough hours at my job. Money was tight. Rick's mother said she wanted to leave me. But instead of doing it the Native way, she hired some lawyer and came after my savings. I had to hand over everything I had. I was so angry that I left the rez and moved here. Rick stayed with his mother in South Dakota. I tried to be a father even though I lived far away. I called, wrote letters."

Reuben folded his hands on the table, his fingers a stronghold amid the wreckage of empty coffee creamers and discarded sugar packets.

"One summer he phoned me. He must have been thirteen or fourteen. Said his

170

mother'd been arrested for something, so he rode his bike over to the jail. When he got there, he said, he heard the police raping his mom in her cell. I didn't know if he was telling the truth, but what could I say? I told him he could come and stay with me if he wanted. I sent him bus money, and he came and lived here for a while. But he didn't know anyone, he was lonely, and he went back to the rez. I could tell he was broken inside, maybe because of his mother, maybe because of me. Every once in a while, I'd get a call from him, asking me to help him out of some jam he was in."

He took his empty coffee cup and turned it on its side, so we could see the bottom of the battered cup, the cracked and faded surface visible beneath the veneer of the ceramic coating.

"I don't know where he is now. He called a few months ago. Said he was in Rosebud, working with some people to set up hemp farming on the rez. Completely legal, he said. Told me I could make some money, but I didn't want any part of that."

I looked over at Marie, who raised her eyebrows slightly.

"Did he say who they were?" I asked.

"No, he didn't mention any names. He did say there was someone in Denver. Is that what this is all about?"

Marie shook her head. "We think some people might be trying to get him involved with, ah, other stuff."

"Rather not know," Reuben said. "I'm sorry if he's done something wrong. I want you to know he was once a good kid. One of our Lakota virtues is compassion — waunsila. I ask you to have compassion. Help him if you can. Please."

Marie and I were subdued on the drive back to the motel.

"You ever hear Rick talk about growing hemp on the rez?" I asked. "It's like marijuana, right? But weaker."

"I think so. No, never heard him mention it."

"You think he was just trying to scam his dad out of some money?"

"Don't know. Possibly. Wait, didn't that dispensary guy say something about hemp?"

"That's right," I said. "He said the grower was making some medicine, I think. Maybe Rick's working with him. Doesn't sound right, though. Rick's never been much of a healer. We need to find this Martin Angel, see what he can tell us."

As we pulled into the motel parking lot, Marie stopped and looked over at me. "So,

I probably shouldn't share this." She paused. "But I know what happened to Rick when he was a kid — what made him change and get so angry. What his dad talked about."

"Yeah?" I wasn't sure where she was going with this.

"So, he got pretty drunk one time, back when we were together," she said. "He told me he'd been abused by some older boy when he was little. Over and over. Wouldn't say exactly how, but I could guess."

"That's pretty shitty. No one deserves that." I studied her face, trying to gauge her feelings. "Was this his big secret? The one you mentioned?"

She nodded. "Yeah. He was really ashamed. I think he thought it was his fault. I tried to talk to him about it the next day, see if I could help him. But he got furious that I mentioned it. So he hit me, right in the face. Hard." She shook her head. "Last time I ever spoke to him."

I didn't say anything, just stared at her.

When we got back to the motel, I decided to go for a walk and clear my head. Heading west on Colfax Avenue, I passed by various groups of street people congregated in the parking lots of fast-food joints. Some of them looked Indian, but it was hard to tell. One homeless guy sitting on the street had a change jar next to a handwritten sign that read GOD HAS CHOSEN YOU. DO THE RIGHT THING IN YOUR LIFE.

Seemed like everyone was telling me what to do. I put a little change in his cup, and he nodded. I kept walking. The stories Reuben had told us about Rick and his childhood had disturbed me. I'd heard a little of this back when we were kids, but had never known the full story. For so long, Rick Crow had been the chief villain of my youth, the one who'd tormented me and made me hate being a half-breed. But he might have been just a sad kid who'd been bullied and abused himself.

Still, just because Rick had a rough childhood didn't change the fact that he was an asshole now. An asshole who'd punched Marie and was bringing hard drugs to the rez. An asshole who'd almost got my nephew killed. Somebody had to stop him, but maybe Marie was right. Even if I took Rick out permanently, the cartel would just find somebody else to move the drugs on the rez. The cop had said that using Nathan to set up the dealers was the best chance to put them in prison. But I couldn't put him in danger. All I wanted was to see him grow up happy, free of the demons that had pursued our family.

All of these thoughts weighed me down, and I decided to take a break. Right then I saw an old-fashioned neon sign attached to a dilapidated building, blinking red and blue: HANGAR BAR.

Without thinking, I opened the door and walked in. About a dozen people were sitting down or playing pool. Hanging up over the bar was a sculpture of an old-fashioned airplane, constructed out of empty beer cans from the 1960s and '70s. Schlitz, Olympia, Hamm's, Falstaff. The bartender walked over and asked me what I'd like.

It had been a long time since I'd had any booze. I remembered the cravings I'd had in the first months after quitting, then the orgy of sugary desserts I'd eaten after the first wave was over. I also thought about the shame I'd felt, back when Marie and I were together, when I'd gotten staggeringly drunk one night, called her a fucking apple, and thrown all of her clothes out of the house. My insult wounded her to the core, as I'd known it would, even in my inebriated state. She'd never felt accepted by the tradish Native crowd, and I'd scorned her for that with my slur, which was ironic, given that I'd always been rejected by those people myself. My words — and my drunkenness — were the last straw for her, and she'd moved out the next day.

Yeah, I'd been a mess, but I'd cleaned up my life, slowly. Now I was facing more problems. I looked over at the people playing pool and talking with each other. They seemed happy.

The bartender waited for me to say something.

"Bud Light and a shot of Old Crow."

I picked the glass up and swirled it around a bit, a few drops of beer spilling out onto the bar. Then I smelled it. It had been a while since I'd inhaled the yeastiness of a beer, the hops and the wheat, and the aroma flooded my mind, triggering a memory from a few years ago, a memory I'd tried to lose.

The empty cans of Bud Light scattered around the living room. The reek of stale beer. The silence. The awful silence.

14

An elder I knew had called me, begging me to go check on her grandchild Mikey, who lived with her son and his girlfriend out by Parmelee. We'd been in one of our terrible snowstorms, temperatures twenty below zero, and she hadn't heard from the child's mother, who wasn't from South Dakota. Nearly all families in the surrounding towns heated their homes with propane, and sometimes people froze to death if they missed out on a propane delivery. She told me that her son was out looking for work in Sioux Falls, but that the girlfriend was staying in their trailer looking after their little boy, who was only two. I'd seen the girlfriend at the grocery store — she was young, maybe twenty-two or twenty-three, with red hair and a nose ring. The little boy was cute; I remembered his Superman T-shirt and big smile.

I'd fired up my car and slowly driven

north, dodging the wind drifts and trying to stay on the road. It took a while to find the trailer in the snow, and there were no street signs or house numbers to go by. The elder had told me that I'd recognize the place by a large painting of Mickey Mouse on the front wall of the trailer. After a while, I spotted it. Whoever had done the painting was no Rembrandt, and it looked more like Bart Simpson than Mickey Mouse, but at least I'd found it. There was a Ford Taurus parked in front, just outside of the fence.

I'd put on my cap, gloves, hoodie, and overcoat to brave the bitter chill. Even though I was only a hundred miles away from my home, it was colder here, and I felt the moisture inside my nose freezing as soon as I got out of my car. I knocked on the door to the trailer, but there was no answer. I waited for a second and banged on the door even louder. It was dangerously cold, and I couldn't wait outside for more than a minute or two. I gave it one more bang and then tried the door. To my surprise, it was unlocked, and I went in.

It was cold inside, but not freezing. That was a relief. I took a look around the small living room. Empty beer cans, Bud Lights, maybe two dozen strewn around. An empty Smirnoff vodka bottle, one of the big ones.

And the stench of stale beer, powerful even in the cold air. No one was around, and I wondered if the girl and her son had gone to stay with neighbors to wait out the storm.

"Hello, anyone here?"

No answer.

I walked over to the bathroom, which was by the small cooking area. No one in there. The door to the bedroom was closed. It wasn't a real door; it was one of those sliding vinyl accordion units that don't give you any true privacy. I slid it back, the vinyl protesting in the chill.

There was a small mountain of clothes on the floor, and a Murphy bed by the wall with four or five blankets on top. I was wondering if I should drive out to the neighbors when I saw the blankets move a little. I tried to remember the woman's name — was it Rose?

"Hey, someone there?" I said, stripping the blankets back.

The mother was under the covers, passed out cold. Her red hair had been dyed green at the tips, and her nose ring was turned up, giving her a comical look. I could smell the alcohol reeking from her, along with some other vile smell. Her skin was even paler than I remembered.

"You okay?"

No response, so I felt her forehead, which was chilly to the touch. She was breathing, but slowly. If she'd drank all the booze in the other room, she must be plastered beyond belief, maybe even suffering from alcohol poisoning. I wondered how I'd get her to the hospital in this storm. I looked around the room for some winter clothes to put on her.

But where was Mikey?

I pulled the entire mess of blankets off the bed, assuming that the child was curled up in there, asleep.

No dice. I looked on the floor next to the bed, under the pile of clothes, and in the small closet.

No child.

I yelled out, "Mikey!"

No response.

I went back to the living room, then the bathroom. I opened up cabinets, looked in trash piles, and behind furniture. I remembered from Nathan's early years that two-year-olds could get into spaces you wouldn't expect, so I tore that trailer up.

No luck.

Then I went back to the bedroom and shook the mother. Hard. I grabbed her shoulders and shouted at her. "Rose, where's Mikey? Did you take him somewhere? Where is he!"

She opened her eyes for a moment. They were going in different directions, so I knew it was pointless to try and wake her up. And then I had a scary thought. Could the boy have wandered outside? I remembered that the front door had been unlocked.

There was no back door, so I ran outside the front and looked around the yard. It was still snowing, but I was able to see. There were no footprints, but that didn't mean anything, given the snowfall we'd had.

"Mikey!" I shouted as I ran around the back and scanned for any snowdrifts. "Mikey!"

It was freezing cold outside, but I didn't notice the temperature. Could he be under the trailer in the crawl space below? I crawled down to the base of the trailer and started digging out snow. It was dark under there, but I didn't see anything. I stood up and looked outside the cheap fence they'd put up, right by their car.

Their car.

The Ford Taurus.

I hadn't looked in there, but it was pointless, right? There was no way the kid could be in there, not in this weather.

I walked over to the vehicle. It was an older model, one of the boxy ones. The windows were iced up, and I couldn't see inside. The driver's side door wouldn't open — it was frozen shut, so I tried the passenger door. With some effort, I was able to pry it open.

I looked inside.

There was a child's car safety seat in the back. Graco model, dark gray with black straps. My sister, Sybil, had bought one of those car seats for Nathan after obsessively researching the safety records of the different brands. She'd worked so hard to keep baby Nathan safe, I remembered the baby-proofing all over the house, the outlet plugs, the padding on sharp corners, all of this work to protect children from their slips and falls, when it was the grown-ups who needed to be muzzled and padded from their own misdeeds and transgressions.

Little Mikey was strapped inside the seat, not moving, stiff. His eyes were open, staring straight ahead into nothingness, not blinking, frozen solid. It was quiet, so quiet, in that car. The falling snowflakes looked like tiny blades in the dying light, and I saw a rabbit skitter across the snow, hurrying for some shelter.

For a second I wondered if I could go back in time somehow, just rewind the last several days, suspend the laws of physics.

Maybe there was something on the internet, or perhaps some famous scientist could visit the rez, showing how it was possible to go back and change events, like a movie running in reverse. Anything so that I wouldn't have to look at this beautiful little boy again, in this car, in this storm.

The last I'd heard, the mother of the child had been charged with felony child abuse and negligent homicide for getting drunk and leaving the child in the car overnight. After I gave my statement to the police, I didn't follow the case. I wanted to forget. But no matter how hard I tried, I hadn't been able to shake the image of that little boy. Sometimes I'd remember his face when I saw little kids playing in the park, sometimes I'd see him when I was driving out in the country. Now he was here again. His sweet face.

I pushed back the full beer and the shot of whiskey, untouched, and walked out of the Hangar Bar.

15

"Hey, where were you?" Marie said when I returned from my journey along Colfax Avenue. The door to her room was open; she was sitting on the edge of the bed, watching television. I could hear the local news broadcasters with their cheerful voices.

"Out for a walk. You get a chance to eat?"

"No, you want to get something? I think there's a pizza place across the street."

"Sure, let me get my coat." I went to my room and got my jacket and cell phone, which I'd left in the hotel while I was out on my stroll. I turned it on and noticed that there were seven missed calls, all from Tommy.

I hit the call button. He picked up right away.

"Homeboy, where you been?" he said. "Trying to reach you all day."

His tone was weird; he wasn't his usual boisterous self. "Just out and about, nothing exciting. What's —"

"You better get back here. Nathan's been arrested. For drugs. They found some stuff in his locker at school."

Marie and I packed up our things as quickly as we could and hit the road back to the rez. Although we'd gotten some information about him, Rick Crow would have to wait. While we drove, I told Marie what I'd learned from Tommy, which wasn't much. Tommy had gone to check on Nathan at Audrey's house and learned about the arrest once he got there. Apparently the school authorities had gotten an anonymous tip and searched the students' lockers. They'd found drugs in Nathan's space, but there was no word yet on what type or how much was found. He'd been arrested at his auntie's house, and they told Audrey they were taking him to the tribal juvenile jail. Audrey didn't have any phone service, so she'd had no way of reaching me.

Marie drove while I made some calls, trying to learn more details. I called the tribal police, but the operator wouldn't put me through to Nathan or give me any information. I tried calling the school, but they were closed and weren't answering. I pounded the dashboard in frustration, and then Marie suggested that she phone her father and have him make a few calls. Of course. The police might be willing to give Ben, a tribal councilman, details and information that weren't yet released. She rang her dad, and I listened to her half of the conversation.

She hung up. "He's going to call the tribal police chief at home and get right back to us."

For once, I was grateful for Ben. I gripped my phone so tightly that my hand turned white. Nathan had told me that his experiment with heroin had been a onetime thing, so what the fuck was this? Had he been lying to me all along?

I stared at the passing scenery and tried to let my mind go blank as we waited for Ben to call back. The mile markers, road signs, and scrub grass blended into each other and created a sort of white-noise buzz in my head, which served as a welcome distraction.

I jumped when I heard Marie's ringtone, a snippet of a powwow drum song. She looked at the phone's screen and handed it to me without a word.

"Virgil, it's Ben. I just spoke with Frank Pourier. Here's the deal. The high school got word about possible contraband and searched the lockers yesterday. They didn't get a search warrant because you don't need one on school grounds, he said. Anyway, they found pills in Nathan's locker, and they —"

"Pills? What kind of pills?"

"Take it easy, and I'll tell you what I know. They're the strong ones, oxycodones — for severe pain. He didn't say how many there were, but it must be a lot, enough for a class three felony possession charge."

"What does that mean? Class three?"

"It means fifteen years in prison. And because they were found on school property, they can double the sentence."

Jesus Christ. "Is Nathan all right? I mean, was he high or anything when they picked him up?"

"Don't know. All I know is that he's in custody at juvenile, but he'll be handed over to the feds next week. You want to prevent that if you can. Frank told me there's no federal juvenile facility here, which means he could be thrown in with the wolves if the feds get him. You get me? Federal prison."

Oh shit.

Ben went on. "More bad news — he said Nathan's right at the age to be tried in court as an adult, not a juvenile. Looks like the age is fourteen for violent crimes or con-trolled substances. You need to contact a lawyer. There's the public defender's office, but I don't recommend them. Call Charley Leader Charge in Rapid City. I've known him for a long time, and he owes me a favor or ten. And he's the best — he'll help Nathan. If anyone can."

Back at the rez, the next few days were a blur as I made countless calls to try and get Nathan out of jail and learn the details of what had gone down. Marie offered to stay with me for a while, and I gratefully accepted. I was too distracted to focus on the everyday details of life, and it was a relief to have her there. She cooked some simple meals and engaged in a full-scale cleaning of the house, top to bottom. I realized with embarrassment that it had been many moons since Nathan and I had really scrubbed the place. I offered to help, but she told me just to focus on getting him home.

I'd been thrown into a world I wasn't familiar with, and it was difficult to know which way to go. I had an appointment in a few days with the lawyer in Rapid City, but I knew there was no way to pay him. I wondered if there was something I could barter for the lawyer's fees. Maybe be some type of enforcer for him or serve legal papers. Ben Short Bear had said I should avoid the public defender, but what choice did I have if I couldn't work something out with the attorney? And what about a bond to get Nathan out of juvie? I knew that bail bondsmen required some type of collateral before they'd put up the full amount of bail, but I didn't own anything beyond three small pieces of land on the rez that I'd inherited, and those couldn't be used anyway, as they were BIA trust properties. They could have my car, but that was worth about a hundred dollars, on a good day.

The only positive news was that, after many phone calls, I was allowed to see Nathan at the juvenile detention center. The facility itself looked like a golf club, with the exception of the fence surrounding the basketball courts. Coils of vicious concertina razor wire were mounted atop the barrier, the blades flashing in the sun.

After a pat-down and a trip through a metal detector, I was ushered into the lobby of the facility, where the director was to meet me. As I walked into the large circular room, I noticed about ten people hunched over armless, legless torsos. I stared at the scene, trying to comprehend what was going on.

"Our annual CPR training. Required by

the state. Don't worry, we get the mannequins sanitized after they're done. I'm Joe, the director here."

A Native man of about thirty-five, sharply dressed in a dark suit and bolo tie, gave me a warm smile and stuck out his hand to shake. I shook it and noticed that he did it the wasicu way: firm, like he was checking for weapons.

"I'm here for Nathan Wounded Horse," I said.

"Sure, I'll take you to him. Let me show you around first. We like to meet with all the parents and guardians, let them know their kids are in good hands."

He motioned for me to follow.

"We're very proud of our facility. We think it's the best in Indian Country, maybe even the best in the state. Thirty-six units in medium and maximum security and about one hundred kids in our transitional program. All of our clients — we don't call them inmates — take part in cultural and rehabilitative training. That's our motto up there."

He pointed to a mural on the wall. There was a large medicine wheel in bright red, yellow, and white. Inside the wheel were these words: WITHIN THE CIRCLE OF LIFE ARE TWO PATHS, ONE OF SORROW . . . ONE

OF HAPPINESS . . . YOU HAVE A CHOICE!

"One of our clients painted that. He's got a steady job now, heard he got married too. All clients join in our talking circles. I'm sure you've heard about the teen suicides around here?"

I nodded.

"Two completed suicides last month, and four attempted. It breaks my heart. The kids here have such despair — they don't think there's anything better for them. But there is! We tell them to have grit. Gratitude, Respect, Integrity, Tenacity. GRIT, get it?"

He led me down a hallway and through a door to a courtyard.

"That's the greenhouse, where we teach gardening skills. Look over there. Those are our bee colonies — we sell our own honey! Real Lakota honey from real Indian bees."

He looked over to see if I'd gotten his little joke, but I wasn't in a laughing mood.

"Over there is our sweat lodge. We purify once a week — parents are welcome to take part. Some of our clients have never taken a sweat, and they say it's the best thing they've ever done."

He shook his head ruefully, and I saw my opening. "Thank you for the tour, looks like a good place. But I need to know about my nephew. Can I see him now?"

191

"Sure. Let me take you down to the visitation room and I'll get him. Here's the resident handbook — you can look this over when you have a chance. By the way, we allow contact visitation here — better for the clients."

He handed me a folder, and we walked down a different hallway, past some heavily fortified cells with bars in the vinyl windows. For all of Joe's talk about the progressiveness of the center, these didn't look much different than the jail cells I'd seen. He took me to an enclosed room with large reinforced windows and two plastic chairs inside. I leafed through the handbook he'd given me while I waited.

Finally they brought Nathan in. He was dressed in a bright orange jumpsuit and sneakers, and looked sad and defeated. I'd been angry at him, but those feelings melted when I saw him. I hugged him, and then we sat down.

"Leksi, I swear to you I didn't do it!" he exclaimed. "They came to Auntie Audrey's house and said there were pills in my locker. They weren't mine, I'm telling you. I've never even taken pills, so I don't know what they're talking about! I wasn't —"

"Take it easy, just tell me what happened. I need the truth, okay?" He seemed genuinely upset, but I was wary. I needed more information from him, and my bullshit alarm was on high alert.

"I am telling you the truth. I don't know nothing about no pills — it's gotta be a mistake or something."

I looked at his face, trying to determine if he was trying to play me. "Do you share a locker?"

"No, I don't share with anybody. It's just mine, so —"

"Anyone have the combination to your lock?"

"No. I mean, I don't think so. The locks are like, built in, part of the door or whatever, so I guess only the school has the combo."

"You don't know what they found or how it got in there?"

"No, I don't know nothing. That's what I've been saying."

I wanted to believe him. But I'd known some addicts back in the day, and I knew that they were liars or worse. Nathan had recently tried heroin, and there was no denying that he'd been mixed up with some bad people.

"Nathan, you know I support you, but this is serious shit. Very serious. If you're covering for someone, I need to know. Now." I crossed my arms. "The guys you got the heroin from, did they give you the pills?"

"No. No! I'm telling you, none of this is right. I know I messed up with the dope, but I never took any pills. There's gotta be a mistake — maybe they looked in the wrong locker or something. It's not true. I swear on Mom's grave, okay?"

Something moved in my chest. I decided to trust him, as much as I could. What choice did I have? If I was able to get him out of here, I'd monitor him, check for drugs in his room, make sure he wasn't lying to me. Trust but verify.

"Okay, I believe you." I touched his shoulder. "But you got to promise that you'll be straight with me, all right?"

He nodded, and I saw some tears pooling in his eyes.

"What'd the police say?" he asked after a moment. "You know, like what's going to happen to me next?"

I hesitated, wondering how much I should tell him. I decided to keep quiet about the possibility of him being moved to the federal holding center, and the fact that he was looking at thirty years in prison if convicted.

"They haven't told me much, just that they found illegal pills. I've got a meeting with a lawyer in Rapid City tomorrow. We'll figure this out and get you out of here. Marie's been helping me — she's staying at our place for now."

"Marie?" His face lit up. "Sweet!"

"So, they treating you okay here?" I asked, not wanting to answer any questions about Marie just yet. She and I hadn't discussed our relationship, if that's what it was. For now, we'd simply enjoyed being together again.

"Yeah, it's all right," he said. "The food's pretty bad, but they let us play b-ball in the afternoon. Have to do schoolwork, too. It's weird, I know one of the other guys here; I was in fourth grade with him, I think. Maybe, I don't know. I don't know anything."

His voice changed, and he stared straight at me.

"Leksi, I really want to go home."

The look on his face was heartbreaking.

"Soon," I said. "I promise you."

The next morning, I left early for my appointment with the lawyer in Rapid City. Indians called it Racist City, due to the countless stories about Natives being harassed by locals or the police for the crime of being indigenous. Just a few years ago, a group of middle school kids from Pine

Ridge had gone to a minor-league hockey game as a reward for making the honor roll, but a group of fifteen white men sitting in a corporate box above them poured beer on the kids and shouted nasty slurs at them. The children were humiliated and left the arena in shame. They identified the men that did the deed and charged one of them — just one — with disorderly conduct. To no one's surprise, the jury acquitted the man, and the kids learned a bitter lesson in how the justice system works in the good old USA. And people wonder why Natives want to stay on the reservation.

The lawyer's office was in the small downtown area of Rapid City, where there were life-size statues of every US president, and also two sculptures of anonymous Native Americans. A few years ago there had been a statue of an Indian with his hands tied behind his back, but protesters had forced its removal, and a more generic artwork of a Native mother and child had been set up in its place. Walking down the street, I saw some graffiti in an alley — a spray-painted picture of Sitting Bull and the words THIS IS NDN LAND below it.

Charley Leader Charge greeted me in the reception area and led me back to his office. He was an older man, tall and expensively dressed in a dark-gray suit and striped red necktie — no bolos here. His gray hair was cut short and gelled, and his handshake was direct and firm. He radiated an aura of authority, reinforced by his voice, which lacked the usual rambling rez cadence and intonation.

I looked around his office, which was dominated by an elegant mahogany desk and an old-fashioned bronze banker's lamp. Various diplomas and certificates were hung on the walls: Georgetown University Law Center, Supreme Court of South Dakota, United States Court of Appeals for the Eighth Circuit, Sicangu Oyate Bar Association.

"Thanks for driving up here," he said. "I've talked to Ben Short Bear a few times about — is it Nathan?"

I nodded.

"Nathan, right. Ben told me what's going on, and I made some calls over to the Rosebud Juvenile Court and the prosecutor's office. He hasn't been formally indicted yet — that should happen soon — but the tribal prosecutor filled me in on what he's looking at. It's not good. They found a substantial amount of narcotics in his locker, and there's potentially a class three felony charge. At best maybe class four. If they use the federal schedule, it's a class C charge — that's a minimum of ten years in prison, no parole. Either way, it's a serious charge, and the tribe doesn't have jurisdiction over major felonies." He leaned back in his chair. "That means he'd be transferred to the federal system and possibly tried as an adult. We don't want that, of course. We want to keep him in tribal juvenile court, but it'll take some fancy footwork to persuade the feds."

No one had yet explained to me what sort of evidence they had. "How do they know it's his drugs? What proof do they have?"

"I don't have his documents and can't get them unless I enter an appearance as his counsel. I don't have any idea how strong a case they have or what probable cause they had to search those lockers. It's tricky in school cases, but we'd likely be looking at a motion to suppress in court. But I can't do anything unless you sign an agreement for me to represent him."

This was the moment I'd been dreading. "Uh, what sort of rates do you charge? I don't have too much cash on hand, but I could possibly —"

"Not to worry," he said. "Ben asked me to help out, so I'd be taking this case pro bono. For free. I just need you to sign this agreement, if you approve. You're his legal guardian, right?"

I nodded.

"Then you're authorized to retain me as his counsel. But let me explain a few things. Juvenile justice is different in some ways from other cases. Even though you're the one retaining me as his lawyer, he's the actual client. That means that I represent his interests, not yours. I'll have an obligation to protect any confidential information he tells me because of attorney-client privilege. I can't even let you see any documents in the case unless he consents. If all that sounds acceptable, read over the agreement and sign it. You have any questions, fire away."

I skimmed the document and signed it. What choice did I have? Here was a solid defense lawyer — and Native to boot — willing to fight on behalf of my nephew and not charge me for it. I was lucky, and I knew it.

"All right, I'll have my assistant file the papers. Now, the first order of business is to get your nephew out of detention. He's really very fortunate to be in the Rosebud juvenile center. They're one of the best — good programs, decent conditions, not like some I've seen."

I jumped in when he paused. "Yeah, I got a tour by the director. Lots of classes, sure, but he's still in a cell. What do we got to do to get him out?"

"I'm getting to that. At the detention hearing, I'll request a PR bond — that means no bail — but it's unlikely the judge will grant it. Given these charges, I'm guessing the judge will set bail at twenty thousand dollars, maybe more, which means you'll have to come up with two thousand for the bondsman."

"Look, I'm not sure I —" The look on my face must have been evident, because Charley stopped me.

"Let's not panic; maybe I can convince the judge to issue a reasonable bond. Nathan doesn't have any past offenses, does he?"

I shook my head, and he wrote something down on a yellow legal pad.

"That'll be my argument. The hearing should be held in the next day or two; sometimes jurisdictional issues slow things down, but the court has a duty to set a bond right away. Two things I need to tell you." He leaned in closer to me. "First, as the legal guardian, you must appear at all court appearances for Nathan — without fail. If you miss even one, the court can issue a warrant for your arrest. We don't need that right now, so you better stay in touch with my office for settings. Second, when Nathan is bonded out, don't let him make any statements to anyone — and I mean anyone — unless I'm there. That goes for searches too. I don't care if some friendly cop comes sniffing by, seems like the nicest guy in the world, just wants to help; *do not* let them search your residence or vehicle and especially his cell phone, unless they have a search warrant. You call me on my direct line if they show up with a warrant."

"I get it. We don't let the cops in the house," I said. "But what if Nathan doesn't have anything to hide? Shouldn't we show that we're cooperating?"

Charley smiled like I was an idiot.

"The police are not your friends. Especially the feds. Right now there's only one person you trust, and you're looking at him. If you haven't figured this out yet, Indians get the short end of the stick when it comes to white justice. I'm going to do my damnedest to make sure it doesn't happen to Nathan."

After the meeting with the lawyer, I needed to unwind for a few minutes, so I headed for the Black Hills, known in Lakota as He

Sapa. As usual, the roads were crawling with tourists speeding to see Mount Rushmore, or, for those who considered themselves to be more progressive, the Crazy Horse Memorial. Few of these people knew they were traveling on sacred ground, lands that had been promised by treaty to the Lakota people forever but were stolen after gold was discovered in the 1860s. Adding insult to injury, Mount Rushmore had been carved out of the holy mountain previously known as Six Grandfathers as a giant screw-you to the Lakotas. Kind of like Indians building a casino in the Church of the Resurrection in Jerusalem.

Even the Supreme Court agreed that the Black Hills had been illegally seized, and the Lakota nation won a big lawsuit against the government in 1980, with hundreds of millions of dollars awarded in damages. But the leaders of the Lakota nations refused to accept the settlement, stating that they wanted the land back, not the money. The government wouldn't hand over the Hills, and the Lakotas wouldn't take the blood money, and so the settlement sits in a bank account earning interest, over $1 billion. If the seven Lakota nations were to accept the money and divide it equally among the people, every man, woman, and child would get about $25,000 each. For a family of four, a hundred grand could ease a lot of financial suffering. But aside from a few complainers, there hadn't been any real pressure from the Lakota people to accept the money. I admit, I'd daydreamed about what $50,000 could do for Nathan and myself. A decent place to live, good food, a chance at college for Nathan. As I drove through the Hills, I felt guilty for thinking about the money again, but I resolved to wise up. What did I care about some rocks and valleys?

I took the back roads to stay away from the tourists, driving past one of the longtime tourist traps, the Cosmos Mystery House. I'd loved that place when I was a kid, and even Nathan had a good time when I took him there. It was a wooden cabin built on the side of a mountain at a crazy angle, so it seemed like the law of gravity was suspended. Water appeared to run uphill, people looked like they were standing at a 45-degree angle, and trees seemed to curve in strange ways. The tour guides told a hokey story that powerful magnetic fields created a gravitation vortex, but the whole house was a giant optical illusion. The best part was the Cosmos Truth Chair, a wooden seat that seemed to be suspended in midair by only its back legs. The tour guide said that anyone sitting in the chair who told a lie would cause it to fall down. A few tourists sat in the chair and appeared extremely nervous as the tour guide asked corny questions like "Have you ever run a red light?" or "Have you ever cheated on a test?" I wondered what questions someone would ask me if I was in the Truth Chair. Maybe "Did you ever stop loving Marie?" or "Do you think you'll ever forgive yourself for the things you've done?"

After a while, I pulled off the road and found a quiet spot away from all of the people. I listened to the wind and the birds and the sound of some water off in the distance, then looked at the mountain across from me, rising up into the sky. It was crazy, but the shape of the rocks — the fractures, fissures, and crevices — looked like the wrinkled face of an elderly Native man. In fact, I thought it looked a lot like my grandfather, who'd lived to be ninety years old. He'd died when I was young, maybe eight or nine. He'd spent most of his later years in a small shack without running water or electricity. And now that shack was demolished, just a pile of old lumber on a deserted road. I thought about him and the kindness he'd shown me, even when he could barely walk or move around. He'd endured so much trauma in his life, and yet he'd survived and found some peace, some acceptance. I stared at that mountain — the rock that looked like my tunkasila — for a long time.

Then it was time to go home.

16

I woke up the next morning to the smell of bread and flour. It had been so long since anything other than fried hamburgers and frozen burritos had been cooked in the house, I wasn't sure what it was at first. I peeked my head around the corner and saw Marie hunched over my tiny stove.

"I made kabubu bread. Want a piece?" she said.

"Sounds good. Don't think we got any butter, though."

She smiled. "I picked some up at Turtle Creek. Grape jelly, too."

As we ate, I filled her in about what the lawyer had told me. She listened quietly, nodding her head when I told her I'd retained Charley Leader Charge and that he'd offered to represent Nathan for free. She listened as I explained about the charges Nathan was facing, the prospect that the judge might set a high bond, and the fact I didn't have enough to pay the ten percent fee to the bondsman.

"Look," she said, "I have some cash in a savings account. I want you to have —"

"No way. You know I can't take your money."

"Lose the pride act for one minute, will you? Nathan needs to get out of that place. Call it a loan — pay me back later, if that makes it easier."

I didn't know what to say. Then she softened.

"Just think about it, okay?" She tore off another piece of bread. "If you're not busy this morning, why don't you come with me to the warehouse? There's a shipment of commods coming in. A food truck, too. Free lunch."

I'd always heard there was no free lunch — that you always pay. One way or the other.

We took off for the warehouse near the tribal offices, which were located about twenty miles away. While she drove, Marie talked about the latest outrage from her boss, Delia. Something about a negative review of a memo Marie had written.

Delia was the bane of Marie's existence. As she told it, Delia took every opportunity to make Marie look bad, stop her proposals, and talk shit behind her back. She'd even written Marie up a few times for missing work. On top of that, Delia had apparently told everyone that Marie only got the job because of her father. Which was partially true, although I didn't point this out. I'd suggested Marie look for another job, but she was too stubborn for that. She was going to defeat Delia at her own game — rise above her and get her own ideas implemented. But tribal bureaucracy moved slowly. I remembered that they'd once been semi-friends years before, but had a falling-out.

"Hey, what ever happened between you guys?" I asked. "You and Delia."

"You mean back in high school?"

I nodded.

"Well, I guess I can tell this now. I found out she was having sex with a teacher. Mr. Joseph? The English teacher? I thought that was pretty crappy, because he was married and his wife was pregnant. So I told her to cut it out."

"That's all?"

"Ah, no. When she wouldn't stop messing around with him, I had to take action."

"Yeah?"

"I sent an anonymous letter to her parents.

She got in pretty bad trouble, I heard. But I was still mad, so I stuck some frozen shrimp behind her locker. When they spoiled, it smelled so bad. There were bugs, flies — everyone made fun of her. It took her a week to figure out that I did it. I still smile about that."

When we got to the warehouse, the trucks with the government-supplied food had just arrived. Marie went back to the office while I helped the staff move the large cartons of commodities inside. When we were done with that, Marie came back, and we started packing the individual food boxes for the people who'd be arriving soon. Each box got big blocks of bland cheese, vegetable oil, cans of beans, instant potatoes, powdered eggs, flour, dry nonfat milk. Then we moved on to the specialty items: canned vegetables, peanut butter, cereal, and the dreaded macaroni pasta, which my mother had always saved until the end of the month, when the pantry was nearly empty. Mac soup was one food I'd vowed to never eat again.

I watched Marie while I helped pack the boxes and label them. Everyone knew her, and she walked from person to person, answering questions and chatting for a bit before going on to the next task. She kept the process moving smoothly, and we made steady progress.

Then I saw someone walk in the back door. Dark-blue tracksuit, long black hair, dangly beaded earrings. Delia Kills in Water. I hadn't seen her in a few years, but she looked the same, pretty much. Marie stopped packing, went over, and started talking to her. I couldn't hear their conversation, but it was clear they were having some words. Marie was frowning and gesturing with her hands while Delia stood aloof, her arms crossed. I moved a little closer so I could listen.

"— said they'll let me know. If you talk to them, maybe they'll do something."

Delia held up her hand. "I already told you, I'm not getting involved. Stupid idea anyway. How we going to keep that meat fresh? You know we don't got no money for freezers."

"Maybe we can use the grant to buy some! Just ask Wayne from council if we can do that. Why not?"

"I'm not bothering Wayne! Not his job."

"But he's on the committee, right? So he's got the authority to approve the purchase."

"I said no. Don't ask me again!" Delia waved her finger at Marie.

"But we can't use the grant if we don't have a way to store —"

"You're the rich girl with the councilman father — why don't you buy some freezers?" Delia shook her head and walked away.

I fumbled with some tape and tried to look like I hadn't been eavesdropping. Marie walked back over to me, anger and irritation playing across her face.

"What was that about?" I asked.

"Let's go," she said. "I need to get out before I say something stupid."

Once we were inside the car, Marie gripped the steering wheel and put her head down.

"Just give me a minute," she said. "Damn it."

I could hear her breathing. It sounded like she'd just run around the track. "Take it easy," I said.

After a while, she lifted her head up. "Sorry you had to see that. I try to keep my temper, but it's hard. She won't do anything, she's so freaking lazy."

"What's the problem?"

"Well, I helped write a grant proposal last year for the USDA. It was my idea, so of course she hated it. Anyway, it got approved, two hundred thousand dollars to bring in bison meat for the food program. You know,

211

better quality than that crappy canned pork we get." She curled her lips in disgust. "We could put five pounds of frozen buffalo meat in every box. Not to mention, buffalo's our sacred food. Great idea, right? The grant even included funds for nutrition education. The money came in months ago, but the tribe hasn't chosen a supplier. There are four or five bison ranches around here, but tribal council won't get off their asses."

I asked the obvious question. "What does your dad say?"

"I talked to him, even though I felt weird about it. He told me there's a committee handling it, and he's not on it. Said he spoke to Wayne Janis — I guess they're soliciting bids before they decide. I'm trying to get Delia to call the committee and get them to hurry up, but she won't do it. Families are going hungry while they fool around."

She shook her head, then picked up her phone and looked at the screen.

"She spends all of her time messing around on social media and texting, barely does any work." She put her phone into her bag and sighed. "Let's forget about this stuff. Like I told you, there's a food truck at the center. It's part of the grant — we're supposed to provide nutrition information, so there's a lecture on healthy cooking after lunch is served. Want to check it out?"

"Uh," I said, "do I have to stay for the lecture?"

"You do whatever you want. Maybe I'll hire you to pound some sense in Delia." She gave me a half smile and started the car.

At the community center, the food truck was already there. It was painted in psychedelic colors, bright red and orange and purple and green, not colors usually associated with Indians, and a giant pink medicine wheel adorned one side. Emblazoned at the top were the words INDIGI-CULTURAL DECOLO-NATIVE CUISINE, CHEF LACKLAND STRONGBOW. There was a crowd in front of the truck waiting to be served, so Marie and I took our places at the back of the line. "You guys brought this in?" I said. "Who is he?"

"We scheduled it a few months ago. To be honest, I don't remember his background." She took out her phone and started typing. "Oh, right. He's the executive chef at a restaurant in California. He calls his food 'decolonized indigenous Native cuisine.' Only uses ingredients that were around before Columbus."

I spotted Tommy behind the truck, holding a plate.

"Should have known I'd see you here," I said. "Free food."

"Yo Virg! Welcome back! Hey there, Marie." He tried to give me a fist bump, but couldn't due to the fact that he was holding a platter of food. I looked at the food he'd gotten; it appeared to be a few tablespoons of beans and rice and some salad.

"Dang, had to walk all the way here from the Depot! I was with Rudy, doin' a little day drinking. But he started freakin' out — said he saw some strange dude in the bar with a blurry face. He said the guy was throwin' off black sparks, like a welding machine or something, so Rudy wanted to get out of there. I didn't see no one like that, think Rudy was just lit up."

He started eating his food, using a little plastic spork. "We tried to leave, but he's got one of them alcohol interlock things in his car — he puffed in it but was too damn drunk, so it wouldn't start. Tried to find one sober person in the bar to blow in the tube, but nobody could get it to turn over."

He looked down at his now-empty plate. "Sheeit, this all the chow they gonna give us? Damn! I need some more." He threw his trash away and turned his attention back to me. "Hey, been meaning to ask you, what's the story with Nathan?"

I didn't know where to begin.

"Been back a few days," I said. "Met with a lawyer in Rapid City. Lots of news — I'll tell you about it after I eat. So what's the deal with the food truck? They serving Indian tacos or what?"

"Hell no. Don't know what that stuff was, some sort of rice and meat pudding."

I noticed a printed sheet taped on the side of the truck. It said:

INDIGENOUS RICE WITH HEIRLOOM BEANS
   AND TOASTED SUMAC LEAVES
WILD ONION, WOOD SORREL, AND CORN
   SMUT SALAD
BISON TERRINE WITH CHOKECHERRY AND
   PINE NUT PESTO

I had no idea what most of that was. "What's corn smut?"

Marie shook her head. "I think it's a fungus? What's it taste like, Tommy?"

"Don't even know which one it was," he said. "The salad was good; meat pudding was pretty banging, but they gave us like only a bite. I'm out, yo. Gonna head over to the gas station, see if they got any of that Chester Fried Chicken left. Catch y'all later."

Soon after Tommy left, a man dressed in a

white chef's uniform stepped in front of the truck, holding a microphone. He was fairly young looking, and had two long black braids tucked behind his ears and trailing down his back. He was wearing leather fringed pants, the kind that Indians supposedly wore a hundred years ago. I'd never actually seen anyone dressed in those, outside of museums and old movies.

"Hello everyone! I'm Lack Strongbow, citizen of the Muckleshoot Nation, and I'm honored to be here. If you don't know, I'm the executive chef at Red Eats in Los Angeles and the leader of the new indigicultural food movement. I hope you all are enjoying the indigenous cuisine we've gifted you. Today we put together a menu using ingredients from the Great Plains! How about a round of applause for my associates, who cooked this meal for you?"

The crowd applauded politely, and I stole a glance at Marie to see what she thought of this. She was watching the chef intently.

He went on. "I want to start by making an important point, something I hope every person here will take to heart." He waited a moment to increase the suspense. "*Put down your frybread!* That's right, I want you to throw away all the flour, dairy, and sugar you have at home. Get rid of it! Frybread isn't indigenous! It's the food our grand-mothers had to invent when the government robbed us of our way of life! I honor our elders for doing what they had to do, but there's a reason diabetes is killing our people."

He held up some type of shrub.

"Indigenous people need to eat indigenous foods, the proteins and wild plants our ancestors lived on. Instead of eating commodity cheese, go out and forage for some edible plants and roots! My friends, we must decolonize our minds *and* our stomachs, and I'm here to show you how. After lunch is served, I'll give an indigenous cooking demonstration, and we'll also be offering short classes over the next week, absolutely free of charge! You can also buy my new cookbook, on sale right here. Thank you again for letting us nourish you — your bellies and your spirits."

The line for the food truck was still long, so I asked Marie if we should leave. She looked at me indignantly.

"Let's try it. What he says makes sense. Less sugar and dairy, more vegetables."

"That sounds good," I said, "but how is a single mother with three kids going to find the time to go out and, you know, pick wild herbs? Won't work here."

Marie grimaced, and I could tell she was frustrated. "I think what he's saying is that Native people need to take more control of their health. Small changes, right?"

"Don't sound like he wants small changes. Get rid of frybread? Not gonna happen. You made some skillet bread yourself this morning. Pretty damn good, too." By the look on her face, I could tell I'd said the right thing. "You stay here and try the chef's food. I'll run over and catch up with Tommy and see you in a bit."

I went off in search of Tommy. He'd said he wanted some fried chicken, and there was only one place on the rez where he could get it. I drove for a while, thinking about the frybread my mother used to make. Was it unhealthy? I suppose, but I'd loved it so much. I remembered the way the house smelled when she was cooking, the damp and yeasty feel of the air, the shape of the little discs of fresh dough, and the crackling of the oil when she dropped them in. While I was reminiscing about frybread, my phone rang.

"Virgil?"

"Yeah."

"It's Ben. Marie gave me your number. You holding up okay?"

"Doing all right. Trying to get things in

order. I saw Nathan day before yesterday, and I met with Charley Leader Charge in Rapid City —"

"I heard. He's a good lawyer, one of the best around. He'll be able to help Nathan out."

"Hey, I owe you some thanks. Charley's not making me pay anything, said he talked to you. Appreciate it. Right now, I couldn't afford any high-dollar attorneys —"

"Don't mention it. Charley and I go way back. I got him out of some jams in the old days, and he hasn't forgotten. Let me know if he gives you any guff, I'll set him straight."

"Okay. Sounds good." I pulled into the convenience store parking lot. I'd finish with Ben and go inside, see if Tommy was there. "I'll let you know if —"

"Hold on. I want to ask you about something else."

"Yeah?"

"Tell me what's going on with Rick Crow."

I'd been so focused on getting Nathan out of jail, it was hard to get my mind wrapped around that situation again.

"Well, we went to this bar in Denver where he usually drinks, but he wasn't there. Then we found his dad — he lives in Colorado. Said he hadn't seen him lately, but he said Rick had called, told him about some hemp-growing business out here. First I'd heard of it — that ring any bells?"

"No," Ben said. "Still against the law, for now anyway. He say who Rick was working with?"

"Didn't mention any names. I can ask around, but not sure where —"

"Marie told me about the cop, the one who's been tracking Rick. What did he say?"

I hadn't realized Marie was sharing all of this information with her father.

"What did she tell you?" I asked. "About the cop."

"Rather hear it from you."

For an instant, I wondered about how much to share. I'd wanted more solid information about Rick and his whereabouts before having this conversation, but I supposed I owed Ben.

"The cop said Rick's involved with some gang in Denver. They're starting to bring black tar heroin here, just like you said. They got some new system — they smuggle the drugs from Mexico and deliver it to the customers themselves. Hand out free samples to get people hooked — some real bad shit. But they need people here, you know, drivers. Indians who can blend in, not attract any attention. The cop thinks Rick's setting up the local sales force."

"What's the next step, according to the cop?"

I paused again while I considered how much to say.

"He wanted Nathan to wear a wire and set up a buy. At the school. He said selling drugs near a school gets you a life sentence or something like that. But it doesn't matter now. Nathan's got these charges against him, so he's out."

"Can they get someone else to do it?"

"I don't know. They wanted to use Nathan, since he already knows the guys. Right now I got to get him out of juvie, figure out what the hell's going on with those pills they found. That's job one. The cops can find some other narc to wear a wire."

I could hear Ben breathing on the other end of the phone.

"You may need to rethink that," he said.

17

The next day I got up early and left while Marie was still asleep. We hadn't talked about indigenous cooking again, and that's where I wanted to leave it. What did I care if Marie wanted to give up frybread and Indian tacos? I had important shit to deal with, and there was no point in getting jealous over some celebrity chef from California.

As I drove, I thought about Nathan's situation. Something about the arrest didn't make sense to me. The lawyer had said that the school authorities found illegal pills in his locker. But Nathan told me he hadn't bought any pills, and if he had, why would he keep them at school? He was a smart kid, and storing narcotics in a school locker was a stupid move. On the other hand, kids did stupid stuff all the time. Maybe he was lying to me and was more involved with the drug guys than I'd known. Dennis had said they were moving black tar heroin, not pills, but they could be selling both.

I decided to call the Denver cop and tell him about Nathan's arrest. I was sure he'd try to sell me again on the wire, and now I had to consider the possibility, given Nathan's situation. Maybe set up a deal. But I'd talk to the lawyer first, get his opinion on whether it was even possible. That was his job. I called the lawyer's office and left a message for him. His assistant informed me that he'd call me back at his earliest convenience. Good to know.

It seemed like I'd done all I could do for the moment, but then I had an idea. I decided to try and find out more about the Denver gang. The ones who'd given Nathan free heroin and possibly the pills. If they were in town, it would be useful to scope them out, see how many of them there were, and if they were moving pain pills in addition to heroin. Useful information for the lawyer, perhaps even the cops, and maybe I could put some pressure on the dealers if the opportunity came up. The problem was finding them. But the rez was like a small town — everybody knew everyone else's business.

I realized I should go visit my friend Bill Ford — probably should have contacted him sooner. Bill was an older guy who owned a gas station and auto repair shop right on Main Street. He was there all the time, selling gas and fixing cars for cheap. What's more, I knew he'd tell me if he'd seen anything out of the ordinary, especially if I told him what was going on. Bill had a hatred of drugs and drug dealers beyond words. His only daughter had gotten hooked on something while living in Rapid City. She'd fought it for years but finally gave up and committed suicide. Bill told me she'd taken a full bottle of sleeping pills, then bound her mouth shut with pink duct tape while she waited to die. The heartbreaking thing was that she'd apparently changed her mind in the middle of it, because she tried to call 911 but passed out before she could dial the last number.

Even though it was early, Bill was at the shop, hunched underneath a car hood.

"Hey Bill, how goes it?"

He looked up from his work and saw me.

"Virgil, long time no see. How you been doing?" He grabbed a shop towel and wiped off his hands.

"Doing the best I can. Aren't we all?"

"Oh yeah. You want a soda? Got some Mountain Dews. Those'll start your motor. Might have a couple of Dr Peppers, too."

He went to the cooler, opened two cans, and handed me one. "Heard about Nathan, sorry about the news. Hope he gets some help. Damn these drug sellers — sons-a-bitches."

"That's why I came by. Cops are telling me there might be some guys moving in, selling dope — real dangerous shit. But they're not from around here. Maybe from Denver, maybe from Mexico. You see anyone like that?"

He paused and stared off into the distance. "How many?"

"Not sure. Could be five or six, maybe more."

He was quiet again. "You know what they drive?"

"Nope."

"What do they look like? Indians, white?"

"Not sure. Most likely from Mexico, so Hispanic, I guess. Rick Crow might have been with them."

"Tough one. This time of year we get some tourists, usually on their way to Pine Ridge. Get some of the charity people and a few going down to the casino. Can't think of anybody like you mention." He took a drink of his soda and frowned.

"That's all right, Bill. Just thought I'd stop by, see if you'd —"

"Wait, you say Rick Crow was with them?"
I nodded.

"Now that I think of it, Rick was here a while back. In some brand-new SUV. You don't see too many of those around here. Don't know if he was with anybody, but I asked him about the car. He said it wasn't his."

"Did he say where he was going?"

"Ah, can't really remember. Shit, I'm trying to think." His face creased as he searched his memory. "Wait, he may have said he was on his way to Valentine. Yeah, I think so. Valentine."

Of course. Just ten miles across the state line from the rez. Small town in the heart of the Nebraska Sandhills, so there were loads of tourists who wanted to hunt, fish, and float down the dark river in a canoe. There were seven or eight motels in the town as well as several campgrounds. And the town was surrounded by farms, so there was a steady stream of agricultural workers moving in and out. Valentine was no Denver, but it was the best place in the area to hide out and blend in.

I thanked Bill and headed due south.

The rolling hills of South Dakota transformed into the flatter terrain of Nebraska during the short drive. Soon I hit the city limits of Valentine, being careful to slow my speed to twenty-five miles per hour so I wouldn't be pulled over. My first stop would be the Derby Bar, where I used to know most of the bartenders and could ask some questions.

I was the only customer in the place, which surprised me, given that it was early afternoon. Behind the bar a large Native woman was hunched over her phone. I'd gone to high school with her about a million years ago, but couldn't remember her name.

"You got Shasta?" I asked.

She shook her head. "Just Coke." She filled up a glass with ice and poured some syrup out of the beverage gun, then went back to her cell phone.

"We went to school together, right?" I said. "Tell me your name again."

"Sharlene. You're, ah —"

"Virgil. Virgil Wounded Horse."

"Oh yeah, I think we were in math class together. Who was that teacher?"

"Shit, I can't remember. Too many dead brain cells. How you been doing?"

She set her phone down and poured herself a beer. "Same old, same old. You still in Mission?"

I took a drink of my Coke. "Yeah, lived in Rapid for a while, ended up back on the rez. What about you?"

"Got a place here in Valentine. Pretty cheap, get to stay close to my kids."

"You got kids? Nice."

"Two. Boy and a girl. Share custody with my ex. He's a real asshole."

"I know him?"

"Nope. Wasicu from Omaha. Hooked up with him after I left my mom's house. Worst move I ever made."

"Sorry to hear it." I motioned toward my glass, and she filled it up again. I slipped a five-dollar bill on the bar.

"All good. I got two great kids out of the deal, more than I can say for others."

"I hear you." I took a sip of my Coke. "Hey, ask you a question? Wondering if you've seen some guys come in here lately — like five or six dudes, they maybe came with Rick Crow. You remember him from school?"

She shook her head. "Lot of people drink here. Don't keep track."

"You remember anyone with some fancy SUV?"

She shook her head again. "Unless they park right in front, I can't see what people are driving."

This was a dead end. "One more thing. If somebody was trying to hole up around here, you know, lay low, where would they stay?"

Now she looked interested. "What's going on? These guys in trouble?"

"No. They might be able to help me with some stuff I got going on."

She didn't look convinced, but I hoped the beer had loosened her tongue.

"Well, I doubt someone trying to hole up would stay in the motels. They rent out mainly to the campers and the hunters. Rooms are pretty expensive; they don't like any trouble. The Econo Lodge just kicked out some college kids that were drinking too much and being loud."

I took another sip. "Anyplace else people might stay?"

"There's a travel park across town, out by Highway 83. Pretty beat up, not many people camp there. I hear they got a few cabins, though. It's called the Pay-E-Zee."

I found the place easily. There was a big sign advertising accommodations with nightly, weekly, or monthly rates. It was an old-fashioned campground, just like the bartender had said. Hookups for campers and RVs, a dilapidated building that probably housed the bathrooms and laundry facilities, and a small main office. I didn't see any motor homes or campers, which made me wonder if the place was still open. I spotted a few cabins down the road. One of them looked occupied. There was a big vehicle parked in front, but I couldn't identify the make or model from a distance. No sense in attracting attention, so I drove my car back through the entrance and pulled around to the rear of the travel park, where I was able to get closer to the cabin. I got out of my car and walked around the outskirts of the campground so I could get a better view of what was parked there. A shiny black Lincoln Navigator with Colorado plates.

Maybe I'd found them, but I needed to be sure. There were plenty of tourists and hunters from Colorado who passed through Nebraska with their fancy trucks and SUVs. I went back to my car and settled in for some surveillance. My view wasn't perfect, but I could see if anyone entered or left the cabin. It was pretty deserted, but if somebody came by, my cover story would be that I'd pulled off to make some calls.

The minutes passed slowly while I staked out the place. I couldn't see any movement inside the cabin, but I had time to kill. While

I waited, I called Marie and updated her on my status. She said she couldn't talk long because she was headed out to the indigi-chef's cooking class. I felt the blood in my veins begin to throb, but kept my mouth shut and told her to have a good time. For the next few hours, visions of Marie and Chef Longhair crowded into my mind, despite my best efforts to focus solely on the cabin.

After what seemed like an eternity, there was finally some action. A man opened the door, went behind the cabin, and urinated in the dirt. Couldn't see him well, but he looked to be young, with short black hair. Half an hour later, another man did the same thing. This time, I was ready and got a better look at him. Definitely wasn't white. Dark hair, shorter guy, dressed in jeans and a plaid Western shirt.

Why didn't they go to the main restroom at the campgrounds? Maybe they were drinking or lazy. Over the next hour, three more men pissed in the back. Now I was pretty sure they were boozing in there, a fact I could use to my advantage if I needed to enter. Of course, I didn't know anything about their weaponry or how many more were inside. For that matter, I still didn't know if these were gang members or farm workers. I decided to continue the surveillance.

About an hour later, a beat-up Ford truck pulled in. By now it was pretty dark, so I couldn't see well, although there was some moonlight. One man came out of the passenger door. From what I could see, he looked to be a little older, maybe in his forties, and carried several duffel bags. Another man came out of the driver's side, carrying what looked like sacks of fast food. The driver was dressed in an old denim jacket and had long black hair. I shifted in my seat to get a better view. It took me a moment, but I realized I knew him.

Rick Crow.

So it was true. Son of a bitch.

For a moment I flashed back to middle school, when Rick had given me the most grief. I remembered one time when his friends had held me down while he pounded my face. I'd tried to fight back, but it was no use. For some reason, Rick had it in for me more than any other kid. Maybe because he knew I had no older brothers or cousins to stick up for me, maybe he just hated me. An old familiar anger flowed through me, and I started to get out of the car.

But I came to my senses and began to

control my adrenaline so I could think this through. It looked like there were seven or eight men in the house, most of them likely drunk. I'd have the advantages of surprise and sobriety if I stormed in, but I didn't have any weapons beyond my Spyder knife and a little Smith & Wesson revolver with a five-round cylinder. If they were armed — and they almost certainly were — it would be a suicide mission.

I felt physical pain as I realized there was no way to get Rick tonight. I'd have to get more guns and ammo, stake out the place again, and wait for the right moment. Tonight I'd regroup and map out a strategy. But tomorrow would be the day.

The day I finally got my revenge on Rick Crow.

18

The next morning, my cell phone rang, awakening me from a deep sleep.

"Virgil? Charley Leader Charge. Are you free? Some new information about Nathan's case has come in that I need to discuss with you."

It took a moment to extricate myself from my dreams. "Yeah, I can talk. Go ahead."

"Better if we do it in person. Can you make it to my office today? I'll clear out my schedule."

"I'll leave right now."

I drove without stopping to Rapid City, wondering what the new info could be. Maybe more drugs were found in Nathan's locker? Or perhaps they'd agreed to drop the charges? As much as I wanted to go back to the gang cabin, I needed to find out what was going on first.

Charley's assistant escorted me directly to his office. The lawyer looked as spotless as before in a gray double-breasted suit and green tie.

"Thanks for coming in," he said, motioning me to sit down. "Here's what's happening. I got a call from the federal prosecutor on a couple of issues. First, it looks like Nathan's involved — tangentially — with something big. The DEA and other agencies have got some investigations going. You know about this?"

I squirmed uncomfortably in my seat. "Uh, not really. Do you mean the cop in Denver?"

The lawyer didn't look happy. "Yes, the Colorado and New Mexico investigations, apparently a task force led by the DEA, from what I can dig up. You didn't tell me you'd been in contact with the police down there."

"That was before Nathan's arrest. Before all this went down. I was going to tell you, honest. Called and left a message for you just yesterday."

Charley tapped his pen on the desk. "You need to tell me everything — and I mean everything — if I'm going to help Nathan. Everything, not bits and pieces. Remember, what you say is privileged, so you don't have to hold back. Let's hear it."

"Okay," I said, "what happened was, I was

trying to find a guy in Colorado — a real asshole — and this cop chased me. Turns out the cop is part of the investigation you mentioned, and he wanted to use Nathan as bait, you know, wire him up and have him buy drugs from these dealers here, but I told him no way —"

"Yes, I've been briefed on the offer to make Nathan a confidential informant. This thing is a lot bigger than you know. They won't tell me much, but it looks like they're going after the cartels. Somehow they got word that Nathan had been arrested here, and the investigator in Denver — the police officer you spoke to — was brought in for a briefing."

"Dennis. That's the cop's name."

"All right. The other news I have is that — as I'd suspected — Nathan's case has been referred to the federal prosecutors by the state. No surprise there. I was hoping the feds might decline the referral, but they didn't. Especially with this big drug investigation. So, Nathan will be prosecuted in federal court. The AUSA — that's the federal prosecutor — told me what they're planning to file against Nathan. I've got to warn you, they're playing hardball."

He opened a folder and pulled out some papers.

"As I'd feared, Nathan will be charged with a narcotics distribution charge and moved to federal detention. The reason a federal charge is so rough is because of the sentencing guidelines. In criminal cases, federal judges have to use these rules for sentencing, no flexibility at all. Bottom line, if he's found guilty, he's looking at a minimum of ten years in prison, no parole, along with some pretty massive fines."

"Wait," I said. "What's the charge against him?"

"Narcotics distribution, class C."

"Distribution? Does that mean selling drugs? Nathan's no drug dealer!"

"Relax. Prosecutors typically overcharge to give themselves some wiggle room for plea bargains. It might not come to that. I hope. Anyway, there's some good news. Maybe a silver lining."

I waited for him to say more.

"So, the feds made an offer. A deal that could keep Nathan out of jail."

"Yeah? What is it?"

"It's called 'substantial assistance to authorities.' If a defendant helps with an investigation, the judge can depart from the sentencing guidelines and issue a more reasonable punishment. Usually that means a lot less time in prison. What this means is, if Nathan helps out with the feds, he'd get a lighter sentence, but he'd have to plead guilty. The other option is to plead not guilty and take our chances in court. I've reviewed the file, and I can tell you there's a pretty strong case against Nathan. I would bombard them with motions to suppress evidence, but I can't guarantee how a jury would decide. Especially if we get a white jury. But maybe we would win — you never know."

He picked up a gold pen and pointed it at the ceiling. "My advice is that Nathan take the deal to assist the investigation."

I started to talk, but he held up his hand.

"Let me finish. I told the prosecutors their deal wasn't good enough, that they'd have to do better. We went round and round, and here's what they're offering now: if Nathan cooperates, the feds will allow the case to stay in state court, no transfer to the federal system. That means he stays in the juvenile court system, no prison, and his record is wiped clean when he turns eighteen. I'd request probation and drug counseling at sentencing in the juvenile court. They even agreed to a PR bond, so he'd be out of detention soon, no bail. Frankly, this is an incredible deal, far better than I thought we'd get."

"You mean he wouldn't go to jail?" I asked. "He'd get to stay in school?"

He nodded.

"What's the catch?" I asked.

"The catch? We'll get all this in writing, if that's what you mean."

"No, I mean what does Nathan have to do? Meet with the cops, tell them what he knows? He can do that."

The lawyer looked at me like I was slow.

"Nathan has to wear the wire and buy the drugs. They made it clear, that's non-negotiable. If he does it, this all goes away. Otherwise he's looking at ten years. Or more."

The drive back to the rez felt longer than the drive out. Ten years in prison with no parole? That didn't seem fair for a teenage offender, but Charley had told me it was standard in drug cases. But there was a magic bullet to keep Nathan out of prison. All he had to do was wear a wire during a drug buy, which I'd been assured would be completely safe for him.

But I knew better than to take them at their word. These were violent criminals who'd protect their business and their profits. And if word got out that Nathan had cooperated with the authorities, he'd be finished on the rez. Not only with kids his own age, but everyone. The lawyer had said we could refuse the deal and take the case to trial. It seemed pretty unlikely to me that a jury would convict a kid only fourteen years old. If the jury found him innocent, then Nathan would be in the clear completely. No juvenile detention, no probation officers, no counseling or therapy. Our family had never shied away from a battle; maybe this was the honorable way to go. Fight these charges in court, let the FBI catch the dealers without our help.

The bitterest pill was the realization that I couldn't go after Rick. Storming in and shooting Rick Crow and the gang now would remove any incentive for the feds to make a deal with Nathan. Rick Crow would have to wait. For now.

The lawyer had said we needed to sign the agreement to assist the feds right away, so there wasn't much time to think things over. I had to talk to Nathan immediately and see how he felt about the offer. He was old enough to weigh in on this decision. But he was also a scared kid, and he'd rely upon my guidance. I had to figure out what I was going to tell him. But I knew who I had to see first.

■ ■ ■ ■

I pulled into the medicine man's camp. Jerome lived outside of town in a small house surrounded by brown, weedy fields and a few defiant trees. He was alone on his porch, drinking some coffee.

"You want a cup?" he asked.

"Sure. Where is everyone?" There were usually numerous nieces, nephews, and grandchildren running around the place.

"Don't know. Kids are probably in town playing with their friends. Rocky's at his mom's house. They invited me over for some wohanpi, but I thought I'd stay here."

I sat down with him on a battered plastic chair. We were quiet for a long time, drinking java and listening to the wind. After a while, I held out a cigarette as a tobacco offering. He took it and lit up, then looked into the sky.

"Thunder Beings off in the distance. Think the spirits might water the grass tonight."

"Looks like it. Better shut the windows," I said, then paused a moment. "Wanted to ask you something." He was quiet, so I went on. "There's some talk about heroin dealers from Denver coming here. Selling some new kind of dope, dangerous stuff. One hit can kill you."

He took a drink of his coffee. "Bad news. Got enough problems with the kids killing themselves, don't need no one else doing it for them."

"They say these guys are from Mexico, might be working with a gang from Denver. They gave Nathan some drugs for free, he nearly died."

"He still over at the kiddie jail?"

I should have known Jerome would be aware of Nathan's arrest. The moccasin telegraph. Everybody knew each other's business and had to pass it on to the next person, and no one ever forgot shit. So now Nathan would be branded as a drug dealer. The past sticks to you on the rez.

"Yeah, he's still there. Cops say they found pills in his locker at school. Lots of them. Could be looking at ten years in prison. Not juvie, federal prison. They'll eat him up in there."

"Aayy." He shook his head.

"Like to hear your thoughts, but need you to keep this under your hat," I said.

A nod.

I told him about the deal they'd offered Nathan. Jerome listened silently, then nodded when I finished. I lit up a cigarette, gave him one, and continued.

"It's a tough call," I said. "Don't like Nathan being involved with the feds. Not to mention, word might get out that Nathan was a snitch. Remember Anna Mae?" Rumors had swirled around the rez for decades that Anna Mae Aquash was murdered for being an FBI informant.

"Yeah," Jerome said, "no one likes rats. But that Annie thing, it was a long time ago."

"Sure, but the kids today are even worse about being a snitch or a bait, whatever they call it. 'Snitches get stitches,' that's what they say. You know, somebody's gotta stop those drugs coming here. But if the gang finds out he snitched, they'll kill him. Or maybe somebody else will. Where's the justice in that?"

Jerome was quiet for a minute while he looked off into the distance.

"I don't know much about justice. But I think the white man has a different idea about it. A lot of our young men are in prison for crimes they didn't do — maybe they were in the wrong place at the wrong time. But the people come to you for justice, right? When the police won't do anything about some winyan who got beat up, you're the one they call. For justice."

He poured another cup of coffee and continued. "I see a lot of Indian wannabes come here, they think we worship the earth, they want to sing our songs and do our dances. But Wolakota means not only honoring the land but protecting the people, too. The hippies and the wasicu longhairs who come here, they don't get that part, that our people are sacred too, not just the land and the water."

He stopped for a second and looked out into the woods. "I think Indian justice means putting the oyate first, healing the community. That's what my father told me, anyway. He was Ikce Wicasa, a man of the people, someone who looked after the oyate. He told me, Jerome, always remember the Lakota values, especially waohola, respect for yourself and respect for the community. You got to act with respect for others — no, maybe he said reverence, I'm not sure if that's the right English word."

He tossed the remains of his coffee into the weeds.

"These drug dealers, they're shitting in their own nest. Don't be a magpie, my father told me, the magpie is the only bird that fouls its own nest. Tell Nathan about Wolakota. Tell him it means living the Lakota way. Think about this, and you'll know what to do."

The next morning, I told Marie about the deal the feds had offered. She listened quietly but didn't offer an opinion. "I'm going to go dig up some wild turnips after breakfast, want to come along?" she said. "Get some fresh air."

"Turnips? Since when have you been a turnip hunter?"

"Well, Lack told me the tinpsila is the most important indigenous food from the Plains. You can eat it raw, roast it like a potato, even grind it into flour and make Indian bread."

"How does he know about Plains food? Being from California."

"Washington, originally. Now he lives in Los Angeles. What difference does it make? He knows about Native foods from all regions, it's his passion."

"What's he still doing here?" I asked. "Thought he was supposed to leave."

"He really likes it here and changed his schedule to stay a while. He says he's tired of the California scene. We're having lunch tomorrow, why don't you come?"

Since when did Marie know this guy well enough to have lunch with him?

"Sure, I'll join you tomorrow. Pass on the turnip hunting, though."

Later in the day, I left to visit Nathan at the juvenile detention center. A staff member led me back to the visiting area. We passed by the medicine wheel mural that proclaimed YOU HAVE A CHOICE! I wondered if any of us really had a choice about our judgments, or if we were forced by circumstances beyond our control into our own orbits, our own pathways.

"Uncle!" Nathan grabbed me in a tight embrace.

"Hey dude, happy to see you. You doing okay?" He didn't look so good. There were dark hollows in his face, and he appeared ten pounds lighter.

"I'm all right. You know. It's weird to be here."

"They feeding you? You look skinny."

"Yeah, I'm eating. The breakfasts are decent — cereal, maybe a boiled egg, but the lunches are pretty gross."

"Gross? What do they give you?"

"Like tuna cakes and mashed potatoes, some old salad. Carton of milk."

Apparently the indigenous food movement hadn't taken root here. "What about dinner?"

"Um, maybe some canned chicken and rice. We got peach crisp yesterday, wasn't too bad. But the portions are really small. I'm hungry all the time."

"Is there a commissary — any way to buy snacks?"

"Naw. There's a garden where they grow stuff sometimes, but nothing's going on in there now."

It pissed me off to hear he was hungry, and I was tempted to have some words with the self-satisfied facility director. But chances were, I'd end up decking him. Best to keep my mouth shut.

"Let's talk," I said. "There's a lot of news."

He looked at me expectantly.

"Best news is we got a lawyer for you. Charley Leader Charge. He's not costing us anything, I guess he owes Ben Short Bear — you know, Marie's dad — some favors. I went ahead and signed the papers, so he's your guy now. I hear he's solid, knows how to work with the whites. At first I thought he might be a hang-around-the-fort Indian, but he's a fighter, I can tell."

Nathan shifted around in his seat, waiting for me to say more.

"Now the bad news. The lawyer got the papers for your case and talked with the prosecutors. The charges against you — it's pretty rough. They want to move you to federal court and charge you as an adult. Means you'd have to leave here, fight the case in Rapid City, I think."

"That doesn't sound so bad." His face looked hopeful, but I was trying to soften the blow that was about to come.

"Well, it means you'd go to federal prison, if you lost the case. No juvie jail."

"Oh. But there's no way that would happen. If I can just explain to them —"

"Nathan, it's bad. They're charging you with distribution. There were so many pills in the locker, they think you were selling them. The sentence for selling is ten years in prison, no parole."

"Ten years! That's not fair!" He stood up and pushed his chair aside. "I wasn't selling no pills! They aren't mine!"

"Dude, take it easy. I believe you. We got to be smart and listen to what the lawyer says. He told me there may be a way to keep you out of federal prison and have the charges dropped."

The hopeful look on his face broke my heart.

"Turns out the federal cops are chasing some drug dealers in Denver, same dudes that gave you that stuff. The heroin. The crap that —"

"But I don't even know them —"

"Let me finish." I stopped for a second. "They want to catch these guys selling heroin on school grounds. There's some major penalty if you sell by a school. So they want your help. To get them off the rez. For good."

It slowly dawned on him.

"You mean, they want me to snitch?"

I nodded, slowly. "It's worse. They want you to wear a wire and buy drugs from the guys, then they'll arrest them."

"I can't do that. Won't happen."

I took a moment.

"What are you worried about?" I asked. "You afraid it'll be dangerous? Or they'll find the wire? A cop told me the wire is really small, you can't even see it —"

"No, that's not it." His face knotted as he struggled to find the words. "What it is, you gotta understand, you can't snitch at school. It's just not done. Anyone who rats somebody else out, the kids hate him. Like, everybody."

It was what I'd suspected. The culture against working with the police was strong with them — even the rap songs they listened to hammered home that message.

"Hey, I get you don't want to be a rat, or like we used to call them, a narc. But listen:

the lawyer said the case against you is strong. I don't want to think about you going to prison. Not juvie, real prison, federal prison, with grown men."

I looked him straight in the eye.

"I can't — won't — force you to do anything you don't want to do. But this is serious shit. The jury finds you guilty — and guess how white juries feel about Indians — you could go away for a long stretch. Doing hard time. You hear me? I believe your story, but I don't know if a jury would."

Did I believe him? I wanted to, but there were so many things that didn't make sense. Like Nathan trying heroin in the first place, and just days after that, morphine pain pills are found in his locker. I wanted to trust him, but it was hard to escape my suspicions. I looked over at him, and could tell by his face he was starting to understand the gravity of the situation.

"What do you think I should do?"

The moment I'd dreaded.

"I think you need to wear the wire."

19

I awoke the next morning to the smell of fried wild turnips. Marie was already awake and cooking, her pillow vacant. The aroma was sharp, nothing like the pleasant smell of hash browns and bacon. It was like a cross between boiled cabbage and burned popcorn, and I crawled out of bed, still partially enmeshed in my dream.

Then the events of the previous day came flooding back. After my conversation with Nathan, I'd been disturbed, worried that I'd given him bad advice. When I got home, Marie had seen the trouble in my face. She didn't say a word, just took me in her arms, and I'd felt some peace then, a calm amid the storm winds.

I sat down at the table, and Marie poured me a cup of coffee. "Sorry, these are taking forever to cook. It's my first time frying them, and I'm trying to get them to caramelize. I threw in some wild onions and a little garlic salt I found in your cabinet."

I didn't know what caramelizing was — it sounded like adding sugary sauce to a dish — but the fried turnips were excellent, a sweet and nutty flavor balanced with a little bitterness.

"I could get used to these," I said.

"See? Told you they were good. Speaking of food, you going to join us for lunch today? Lack will be there, remember? I should warn you, though, my mother is going to come."

Oh boy. It made sense that Marie's mother would want to meet the celebrity chef. Anastasia Freeman Short Bear, Ann to her friends. A light-skinned Osage from a wealthy family in Oklahoma, she'd met Ben at some Native conference and then followed him to South Dakota, which she detested. Tall, thin, elegant, she wore her short hair styled in a modern bob cut and shopped for her clothes in Santa Fe, San Francisco, and Dallas. Marie once told me that she'd demanded a monthly clothing allowance from Ben in excess of what most people made here in a year.

Needless to say, she'd never liked me and hadn't been shy about expressing her opinion. She felt Marie should follow in the footsteps of her older sister, who'd left the rez and worked in banking somewhere on the West Coast. I suspected that Marie's med school applications were largely driven by Ann's maneuverings. I had no desire to eat lunch with Ann, but I thought I'd better meet this Chef Lack.

"Yeah, I'll meet you guys there. Sounds fun."

I had one call to make before I did anything else.

"Charley? It's Virgil Wounded Horse." I'd called his direct line and was surprised that he picked up on the first ring.

"Virgil, how you doing? I've got about five minutes before I head out for a deposition."

"Won't need that much time. I'm calling to let you know I spoke to Nathan. He's willing to wear the wire. Go ahead and set it up."

I heard rustling noises in the background, like he was moving papers around.

"That's great, I think it's the right decision. Hold on, let me take some notes. First step, let's get Nathan out of the detention center. I'll call the ADA right away, get everything going, and I'll nail down the terms in writing. This may take a couple days, but I'll be in touch as soon as the agreement is finalized. We'll need a judge to

253

sign off on the PR bond, but that won't be a problem. Worst case, he has to stay in there for a few more days."

"That's great," I said, "but will there be something in there about keeping Nathan safe during the buy? You know, what they'll do to protect him?"

"No, these agreements never specify the details of how the CI will be utilized. They probably don't know themselves yet. Don't worry, these guys know what they're doing. They follow a safety protocol, and they'll be even more careful given his age. They have every incentive to keep him safe so he can testify in court. Trust me, there's nothing to worry about."

Trust me. I kept hearing those words.

I needed some smokes, so I rode my motorcycle into town early. After stopping at the gas station for supplies and nicotine, I pulled over. A new coffee spot had opened up in the old warehouse building, the one with the ghost sign, the former owner's name still visible in the fading paint. GRABLANDER, it said. I'd never grasped the bitter irony of the long-dead wasicu's name on the sign before, and I stared at the lettering, trying to remember when I'd first seen it. It was one of those familiar sights, the kind that you stop noticing until something makes you see it in a new way. I leaned on my bike and lit up. The coffee shop — called Buffalo Brew — was crawling with teenagers. As I smoked, I watched the kids inside gossiping and chattering with each other, and wished Nathan was one of them.

After I was done smoking, I decided to go to the casino early. Our little gaming house was nothing like the huge Indian casinos in Connecticut or Minnesota. Those casinos were near big cities, so they had a massive population to draw upon for their customers. The closest town to our local gambling den was Valentine, population two thousand. Not only that, but there was another casino over in Pine Ridge and plenty of them up in Deadwood. Some wasicus believed all Natives were rich because of casino earnings, but our casino barely broke even, much less provide any profits to tribal citizens. But I liked our little gambling house. It was a good place to relax and visit with people, even though I didn't drink anymore.

I showed my ID and entered the main room. A cloud of cigarette smoke drifted over the gamblers like a cancerous veil. I sauntered past the slot machines to the tiny bar to get a Coke. The one advantage we had over the neighboring Pine Ridge casino was that we served booze, although there was no real bar area or any place to sit down with a drink. As I approached the bar counter, I saw Tommy. Even though it was late morning, I could tell he was already three, maybe four sheets to the wind.

"What are you doing here so early?" I said.

"Hey Virg! Shit man, good to see you! I'm playin' some slots, trying to get on a winning streak. I'm hurting for coin, trying to win a few dollars. Got a shutoff notice, had to pawn my guitar. You playing blackjack?"

The blackjack tables were closed.

"No, just hanging out. But I'll watch you play. Let me get a soda."

"You spot me a beer? I hit the jackpot, pay you back."

I came back with the drinks and watched Tommy hit the buttons on the slot machines.

He won a little bit and kept playing. Eventually he hit a pretty good jackpot — fifty dollars.

He turned to me excitedly. "See, I told you, homeboy! I knew I'd win, just gotta have faith." He started singing. "You gotta have faith, faith, faith. Who was that song by? George Carlin? Sheeit, I don't know, let's go get a drink, on me."

I sipped a fresh Coke while he downed a

Bud Light.

"Never seen you drink a light beer before. What's up with that?"

He laughed and spilled a little beer down the front of his shirt. "Watching my weight, am I right? Naw, I was drinking with my friend Ivan last night, he picked up some light brews at the off-sale, I kind of liked 'em. You know Ivan?"

I shook my head.

"He's a cool cat, I think he's Navajo, Pueblo, you know, one of them desert Indians. Met him at the Depot. Dude really knows about music, played me some shit I never heard before. But he started freaking me out. Said he could start fires with his breath, 'cause he's a, uh, pyrocardiac, something like that. Told him to show me but he wouldn't do it, said he might burn us. Sounded like some booshit, but I got outta there anyway."

"Crazy," I said, and looked at my watch. I had to get to lunch with Marie, her mother, and the chef. But then I had an inspiration. "Hey, you want to come along for lunch? At the restaurant here? Marie and her mom are meeting with that chef guy from California."

I realized having Tommy along could take some of the pressure off me. I also knew that Marie's mother detested Tommy — she thought he was a buffoon — and it tickled me to bring him along, just to irritate Ann Short Bear.

"The dude with the food truck? In the house? Hell yeah, I'll go."

We made our way to the other end of the casino. The restaurant was a large room with banks of pulsing fluorescent lights overhead, and about twenty plain tables. Marie's group had already been seated. Marie was sitting at the corner, wearing a floral print blouse I hadn't seen before. Next to her was Chef Lack, dressed in a black cook's uniform with a silver pendant in the shape of a turtle. Then there was Ann Short Bear, wearing an expensive-looking brown pantsuit and a large turquoise necklace, along with her dog, Ava. Of course dogs weren't allowed in the restaurant, but Ann claimed that she was an "emotional support animal," and no one dared tell her she couldn't bring her mutt wherever she wanted. Ava was a bichon frise with fluffy white fur and a perky, happy disposition. This was no rez dog, living on the streets and scrounging for scraps, but a pampered, happy canine. I liked the tiny dog and was glad Ann had brought her.

"Hey there," I said, "room for two more?"

Tommy and I pulled up chairs and sat down. I hugged Marie and greeted Ann, who responded with a curt nod.

"Virgil, Tommy, this is Lack Strongbow," Marie said.

I shook Lack's hand, and Tommy stuck out his arm for a fist bump and said, "How you doin'? I liked that food you was serving the other day, especially that meat pudding! You gotta show us how to make that stuff, it was the bomb!"

Lack smiled. "Thanks, that was bison terrine. I make it with salt, sage, and the secret ingredient, a little wojapi."

"Lack, tell us again what wojapi is," said Ann, beaming at the chef.

"It's chokecherries, simmered with some honey or maple syrup."

"I think my grandmother used to make that," Marie said. "I remember eating it when I was a kid."

"I'm not surprised. It's the traditional berry soup that most Natives used to cook. My people made it with chokecherries, blackberries, and red currant."

"Who are your people?" I asked. Marie frowned at me.

"I'm Muckleshoot — from Washington — but as a food justice warrior, I've studied the indigenous lifeways and nourishment customs of Native peoples from all regions of this hemisphere. I've always loved the food of the Plains; you have such riches here."

Riches? Had he driven around our reservation at all?

"What do you mean?" I asked.

"You have amazing herbs, seeds, vegetables — all growing right outside your door. Where I live, in LA, it's a wasteland for wild foods. I have to go inland or to farmers' markets to get what I need. You Lakotas are lucky to have such a bounty of traditional foods here."

I didn't feel lucky, but I knew it was better to stay quiet.

"Lack, how long are you staying in South Dakota?" asked Ann.

"Well, we're funded through this week by a grant program. After that, I was planning to drive down to New Mexico — Santa Fe. I'm thinking about opening a second outpost of my restaurant there. But you guys have shown such hospitality that I thought I'd stay for a bit, give my employees a break. The hotel here at the casino comped our rooms, really nice of them."

Ann touched Lack's arm. "I love Santa Fe. The city has such beautiful architecture and history; we love to walk around the plaza and explore the shops. Marie, didn't you apply to medical school in New Mexico? She's planning to become a physician."

Marie, uncomfortable, said, "Yes, Mom, but the med school's in Albuquerque, not Santa Fe." She looked over at Lack. "I'd like to stay here, but New Mexico has one of the best internal medicine programs in the country. I'm waiting to hear back where I'll be accepted. If anywhere."

"What type of medicine do you plan to specialize in?" Lack asked.

"Probably general practice. But I want to combine traditional indigenous healing customs with Western medicine. Native people have always known you have to heal the spirit as well as the body. I want to use ceremonies, herbs, and prayers along with allopathic cures to help people walk in beauty."

"Walk in beauty! I love it," said Lack. "That's exactly what I'm trying to do with indigenous food."

"I didn't come up with the concept," said Marie. "It's Navajo. Not that I'm any expert in their culture."

"Well, it's a marvelous way to express it. The idea that we can combine traditional indigenous customs with the technology of the twenty-first century." Lack looked over

261

at me. "Virgil, what do you do?"

I hated that question. It was such a white way of looking at the world, that a person is judged by their job, not their character. While I was thinking about how to reply, Ann chimed in.

"Virgil is our local hired thug."

"Mom, you know that's not true," said Marie. "Virgil does a lot of things. Construction, odd jobs, raising his nephew."

"You're a pretty big guy. Maybe I can call you if anyone gives me a hard time around here," Lack said with a half smile. "Tommy, what about you? You work around here?"

"I'm between jobs right now," said Tommy. "Looking for the right fit. You hiring?"

Lack laughed. "Maybe. My crew's pretty intense, I got to warn you."

Right at that moment, a drunk and dirty Indian stumbled into the restaurant. The stereotype — a skinny dude on crutches, with long greasy hair and wearing an old green jacket. He spotted our group and started limping over to our table.

"Oh no," Ann said.

"Hey, can you lend me some money? I lost my wallet, need a few dollars to get home."

Lack, Ann, and Marie looked away from

the man and were quiet. The little dog wagged her tail, hoping for some affection from the guy. I quickly got up and led the man out of the restaurant into the hallway. I put a few bucks in his hands. He didn't thank me, just wandered off down the hallway, past the hanging portraits of Chief Spotted Tail, the great leader of our tribe. Spotted Tail, who'd been killed by one of his own people, ambushed and shot before he could return fire.

When I got back to the table, Lack said, "Do you know him?"

"Not really. His name's Russ, he served in the army a while back. Got sent overseas to fight in the war. Had his leg blown off by one of those land mines. That's all I know."

There was silence at our table for a while, then Lack jumped up and hurried out of the restaurant.

"We can't even have a nice lunch around here anymore," said Ann. "Now we've offended Lack."

"Should I go after him?" asked Marie, looking out into the hallway.

Lack walked back in to the restaurant and sat down again.

Ann said, "Lack, we're sorry that man bothered you —"

"It's fine, no problem," Lack said.

"Where did you go?" asked Marie. "Did you say something to him?"

"I told him to come around to the food truck later if he was hungry. Gave him a hundred dollars."

I knew I should be jealous of Lack. That he could give so much more money than me, hand out free dinners and lunches. That he got to look like the hero in the situation. I wasn't sure what I was feeling, but jealousy wasn't it.

"Perhaps we should get our food before this place fills up," Ann said.

We walked over to the serving area. The casino restaurant featured a buffet, serving roast beef, fried chicken, spaghetti, and other standard American fare. I guess the casino wanted to appeal to the midwestern farmer palate. I filled up my plate with slices of beef, a fried chicken breast, mashed potatoes, macaroni and cheese, and then sat down with the others at the table. I looked over at Lack. His plate was largely empty — there was only a small piece of fish, a dollop of mac and cheese, some steamed vegetables, and a tiny portion of white rice. I started eating, the little dog Ava looking up at me pleadingly. When no one was looking, I slipped her a piece of roast beef, which she ate in one gulp, not even chewing it.

Suddenly Lack stood up. "This is terrible. A disgrace."

We all looked at him.

"The food. Bland and tasteless." He strode off toward the back of the restaurant, to the kitchen area. I looked over at Marie, who made a shrugging motion. Tommy was the first up; he followed Lack to the kitchen. Marie and I stood up too, slowly, and Ann tied the little dog's leash to the chair leg. The three of us got up, not sure what Lack was doing.

We opened the door marked EMPLOYEES ONLY and discovered Lack talking to two bewildered kitchen employees, presumably cooks. He noticed us watching him and held up his hand.

"Give me one hour," he said to us. "I'm going to see what I can do with the food here, show them a few tricks. Tommy, you still want a job? This is your audition."

"Wait, can I help, too?" said Marie. "I've done some kitchen work before."

Lack motioned her in.

"Text me when you guys are done," I said to Marie. "I'm going out for a smoke."

It took longer than an hour, but Chef Lack brought out a spicy mac and cheese, roasted potatoes and vegetables, corn cakes, bowls of fresh salad, and beef ribs with a sage and berry sauce. I had to admit, it was some of the best food I'd had in a long time. I ate seconds and thirds.

"Lack, thank you so much for showing our local cooks how to do it," said Ann, who'd eaten half a corn cake and some salad.

"You're welcome," he said. "Thanks for the help back there. Marie, you're a natural in the kitchen. I mean it. And Tommy, you're a hard worker. You really knocked out the vegetables today. There's a job for you if you want it."

Tommy grinned. "Hell, yeah, I do! And big wopes for that meal, good stuff. Think I'm gonna take a nap now. Toksa, y'all."

I looked over at Marie. She gave me a smoky look, a look that may have said *I told you so,* or perhaps *Let's go back home and be alone.*

Either way, I was all in.

266

20

The next few weeks passed slowly as I waited for word from the attorney about Nathan and the drug sting. Charley had said it was going to take some time for the cops to set everything up, but it was hard to wait and do nothing. I was tempted to do more surveillance of Rick and the gang, but I didn't want to risk being spotted and ruining the buy.

The best news was that Nathan was released from the juvenile detention center, just as the lawyer had promised. The district attorney had agreed not to object to a personal recognizance bond, which meant that I had to go down to the courthouse, sign a form promising that Nathan wouldn't commit any "delinquent acts," and agree that Nathan would show up for all court hearings. If Nathan violated either of these conditions, a warrant for his arrest — and mine — would be issued.

"Welcome back," I said, opening the door and letting him in. Marie was already there, standing in the kitchen with a smile. She'd started to split her time between my little shack and her own place, although we hadn't had any discussions about the status of our relationship. If that's what it was.

"Looks different in here. Where'd those come from?" he said, pointing at the wall. She'd added some decorative touches. Framed posters of Sitting Bull and Red Cloud, nautical-themed window curtains, and bright orange place mats on the tiny kitchen table. I had to admit, a little bit of cleaning and interior decorating made a big difference.

"Marie hung them up," I said. "Look what else she got." I pointed at the large double chocolate cake she'd bought at the Turtle Creek supermarket. She'd even inscribed WELCOME HOME NATHAN! on top with a cake decorating kit. She'd remembered that chocolate was his favorite.

He looked at the cake on the table and began to cry, the tears rolling down his cheeks.

"Thank you. That's, like — I'm sorry, I'm just really happy to be home." He sat down at the kitchen table, drying his eyes. "Can I have a piece now?"

"Sure," I said, and got out some plates and silverware. Marie began cutting the cake, but Nathan stopped her.

"This looks really good, and I'm like, so hungry. But can we save a couple pieces? I kind of became friends with this guy in juvie. His name's Charles, but he wants everyone to call him Snagmore. Stupid, right? But he's been telling me about his family. I guess he's got some little brothers and sisters; he's worried about them, you know, that they're not getting enough to eat. I guess his mom has some problems or something. Can we give some of it to them?"

I looked over at Marie, who was now tearing up herself.

"Yeah, we can do that," I said. "We'll go over there right now."

After his return home, Nathan put his head down and worked in school to make up the ground he'd lost while he was locked up. I tried to talk with him about the arrest and his incarceration, but he wouldn't say much. I asked if he'd shared anything with his friend Jimmy, but he just said, "Not really." I assumed that word had gotten out at his school about the pills and his arrest, and wondered if he was getting any grief there. Knowing Nathan, I'm sure he wanted to speak out in his own defense, but he'd been instructed by the lawyer to keep absolutely quiet about all of these matters.

To my surprise, Marie started volunteering at the casino restaurant, where Lack was working to train the kitchen staff and design a new menu before leaving for New Mexico. I was wary of this arrangement, but what could I do? She said she wanted to learn more about indigenous cuisine, so she worked a few nights a week in the kitchen as an unpaid trainee. The good news was that I got free food at the buffet on the nights she was there. Because I didn't want to be a freeloader, I helped out by washing dishes if I'd had a meal. I got to hang out with Tommy as well, as he'd started working on the evening shift as a prep cook and dishwasher.

Besides that, I took on a couple of day jobs in Rapid City for my friend Ernie, who ran a construction company — roofing work, construction cleanup, anything that needed to be done. Ernie paid me under the table, which kept me in gas money. I got a few calls for what Ann had called "hired thug" jobs, but it didn't seem smart to take those on. I don't know if it was because of Nathan's situation or something else, but my gut told me to lay off the beatings — for now.

Finally, I heard back from the lawyer. He called and told me to come to his office and bring Nathan. When we got there, I was surprised to see not only Charley but also Dennis, the cop from Denver, the one who'd nearly shot me, and another person I didn't recognize. It was strange to see Dennis in South Dakota; it felt like he didn't belong here, or like maybe I was the one who was in the wrong place.

Charley led us to a conference room. "Virgil, you know Dennis." He nodded at me. "This is Stan Dillon, the AUSA for our region. And this is Nathan, gentlemen."

"AUSA?" I asked.

"Assistant United States attorney," Stan said. "I'm based in Pierre, but I came down to help out. We want to go over some things, make sure everyone's on the same page."

So this was one of the feds, the guys who couldn't be bothered to prosecute the vast majority of violent crimes committed on our rez. The reason I made a living. But of course he was eager to go after a foreign drug cartel, a bust that would get major news coverage. The arrest of a child abuser or rapist wouldn't bring the same publicity, so those cases went unprosecuted. I wanted to ask how he was able to sleep at night after letting countless criminals go free, but — again — I forced myself to stay quiet.

Charley pulled out a red folder. "Couldn't agree more, Stan. Let's get it all in writing. You gentlemen have had a chance to read this. You know the deal: Nathan does one buy as a CI — one buy only — and his case stays in the state juvenile system, no transfer to federal."

The expressions on the two government men's faces told me they didn't like the deal that had been struck. It also told me that I'd done the right thing by bringing Charley Leader Charge in as Nathan's attorney.

"Charley, we've been over this," said Stan. "We need Nathan to do a trust buy before we give him the device. How do we know they'll even sell to him now?"

"What's a trust buy?" I asked.

"They want Nathan to make one purchase before putting the wire on him," said Charley. "To gain their confidence."

"I don't understand. Why not just wire him up for the first buy, then arrest the guys?"

Dennis jumped in. "Because these guys aren't stupid. They may have heard that Nathan was arrested at school, and they may not sell to him at all. Or if they do, they may use somebody else to make the sale, someone that's not in their group. We'd be wasting our time."

I was beginning to grasp the problem. "What if they won't sell to him? The deal's still on, right? Because he tried."

Charley looked over at me and shook his head. "That's the bone of contention here. Our position is that we're cooperating fully, and we expect the government to honor their side of the deal. If the dealers won't sell to Nathan, he can still provide valuable information —"

"You know it doesn't work that way," said Stan. "We can only reduce the charges if there's full compliance, and that includes a trust buy and controlled buy. Otherwise, no deal."

Charley, Stan, and Dennis all started speaking at once.

"I'll do it."

Everyone stopped talking and looked at Nathan.

"I'll do the, uh, trust buy. It's no problem," Nathan said.

His unexpected willingness to cooperate threw everyone for a loop, and Charley asked to meet with Nathan and me in private. We had the government people leave the room while we talked it over. Nathan was willing to make two buys from the dealers; he said he didn't care. Charley made some changes in the written agreement to reflect Nathan's willingness to take part in several purchases as a CI, and the feds came back in.

"All right," said Charley, "I've amended the agreement to show that my client is willing to take part in two buys — one controlled, one uncontrolled — and that his criminal charges stay in the juvenile system even if the suspects won't sell to Nathan, for whatever reason. We all good?"

The AUSA looked like he was sucking on a lemon, but he signed the agreement, followed by Nathan and myself.

"Now we need something from you," said Dennis. "Nathan, I need you to say out loud that you are cooperating with us willingly in this investigation. It's just a formality, but I need you to speak into this thing."

Nathan nodded and said the words into a little tape recorder. I didn't understand why they needed a verbal statement as well as a written one.

"Okay, let's get this deal going. You ready?" Dennis said to me.

I nodded.

He took out a cell phone and gave it to Nathan. "This is a burner phone, can't be traced to anyone. You don't call anyone else with this phone. There's one phone number programmed in there: mine. We need you to start frequenting with the dealers again. Talk with them, hang around or whatever, but don't be obvious. Just act normal. You see them lately?"

Nathan shook his head. "No, they usually kick it on the picnic tables behind the football field. Since I got back, I been going straight home after school."

"All right, start visiting with them again, but ease into it. When you're ready, ask to buy a small amount — one hit. Don't ask to buy heavy weight. Then call me the day before the buy so we can get everything in place. I'll give you some money, go over a few things. You won't wear a wire for that buy, but I'll need to get a statement from you after it's done. Also, whatever you buy from these guys, save it and give it to us for evidence."

Nathan had a bored look on his face.

"And one more thing. You can't get in any more trouble, so don't take any drugs. No pills, no junk, no pot — from anyone. You get busted again, we can't do anything for you."

"I'm done with that stuff," Nathan said. "I told you, it was only one time!" I knew he'd fooled around with weed in the past, but I'd talk to him later and make sure he kept clean.

"Just letting you know. After you do the first buy, you'll set up the next one. Maybe go back a few days later, ask if you can get more. That's what they want, they're trying to get regular customers. Call me on the burner after you talk with them and we'll meet again. We'll give you the device then. It's not actually a wire, that's just in the movies."

Dennis held up his hand. "Okay, last point, and it's important. If there's a problem or you need help, anytime, you call me on this phone and say, how about, 'Going to a friend's house,' and we'll come right away. Got it? *'Going to a friend's house.'* That's the emergency code."

I didn't like the sound of this. "What kind of problem? What do you mean?"

"Standard procedure, it's just a way to signal us if there's a need. The deal will go smoothly, but we always build in a way for a CI to contact us. Think of it as added protection for him. Like an insurance policy."

This sounded like *Trust us, Indian people*

again, but what could I say? The wheels were turning as Nathan began his transformation to criminal informant.

"Will I be able to listen in?" I asked. "In the van, or whatever you guys use?"

Dennis looked at the prosecutor. Stan made a little movement with his head.

"All right. Because I know you and given that he's a minor, you can ride along. But we'll need you to keep your mouth shut."

We'd see about that.

The next day, Marie came by the house right after Nathan had gone to school. I wanted to tell her about the meeting with the lawyer, but something in her face made me wait.

"Hey, aren't you supposed to be at work?" I asked.

"No, I'm driving out to Pine Ridge. Got a meeting with a buffalo company — one of the biggest ranches around. They're willing to sell us bison! For the commod boxes. Remember, the grant we got?"

I threw away the last bit of my toast. "Yeah, I remember. That's good news. Did you sign a contract?"

She shook her head. "No, I'm waiting on Wayne from the tribal committee to approve the deal. But there's no reason not to go with these guys. They're giving us a great price and it's grass-fed bison, humanely slaughtered. And they're a minority-owned business — could be a tax break. Looks like we'll finally get some decent meat in the boxes."

I toasted her with my coffee cup. "Nice job. Maybe they'll make you the manager of the program, get rid of Delia."

"I hope," she said. "Hey, you mind if I put on some tea?"

She took out some of the tea she had stashed in her bag. I wondered if something was up besides the buffalo meat. Back in the day, whenever Marie had wanted to sit down for a talk, she'd brew some funky tea, a blend called Sparrow's Tears her mother had bought in San Francisco. She said the tea calmed her. I knew we were in for a long discussion whenever I saw the bird tea come out. Now it was steeping in the little pot.

"You want some?" she said, pointing with her lips at the tea.

"No thanks, I'll just finish off the coffee." I poured the dregs into my cup as I watched her out of the corner of my eye. The coffee had been simmering so long, it looked like black asphalt and smelled like old cigarette butts. She sat down at the table.

"So, I got a letter in the mail."

"Yeah?"

"You remember I applied to medical school?"

How could I forget?

"Well, the University of New Mexico gave me their answer."

By the look on her face, I could tell it was bad news. "Hey, don't worry about it; there are other schools —"

"I got in. And they offered me a partial scholarship."

It took me a moment to process. Scholarship in New Mexico?

"Congratulations," I said. "Where's the school again?"

"Albuquerque. About ten hours by car."

"That's not so far." It seemed like a million miles away.

"I guess so. Never been there. I applied because they've got one of the best internal med programs around. Honestly, I didn't think I'd get in, much less a scholarship. Thought I might have a chance at USD, but not New Mexico."

"You don't seem too excited."

"It's a lot to take in. And there's something else. The scholarship requires you to stay in New Mexico after graduation."

"You have to do what?"

"To get the scholarship, I have to agree to

practice medicine in New Mexico for at least five years after I graduate."

"Oh." I was beginning to understand. Marie was telling me that she'd be leaving the rez for a long time. "Did you tell them yes?"

She finished the rest of her tea. "Not yet. The deadline to send my deposit is two months from now. I've got some time to think about it."

Even though I usually drank my coffee black, I added four teaspoons of sugar to my cup, took a sip, then dumped the whole thing into the sink. I watched the sugary mess flow down the drain.

"Why don't we celebrate?" I said, looking at my empty cup. "We could go out to dinner, drive to Valentine or Rapid City."

"That's sweet of you, but how about if I cook? I've been learning some things at the restaurant, like to try them out. I need to tell my parents too. Maybe we should have dinner there, Saturday night."

And so we went to Marie's family house, the one she'd grown up in. I'd been there years ago and remembered it well. It was located a long way from town and was spacious and modern, unlike most houses on the rez. Their place wasn't constructed by the government, but had originally been built by a white ranching family. A lot of people who've never been on a reservation probably assume that the entire population consists of Indians only. In reality, a large number of wasicus had gotten reservation land during the allotment years in the late 1800s, when the federal government passed a law dividing most reservations into 160-acre parcels, awarding the majority of the plots to Natives but giving a sizable number to — surprise — white farmers and ranchers. So much for "This land shall be yours as long as the grass shall grow." Decades later, Ben Short Bear had managed to purchase his little piece of land from the white owners. He'd renovated the house and raised two daughters there, all on a tribal councilman's salary, supplemented by his wife's family money.

I rang the doorbell, Nathan trailing behind me. I'd made him ditch his hoodie and wear his cleanest shirt, a checkered red flannel button-up two sizes too big for him. I'd dug up an old Dickies denim shirt, the best I could do. Marie was already there, having started cooking earlier in the day.

Ben answered the door, leading us into the large family room, where Ann, Marie, and Lack were already seated and drinking white wine, along with two people I didn't recognize. I was introduced to Brandi Little Moon, who'd been brought by Lack, and her daughter Shawna. Brandi worked at the casino and had recently transferred from the front desk to a job in the restaurant. She told me that her daughter went to St. Francis Indian School, the former Catholic high school now operated by the tribe. Shawna had bright pink hair, two piercings below her lower lip, and looked bored stiff while the little dog Ava nestled in her lap. I introduced Nathan to Shawna and they immediately ran off to the backyard together, followed by Ava.

Marie brought me a soft drink — some organic soda I didn't recognize — and excused herself to get back to the cooking. Lack went with her, which left me in the uncomfortable position of being in the conversation with Ben, Ann, and Brandi.

"How old is Nathan?" asked Brandi. I could tell from her clipped rez accent that she was from here. Long black hair, slim, Native print skirt. She'd dressed for the occasion. I wondered what the deal was between her and Lack.

"He's fourteen, in ninth grade at TC." I wondered how much Ann had told Brandi about Nathan's legal problems.

"Does he like it there?"

"Yeah, I think so. He's been bullied by some of the older kids, but he's doing okay. He won't tell me much."

"It's the same with Shawna. I don't know, it's like some kind of law with kids — when they get to be teenagers, they stop talking to their parents."

Ann piped in. "Virgil isn't Nathan's father; he's a legal guardian."

Shit, what did that have to do with anything? Ann Short Bear didn't like me, that was clear, but I'd hoped maybe I'd get a pass for just one day.

"Does Shawna like it at St. Francis?" I asked.

"She likes it better now that she's on the cross-country team. She has practice after school every day and some mornings, too. She's so tired in the evenings that she falls asleep at eight thirty."

Interesting. I wouldn't have guessed that from the kid's appearance — she didn't look like the sports type.

"I'm really glad she joined the team," Brandi continued. "She came in fourth place at her last meet; now she's talking about running at college. Maybe at USD, she's not sure yet."

Ann poured herself another glass of wine. "Our older daughter went to Dartmouth and was very happy there. She originally wanted to major in Native American studies, but we convinced her to switch to economics. Dartmouth doesn't have an undergraduate business program, which is a little outrageous, given what they charge for tuition."

"Dartmouth?" Brandi said. "Where's that?"

"New Hampshire, dear."

I knew it was time to take a break, so I excused myself to go to the backyard and smoke a cigarette. I found a spot where I could be alone for a few minutes and lit up. The little dog sidled up to me and I stroked her head, her eyes closing in sheer contentment. After a few puffs, I realized that I could hear some people talking faintly but couldn't see who it was. Then the wind shifted and I could hear a bit more clearly. Shawna and Nathan.

You know St. Francis is mostly Indians there's like one white kid in the whole school

Todd County is I don't know a mix I chill with pretty much anyone

What are you gonna do after graduation you gonna work or go to college

I don't know just trying to get through this year I was thinking about Sinte a while back

I got my CDIB it was stupid why do I have

prove I'm Indian but I guess I need it for scholarships or whatever but I'm on the cross-country team maybe I can get a running scholarship

That's cool

I started running last year my best friend killed herself I just felt like sad all the time so I joined the team I don't know why

Yeah we had two kids kill themselves last year it sucked

You know our ancestors didn't have to go to college or worry about stuff they just hunted and lived life

Yeah but like what are you gonna do go hunting for buffalo right

I'm like really scared to leave the rez for college my mom wants me to stay but there are like no jobs here what does your dad say

He's not my dad he's my uncle

Oh sorry

It's cool I didn't really know my dad my mom died in a car wreck like years ago

Sorry

It's all good he's like my dad now but I really miss my mom you probably think this is stupid but I try to think of her every night before I go to sleep I hit up my memory and try to come up with one thing to remember about her I make sure I remember it in the morning when I wake up

At that point I had to leave. I went back to the living room, where Ann was telling Brandi about New England airports and how terrible and uncomfortable air travel had become. I had nothing to add to this, so I looked around the room as I listened, noticing the large collection of Native art and artifacts displayed on the shelves. There was one large series of photographs hanging up that showed a man in profile. On one side he looked Indian, clean shaven with long hair. On the other side, he looked Latino, with shorter hair and a mustache. In the middle was a pic of the guy head on — he had long hair on one side of his head and short hair on the other. Half a mustache, too. Ann saw me looking at the prints.

"James Luna. It's called *Half Indian/Half Mexican.* That's the original."

I didn't know what she meant, but kept looking at the pictures. The guy in the photos reminded me of some dudes I used to work with at a construction site in Rapid City.

Marie returned to the family room then and told us the meal was ready. Brandi retrieved the teenagers from out back, and we all moved to the formal dining room, where there were complicated place settings on the distressed wood dining table. In the center was an elaborate wicker basket that looked Native, although it had a different design than I usually saw around here. Ann saw me looking at it. "That's a handwoven Navajo protection basket," she said. "We got it while visiting friends in Shiprock. It's over a hundred years old."

"Jeez, Mom, couldn't you buy art from some of our people?" Marie said.

"Thank you, dear, for your input. As you know, I do support local Lakota artisans. But that basket is beautiful and historic."

Lack walked in, carrying a tray of food. "Today we have a wild green salad, locally sourced turkey with braised acorn sauce, and roasted tinpsila with sage — wild turnips that Marie located. Bravo to her for her turnip-hunting skills. I'm happy to tell you that Marie prepared the entire meal today; I just gave her some direction. She is a very gifted cook."

"Lack, you are too sweet," said Marie. "This is your food, no matter what you say, and we're grateful you're starting to change indigenous cuisine. I'll let you all know that I've cleansed my kitchen of wheat and gluten and sugar. From now on, I'm only eating real food."

The meal was served, and it was excellent, just as Lack had promised. Nathan didn't say a word during the feast but ate an astonishing amount. I had to remind him to make sure everyone had been served seconds before he inhaled the rest. Marie made coffee — some brand I hadn't seen called New Mexico Piñon — and Lack served small dishes of fresh berries for dessert.

After we finished with the fruit, Brandi turned to me and whispered, "Can we get wateca?" Knowing Ann and her feelings about rez customs, I shook my head a little. There was no way Ann would let people take home leftovers. She'd rather die than allow a wateca battle. Brandi looked at me with an expression of pure sadness.

"Uh, I suppose I have an announcement, everyone," Marie said.

The whole table looked at her. Ann had a look of distress on her face, and I could guess what she was expecting Marie to say. Something about our relationship. She was probably imagining that Marie was pregnant or engaged or tied to me in some way.

"I think most everybody here knows I applied to medical school about six months ago. Brandi and Shawna, sorry about this boring stuff." Brandi raised her hand and smiled. "So, I've been accepted at U of New Mexico med. In Albuquerque. That's all."

Ann let out a loud shriek that startled us all. "Congratulations! I knew you could do it. Your sister will be so proud. We'll start packing right away."

"Mom, I haven't accepted their offer yet. It's a big decision, because I'd have to do my residency in New Mexico and stay there five years after that. I don't know I'm ready to leave Rosebud for that long. I mean, the whole point of becoming a doctor is to help our people."

I could see the irritation blooming in Ann's face. "Don't be ridiculous. This is your chance to get out of here and become a professional. Someone respected. You can help the Indians in New Mexico and then come back here if you'd like. There's no question you are going to move there for your schooling."

"Mom, we can talk about this later. I'm excited, but I need to think this through, decide if it's the right time. And I'm still waiting to hear from South Dakota's med school."

"My dear," said Ann, "there is nothing to think about. Tomorrow you will send your confirmation or your deposit or whatever it is you need to send. And that's that."

I thought I should let Marie and her mother have their discussion without me, so I sneaked out back for another smoke while the conversation swirled.

"Let's go over there."

Startled, I looked behind me and saw Ben Short Bear. We walked behind a tin tool-shed.

"Wanted to talk to you before you left. Seemed like a good time. They'll be in there a while fighting. Nothing new. So, what's the deal with Nathan and Rick Crow? I called Charley Leader Charge, but he says he can't talk to me now that he's Nathan's lawyer."

I knew Ben and Charley were friends, but it was unsettling to learn Ben was pumping the lawyer for information. But again, I didn't see how I could freeze Ben out, given what he'd done for us.

"Nathan's assisting in the investigation. I'm staying out of it, letting the feds bring the heat. Rick's a scumbag, and he can rot in prison."

"Assisting in the investigation? Does that mean he'll wear the wire?"

Did he really not know about this, or was he testing my honesty? My gut told me to tell as few people as possible about Nathan's status as a CI. But I couldn't see how confirming this to Ben could hurt.

"Yeah, he's going undercover. That's all I know."

"Glad to hear it. Long past time to get rid of the bottom feeders around here. Can I get one of those?" he asked, pointing to my cigs. I was surprised. I didn't think Ben smoked, but I gave him one and he lit up.

"You know," he said, taking a puff, "I was the one who exposed that dimwit who was pocketing the housing money. You remember that, about ten years ago?"

He didn't wait for me to respond.

"Moron was taking housing vouchers from the government, depositing them in his own account. Idiots on the tribal council didn't know, or maybe they were in on it. I was the only one with the smarts to notice something was wrong, so I went straight to the BIA, stopped the scam. Now we got hundreds of people in low-cost housing. Some of them are bums, sure, but not all. Point is, I did some good. That's when I decided to run for tribal council."

He took another drag.

"People around here think tribal politicians just want a paycheck and a per diem. But believe it or not, some of us are trying to do the right thing. Not always easy — we got to balance the BIA, OST, and the state blockheads. The paperwork, Jesus. But there's a chance to make some changes if I get elected tribal president. I need your help — don't let me down, all right?"

He crushed the cigarette with his shoe.

We returned to the dinner, where the conflict between Marie and her mother had apparently ended and the party had devolved into separate conversations. Marie and Brandi were talking while Ann conversed intensely with Lack.

I was ready to leave the party, but noticed that Shawna and Nathan were over in the corner, engaged in rapid-fire teen-speak. I saw him make some big gesture with his hands, and both of them erupted in laughter. He looked happy. He'd had so much of his childhood taken away, and there were so many problems to face in the next few weeks. Without anyone noticing, I slipped out to the backyard again and lit up a smoke.

He could have his time.

21

The following days passed quickly, and I felt a charge in the air, almost a vibration, as things began to happen. As he'd been instructed, Nathan began to spend more time with the group of kids that took drugs. He said they mainly smoked weed, but they'd sometimes dabble in harder stuff. His arrest had apparently gained him some cred, because he was immediately accepted back into the circle of chemical abusers. Once we had talking circles; now Native kids had circles of a different kind. He told me he'd been able to avoid using any substances and escape suspicion by drinking beers with the group instead of taking drugs.

I asked Nathan about the heroin dealers and whether he'd seen them again. He said they were still around but keeping their heads down. Apparently they'd wised up and stopped selling most of their dope on school grounds. I wondered if this would affect the sting, given that the cops had emphasized arresting them on school property. Once the dealers trusted you, Nathan said, they'd deliver to you if you called them. He'd heard that they'd usually meet buyers in the parking lot of the supermarket, where there were always plenty of cars.

Nathan said the banger called Loco was still around, and word was that you didn't want to fuck with him. Stories were circulating that he'd use a baseball bat on your legs or carve a double X on your face with a knife if you crossed him. It was tough to know how much of this was truth and how much was teenage gossip. One thing that'd been confirmed: Loco had a scar on his face like a crooked lightning bolt, so he'd be easy to identify.

One afternoon I came back to the house and found Marie sitting at our small table. I could tell something was wrong. She was twisting the beaded cuff on her wrist around and around.

"Hey, what's up?"

"Oh, nothing really. I got a letter from the University of South Dakota med school. They rejected me."

"Damn. That really sucks. They say why?"

She sighed. "No, just a standard form letter. 'We received many strong application packages,' blah, blah, blah. I'd heard they might be biased against people who graduated from tribal colleges like Sinte. You know, the teachers supposedly aren't as good, the standards are lower, whatever. My classmates told me the rumors, but I didn't want to believe it. Maybe I should have gone to Dartmouth like my parents wanted." She got up and threw the letter in the trash. "I don't know, maybe they didn't reject me because I went to Sinte. Maybe they rejected me because I'm not smart enough."

I went over and put my hand on her shoulder. "Bullshit on that. You are the smartest person around here. You got accepted to that med school in New Mexico, with a scholarship, too. I don't know why they didn't take you, but it wasn't because of that. The hell with them."

"You're sweet," she said. "Not sure why I feel so bad. It's not like being a doctor is my lifelong dream. It's just that there's so much misery sometimes. I want to help, that's all." She sniffed. "Well, like my grandma used to tell me, ceye sni yo, stop your crying."

"So what does this mean?" I asked. "Are you going to accept at the med school in

Albuquerque?" I wasn't sure I wanted to hear the answer.

"Don't know yet. I've been trying not to think about it, because going to USD would have solved so many problems. Now I've got to sit down and figure it out." She poured herself a glass of wine. "How about if we put this stuff on hold?"

"Sounds good."

"Oh yeah, Velma called. She offered to take me out to the Depot later to cheer me up. Drink a few beers, bitch about stuff." She scratched my back with her nail. Her touch was like the tail of a comet. "When's Nathan getting home?"

"Not for a few hours."

"Excellent," she said, taking my arm and leading me away.

Later that evening, Velma came by to pick up Marie. I hadn't seen her for a few years, and if anything, her look had gotten even more extreme. Electric-blue hair, various piercings, knuckle tattoos. She was wearing a cutoff jean jacket with numerous patches sewn on: WARPONY, DEFEND THE SACRED, ARM THE HOMELESS. Marie had told me that she played bass in a local band, the Rez Dawgs, when she wasn't working at the dollar store.

"Hey V, long time no see!" She enveloped me in a bear hug. "You look good, dude! Why don't you join us tonight? Raise some hell, yeah?"

"Thanks," I said, "you two go out and have fun. Nathan and I'll watch a movie."

"All right, bro. Your loss."

Marie gave me a hug, and they took off for the bar. I settled in with an old TV show, something about parallel universes and rogue scientists. The story didn't make sense to me, so I laid back and listened to the characters speak while I stared at the ceiling, the voices on the television mixing with the sound of Nathan's music coming from his room.

I jumped up at the sound of my phone buzzing. The screen showed it was 12:30 a.m.

"Hey, what are you doing? You're not asleep, are you? Sorry! You there?"

It was Marie. I could hear music in the background, so they were likely still at the Depot. "What's going on? You guys okay?"

"We're fine! You won't believe it, but we won at pool. Velma and me. We beat these guys, they thought they were so good. But they scratched on the eight ball. Too bad, right?"

Not good, for sure. I knew what it was like when the bar closed. That's when all the shit went down. And she sounded pretty loaded.

"Where's Velma? You coming home?"

"She's in the bathroom. Just want to tell you I miss you, that all right?"

"Hey, I miss —"

"And also, can you come pick us up? I've had a few drinks, not feeling so good; don't want to drive when I'm —"

"Stay right there. I'm leaving now."

I got to the Depot as quickly as I could. Marie and Velma were sitting outside, smoking cigarettes. I couldn't remember the last time I saw Marie light up.

"Can I get one of those?" I said.

"Virgil!" Marie jumped up, stumbling a little, and gave me a hug, holding her smoke out in the air. Then she gave me a deep kiss. I tasted beer and tobacco, which made me want some of both.

"Thanks for coming. You're a great guy —"

"Don't I get a hug? What the fuck!" Velma put her hands up like a boxer.

"Hey Velma," I said, and she came over and squeezed my shoulders.

"You guys," Velma said, "look what I

298

snagged when no one was watching." She opened her purse with a little flourish and revealed a bottle of Jägermeister.

Just looking at it gave me a headache. "I think you all had enough. Hop in before we get in trouble."

They piled in the back seat, and I drove off before anyone noticed Velma's larceny. They were laughing and talking, and I saw Velma furtively open the Jägermeister, take a drink, and hand it to Marie.

"You know I can see you, right? Just keep it down if there's a cop."

"Cop!" Velma yelled. "Shit, I fucked half of them limp-dick assholes! Bring 'em on!"

This provoked a round of riotous laughter, and I resigned myself to a rowdy drive. I dropped Velma off at her little shack, along with the remains of the Jägermeister. Marie gave her a kiss on the cheek and then joined me in the front. She fumbled with her seat belt, and I could see she was really smashed now.

"I wanna tell you something," she said, her voice jagged and potholed.

"Yeah?"

"You changed, you know? In a good way, I mean. I was tellin' Velma that tonight. I don't know if it's Nathan's stuff or what, but you're different. Now."

Changed? I didn't think I had, but maybe you can't see your own transformations, and that might be a good thing. I wanted to ask her more, but I stopped, afraid to hear it. It was too late in the night for any drunken revelations. Best just to get her home.

"You see anyone at the bar?" I asked.

"Yeah! Your friend Tommy. He was there. I bought him a few, then he played pool with Velma. They were, uh, kind of hitting it off."

Tommy and Velma? Well, stranger things had happened at the Depot.

"Then Lack showed up, with that woman. Brandi. Talked with her for a little bit, asked her about her kid. What was that girl's name? Can't remember."

"I think it was —"

"What do you think about a kid? Child, I mean. You know, having a baby? Maybe it's time. How the fuck are all these women having kids? I mean, what's wrong with me?"

This was unexpected. We'd never talked about kids before, and I wasn't sure it was the right time to discuss the subject, with Marie being four sheets to the wind. But she deserved something from me, some response.

"Is this something you thought about?" I

asked. "Something you want?"

No answer.

"Marie?"

I looked over and saw that she was sound asleep. I kept driving, the road unfurling before me like a dark tunnel, leading somewhere I couldn't imagine.

22

What I'd been waiting for — dreading —
finally happened. Nathan came home from
school and told me he'd talked to the heroin
dealers. They'd agreed to sell him some
black tar.

"What'd they say?" I asked.

"Well, I recognized one of the guys from
before. He was like, come hang out with us
at the house. I guess they got some place
outside of town. So I was like, you got any
eagle? He said, sure do."

"Eagle?"

"Kids are calling it black eagle or just
eagle."

"Okay. You set up a time?"

"Sort of. He said I could go out there
Friday, after school."

Friday. Just a few days away.

I called the lawyer and told him the situation. Charley said he'd contact the feds im-

mediately and that I should sit tight until I heard from them. Sitting was out of the question, so I went to the casino restaurant. It was early, before the dinner rush, so there weren't any customers yet. I spotted Tommy by the dish machine and signaled to him. He took off his apron and came over to my table.

"Homeboy! What you up to?"

"Nothing. You on dishes tonight?"

"Little prep work, little dishwashing. You want some pejuta sapa?"

Black medicine, wakalyapi. He came back with two steaming cups of coffee.

"So listen to this," he said, "I was chillin' with some dudes the other night, Waylon and Chepa; you know Chepa White Plume? He's a smart dude, reads all the books, told me about some new history textbook, first one ever written by an Indian — I know, right? — and he's tellin' me about something they had in the old days. Check this out, you hearing me?"

I nodded.

"The US had this deal for white settlers, called, ah, depredation claims. Turns out, if you were one of them settlers moving to Indian Country and you got attacked — got your horse stolen, cabin burned down, whatever — you could file some paper with the government and get paid back. In full."

"Yeah, so?"

"Well, I been thinkin'. What about an Indian depredation claim? Why don't we submit some claim sheet asking for what's been taken from us? Our land, our kids; shit, what about the buffalo? Waylon told me the wasicus killed fifty million buffalo! Buffalo we needed to survive! Tatanka, you know what I'm saying?" He made little buffalo horns with his fingers and put them on his head, simulating a bison.

"Tommy, the government isn't gonna give any money to Indians, not ever. Best we can do is hold on to what we got."

But as I thought about it, I liked the idea more and more. Depredation claims. If something was stolen from you, all you had to do was file a claim and your losses would be restored. How about a depredation claim of the heart? Maybe I could file some form to get back the years I'd grieved for my mother, father, and sister. Or maybe I could submit a claim to have our dignity returned to us, sealed in an official envelope, the sins of the past magically wiped out, gone like the buffalo.

The next day I heard from Dennis, who was handling the details for the trust buy. He told me Nathan wouldn't wear a wire for this transaction; this was a small purchase so Nathan could gain some cred with the dealers. Nathan would buy the black tar — just one hit — and bring it back to the cops, who'd verify it was heroin. Dennis said this small amount wasn't enough to build a full-scale case against them; they needed either a larger purchase of dope or a sale on school grounds. That would come soon after the first buy. I'd asked if I'd be able to watch the purchase from a distance, but he said no. There'd be no cops at the scene, to preserve Nathan's credibility, but he'd have the burner phone with Dennis's number on it. If he felt anything was going wrong, he was to call the number and say the emergency code. If the cops heard that message, they'd immediately go after Nathan. Safe words.

The plan was that Nathan would buy the drugs right after school, then bring the stuff back and make a statement on the record. Dennis would come to my house so that Nathan didn't have to drive to the police department after the buy. That made sense, because there was no point in risking a sighting of Nathan with the police. Word traveled fast around here. The moccasin internet.

305

On Friday afternoon, there was a knock at the door, and Dennis walked in, dressed in street clothes. Jeans and a T-shirt embossed with an image of Mount Rushmore on the front. If he was trying to blend in on the rez, he was doing a pretty piss-poor job.

It was strange to have him in my little shack. Marie brewed some coffee and set out some sunflower and dried berry cookies she'd made. The weeks she'd spent at the restaurant with Chef Lack learning how to cook indigenous foods had paid off. She was constantly experimenting with new dishes, and the pantry was stocked with varieties of wild rice, flours, and nuts. It had taken me a while to appreciate some of the stranger dishes she cooked, but I liked most everything.

"Any idea how long he'll be there?" I asked Dennis.

"No. I told him to act natural. Maybe he'll stick around a while, listen to music, play a video game. But don't worry, he knows to call if things get weird."

"How many people are there at the place?"

"From what we can tell, about six or seven. We've been surveilling them and doing trash analysis for the last month. Your guy Rick Crow comes and goes, two locals from the reservation, and four gangbangers from Denver. We've positively identified one of them, the one called Loco."

"Yeah, Nathan mentioned him. Thinks he met him before. Said he's got a pretty bad rep."

"I'll say," said Dennis. "We're not sure what he's doing here. He's the tax collector for the Aztec Kingz back in Denver."

"Tax collector?"

"The guy who collects money people owe to the gang. The enforcer. Customers, people in the gang's territory, affiliated gangs, gang members themselves. They have to pay what's called a 'gang tax.' That's the cash they owe for the right to call themselves an Aztec King."

"What happens if they don't pay?" asked Marie.

"If you're lucky, he just roughs you up. If you're not, you get shot or tortured. There're a lot of stories about necklacing and all that, but that's not really done here."

"What's 'necklacing'?" asked Marie. "It sounds bad."

"Uh, yeah. It's when a tire is filled with gas and slipped around the vic's chest and lit on fire. The Mexican cartels do that when they're in a turf war. They're pretty creative when it comes to executions. Acid baths, decapitations, boiling alive, they do it all.

But that stuff's just for show. In the States, gangs don't have the time or energy for that crap. I've never heard of it happening here. Well, once."

Necklacing. I wondered what I'd gotten Nathan involved with.

We drank coffee, ate, and waited for Nathan to come back. Dennis went out to his car to make some calls.

"What are you doing tomorrow?" Marie said. "Maybe you want to come by the restaurant for dinner. I'll make you a bison burger and some wild rice soup."

"Sounds good," I said. "Will Lack be there?"

"I think so. Don't know if you heard, but he's leaving in a few days, going back home. He's done training the staff and finalizing the new menu. And they're going to give the restaurant a real name instead of just 'Dining Room.' "

"Yeah? What's he going to call it?"

"He's leaning toward Strongbow Feast House, or possibly Red Grub. He's thinking about opening a chain of these at Indian casinos across the country. Spread the message about healthy indigenous food. What better places than casinos? And ours will be the first one! Lack says the casinos will have to agree to hire at least fifty percent Native workers and source at least half of their food from indigenous or local suppliers."

Well, shit. I had to hand it to him, he had some good ideas. Even if he was Muckleshoot and not Lakota.

She went on. "This is just the first step. He's hoping to get a TV show on the Food Network to spread the word. Lack says real indigenous cuisine will cut diabetes and heart disease rates for Natives by twenty-five percent. But I think he's being too modest."

I'd heard enough about Lack by now. "Sounds good. Sure, I'll come by tomorrow, if I can."

Dennis returned from his phone calls and joined us inside. After polishing off the cookies, Marie and Dennis engaged in a conversation about baseball. I listened quietly, trying to keep my mind away from Nathan's situation. It turns out Dennis had played college ball before getting injured. To my surprise, Marie knew quite a bit about pro baseball and the Denver team, the Colorado Rockies. Dennis was passionate about the Rockies and talked about the lack of respect the team got around the country. According to Dennis, people believed the high elevation and dry climate in

Denver changed the nature of the game and made the ball travel farther when hit. He said the Rockies stored the balls in a cigar humidor to counter this effect and slow them down. The moisture changed the nature of the balls, turned them into something different. I wondered if there was a way to accomplish this for other objects. Old cars, rotten food, eviction notices. Broken hearts.

The discussion lasted through two pots of coffee and another round of cookies. I was happy to sit back and listen to their debate, even though I didn't grasp most of it. Then I saw some headlights in the distance shine through into the kitchen. I'd never been happier to hear the coughing and stuttering of my old car, which he'd used to get out to the dealers' house. The front door opened and Nathan entered. He looked at us in surprise, as if he'd expected to come home to an empty house.

"You okay?" I asked.

"Yeah, I'm good," he said, hesitantly.

"Tell us what happened."

He took off his jacket and sat down. "You know, I just chilled for a while. It was cool, no problems."

"Who was there?" asked Dennis.

"Uh, couple of dudes I don't know. And

some other guy, name of Shane, I think."

"Rick Crow?" I asked.

"No."

"How about Loco?" asked Dennis.

"Yeah, he was there."

Dennis said, "Let's see it."

Nathan pulled a tiny red balloon out of his pocket. Dennis took a picture of it with his phone. It looked like a cough drop or a small piece of hard candy. Then he opened it and took a picture of the coal-black heroin.

"I need to record a statement from Nathan," Dennis said. "You mind if we do that in back?"

"Go ahead."

They went into the bedroom to tape his statement, leaving the tar on the table.

"I've never seen it before," Marie said, looking at the drugs. "It makes me sad. Why do people want to take that stuff?"

"Slow suicide."

"I'm not stupid, I get wanting a temporary escape. Get away from your problems. Go ahead, have some drinks, sure. But this stuff is so dangerous. Why lie down and die? Why not fight to make things better?"

I shook my head. "They gave up. Don't see any future here. Got twenty dollars, can't pay the rent or buy a tank of propane, but you can fade away for a few hours."

She sighed. "Yeah, I see that with some of the older people. But the kids? Shit."

Frustrated, she went to the tiny kitchen and started washing some dishes. I tried to listen in on what was being said in the bedroom, but the door was closed.

After a while, Dennis came out of the bedroom, Nathan behind him.

"Got what I need."

"What happens next?" I asked.

"Nathan and I went over this. Basically, he's going to stay in contact with the dealers. When the time is right — maybe a few days, maybe a few weeks — Nathan's going to ask to buy some scag, but more weight this time. He'll ask to have them deliver it at the school. We'll need a day's notice to put the device on him and set up a ghost car."

"Ghost car?" said Marie.

"Unmarked police vehicle. We'll have the ghost near the scene and also a van with the electronics to monitor the buy."

Ghost car. I couldn't help but think of the Ghost Dance and the ghost shirts. A long time ago, an Indian named Wovoka had prophesied that, if enough Natives performed the ceremonial dance, all evil would be swept from the earth, the white people would leave North America, and those wearing the sacred shirts would be bulletproof. The Ghost Dance swept across the country, scaring the shit out of the US government, which sent troops to stop Indians from taking part in the ceremony. And the Natives who believed they'd be safe from the soldiers' bullets? They learned otherwise.

The next day Nathan was quiet and withdrawn, even more so than usual.

"You okay?" I said, lighting up a smoke.

"Just tired."

"Want to make sure you're okay. We'll get back to normal when all this is over."

"Yeah, I been thinking about that," he said. "Like, what happens when this stuff is done. You know, the high school sucks so bad. I'm not learning anything. The teachers don't care, they're just losers who couldn't get jobs in the city, so they come here for a paycheck."

This wasn't really true. Rez schools got some bad apples, sure, but we also got the idealistic young teachers who wanted to change the world. Most of them burned out after a few years, but some stayed.

"Since I got arrested, the kids at school have been really shitty. Worse than before.

313

Now even Jimmy — you know, like my only real friend — can't hang with me, 'cause his parents think I'm a bad influence or whatever."

I hadn't known that.

He went on. "My only friends now are the stoners and the freaks. They're not even really friends, just dudes I gotta rat out. The other jerks make fun of me. You know what they call me?" He hesitated, as if I'd be angry to hear of the taunts cast by his classmates.

"Chief Iyeska. Like, to 'chief' some weed is to smoke a bowl without passing it around. And iyeska, I been called that since the day I was born. You know, it's like I'm not Indian enough for the full-bloods, but too Native for the white kids. I don't fit in nowhere."

Iyeska. Originally, the word meant "translator," and also "speaks white." But over time, it became a nasty insult, shorthand for half-breed.

"Nathan, listen," I said. "I got the same sort of crap when I was in school. Plenty of assholes here, I know. They always find some way to insult you." I tossed my cigarette butt in the trash. "But you can't let those guys get you down. Maybe they grow up and stop being assholes, or maybe you move on with your life and ignore them. You hear me?"

"Easy for you to say," he said. "You don't have to be with them every day. When you were in school, they didn't have social media stuff. Kids are on their phones all the time, posting nasty shit about people they don't like. Everyone reads it! What'll happen if word gets out about the snitching? Everybody will really hate me!"

He was beginning to tear up, although I could tell he was trying to fight it.

"So I guess I decided," he said. "I want to drop out in two years. When I'm sixteen. I can get a job somewhere, maybe Rapid City. Get away from those losers."

Drop out? He'd been talking about college just a few months ago, now he was planning to quit school and work some bottom-rung job. I wondered what sort of life he'd have if he left school. Would he end up like me, with ten layers of scars on his knuckles from punching out dirtbags?

"Nathan, I know this is a hard time. A lot of bad shit has gone down. But don't let them win. You finish school, then you make up your mind about getting a job or going to college. You got to hang on, okay?"

A few tears spilled out. "It's just that, you know, I can't sleep or focus. Sometimes I

315

wake up at four in the morning and my mind goes to bad places. Like, I think about all the stuff that's happened, not just at school but with Mom dying and all that. Then I start thinking that maybe it would be better if I'd never been born."

Now more tears came. He turned his head so I couldn't see him, but I glimpsed his misery. He looked desolate and over-whelmed. I didn't know what to say to comfort him.

Then I had a thought.

I went to the bedroom, where I had some boxes stowed in the back of the closet. It took me a few minutes to find what I was looking for, but eventually I located it, wrapped in some newspaper at the bottom of a box full of old photos and ancient comic books.

"This is for you," I said to Nathan. "My mom — your grandma — gave it to me a long time ago. My medicine bag."

I handed it to him, the bag I'd had since I was six years old. It was a small beaded leather pouch with a rawhide cord so it could be worn under a shirt. My mother gave it to me, said that it would bring me strength and protection. As a kid, I'd car-ried it daily for years, but I put it away after my father's death. I hadn't looked at it since then.

"What's in it?" he asked.

"Honestly, I don't remember. Open it."

Inside, there was some dried-out sage, a few tiny rocks, and a small feather. Vague memories of gathering those items came back to me, half-remembered images from my childhood.

"What do I do with all that?" he asked, pointing to the little tangle of objects he'd poured out on the table.

"Give 'em to me," I said. "You need to make your own bundle. Put stuff in there that means something to you."

"Like what?"

"That's up to you. Anything you care about."

"Like Mom's ring?"

I'd forgotten he had Sybil's ring, a small silver piece that she'd loved and worn for years.

"Perfect."

He ran off to his room, and I looked at the little pile of items on the table. The sage, rocks, and feather — objects I'd carried as a child faithfully. I stared at them for a moment, then scooped the pile all up and put it in the pocket of my denim jacket.

Later in the evening, I called Tommy to see if he wanted to grab some food. I agreed to pick him up, and he offered to pay for the meals, having won some money again at the casino.

I honked my horn outside his little house.

"V dog! Good to see you. Where you wanna eat? Can't go to the casino restaurant 'cause they might put me to work. How about the Depot? Kitchen's open till nine. Pretty good burgers."

"No, I don't want to go there," I said. "Too many people, too many problems."

I never knew what sort of reaction I'd get at that place. Some people viewed me as a champion, others wanted to avenge a beating I'd laid down. "How about we drive down to Valentine?"

"Naw, that's too far! Hungry like a mofo. Come on, let's just run over to the Depot. You can go there once without getting in a fight, can't you?"

"All right, fine," I said. "You got cash?"

"Oh, yeah. Hit a pretty good jackpot, won at blackjack too. Still got a hundred left — bought all the drinks after my big win. Everybody wanted to be my friend, start up

318

some skinships."

"Heard you were getting friendly with Velma few nights ago."

His face lit up. "Velma, yeah! She's a real chili pepper — red and hot. Might go check her out at the dollar store tomorrow. But yo, there were some crazy cats at the bar last night."

"Anyone I know?"

"Don't think so. Some dude from Pine Ridge, he was tellin' us that the Republic of Lakota is gonna happen soon."

"What's that?" I looked over at him.

"He said they filed some lawsuit to get back the land promised in the treaty of . . . 1869? 1864? Don't know, but he was saying we're gonna get South Dakota back, most of Nebraska and Montana too. And Wyoming! I forgot."

"Right," I said. "Where are all the white people gonna go?"

"That's the best part. He said the Lakota government will set up reservations for the wasicus, give 'em commodity foods and open boarding schools for the little kids. Sheeit, I almost busted a gut! Taste of their own medicine!"

He laughed so hard that I had a hard time focusing on the road.

"All right, very funny," I said.

"And oh, I forgot. There was some real strange dude there. He didn't have no arms. Had a wooden arm and one of those metal ones with the hook."

"Was he in the war or something?"

"No, that's what I thought, too. He said it happened a long time ago. Told me he put his arms down on the railroad tracks, let the train cut 'em off. Dude said he had to sacrifice them to keep the world safe."

"You messing with me?"

He shook his head. "Naw, it's the truth! He was making all kinds of jokes, too, like sayin' his piano playing wasn't any good now. Wasn't funny, kind of creeped me out."

I'll say. "The guy from around here?"

Tommy shook his head again. "No, white guy from Denver. Said his name was Gabe, Abe, something like that."

In my head, I envisioned a man laying his arms down on the railroad tracks and having them taken off. How could a person do that?

"Was he drunk? I mean, not last night, but when he did it?"

"No, I asked him that. He didn't mind talking about it, he wasn't embarrassed or nothing. Said he wasn't drunk or high, he was having a vision. Must have been some strong motherfuckin' vision."

A vision. I wondered if I'd have the strength to follow a vision like that.

We walked into the Depot. I hadn't been there since I'd knocked the shit out of Guv Yellowhawk. I usually stayed away from the joint, but the hell with that. I had a right to a burger and fries.

We grabbed two spots at the bar. The place was already packed, and the noise level was deafening. CCR was blasting from the speakers, John Fogerty telling us he ain't no fortunate son. I looked around the bar, didn't see anyone with a major complaint against me. Yet.

"That crazy dishwasher still working here?" I asked Tommy.

"Who? Melvin? Don't see him."

Melvin Two Bulls had been working at the Depot for years, getting paid in food, beer, and a few bucks under the table. His only drawback as an employee was that he had the habit of taking a shower by using the spray hose by the dish machine, so you'd occasionally get a glimpse of a naked man hosing down his parts.

"I'm getting a cheeseburger. Rare. What about you?" I said.

"Yeah! Some french fries, too. But good luck gettin' a rare burger here."

"I thought maybe you were getting spoiled

by that fancy food at the casino."

"That's some good stuff — most of it — but you can't beat a burger, am I right? Lack don't serve no beef, says it's the food of the suppressors."

"Suppressors?"

"Suppressors, oppressors, whatever. Just gimme some cow. Dang, I'm starvin'."

We gave our orders to the bartender. Tommy ordered a Bud, I got a Coke.

"Yo homes, how's it going with Nathan?" said Tommy. "He okay?"

"No, he's getting some shit at school. They're pulling that iyeska crap on him. Told me he wants to drop out."

"Yeah, and do what?"

"Get a job, I guess."

"Not easy to find a job around here. Might be something at the casino. Hey, I'm sorry the little dude is takin' some grief with that half-breed stuff. Seems like things never change. Mixed-blood messages, right?"

I just shook my head. Our burgers came and we tore into them. I was looking around for some ketchup when Tommy said, "Look who just came in."

"Who?"

He pointed with his lips toward the door. "Remember him? From high school? Now he's the security dude at the school."

Ray Sits Poor. I'd heard he was the security officer at the high school now, the one in charge of safety; the person who ensured that bullying and harassment were kept to a minimum. It was pretty ironic he'd been hired for the job, because he'd been one of the biggest bullies when he was in school, one of the assholes who'd run with Rick Crow. Now he was the guy keeping the peace. Supposedly.

"Don't go startin' nothing," said Tommy. "Not done with my burger yet."

I walked over to Ray's table. He was seated with two other guys who I didn't recognize. I saw that he'd cut his hair and wore a military-style buzz cut now. He looked like a low-rent mall cop.

"Ray?" I had to shout to be heard over the music.

"Yeah?" He looked over but didn't recognize me. That wasn't surprising — we probably hadn't spoken in about twenty years.

"I'm Virgil. Wounded Horse. I'm Nathan's uncle. Nathan from the high school."

Recognition spread across his face. But there was no friendliness there.

"Right. What's up?"

"I know you're off duty, but I'm wondering if I could talk to you. About some stuff at the school."

323

"Look, we just got here."

"Take only a minute, I promise."

"All right," he said with a scowl. "Get me one of them Mexican beers, will you?" he said to his companions. "A Tecate." He pronounced it *Tee-Kate.*

"You want to go out front?" I said. "Too loud in here."

I followed him out the door. He was still a big guy, but the years hadn't done him any favors. His once muscular frame was covered with a layer of fat. Not that I cared. I was just going to talk to him, see if there was anything he could do to help Nathan out. We stepped onto the sidewalk, and I lit up a cigarette.

"So, my nephew's been telling me that some of the kids at school are giving him a bad time. Calling him iyeska, some other shit. You know anything about that?"

He spat on the sidewalk. "I stay out of their problems. Don't want no part of it. I only get called in if there's a fight. He been in any of those?"

"No, he keeps his nose pretty clean."

Ray made a weird sound. I couldn't tell if it was a sneer or a chuckle.

"You got something to tell me?" I said.

"I was the one that opened up his locker. Found them pills. Seems like he deserves whatever he gets, bringing that crap to the school."

Maybe I'd made a mistake by speaking to this guy. I tossed my cigarette and ground it out with my shoe. "I'm not going to talk about that. Just want to know if you've seen or heard anything about the bullying."

Ray spat again, right by my shoe. "Yeah, I heard something. I heard he's another fucking iyeska like you, a piece of trash that sells drugs. Good riddance; I hope he enjoys prison, where he'll get pounded in the —"

That was it. I took hold of his arm, and he immediately grabbed mine as a reflex. Exactly what I wanted him to do. He'd opened up his hand, and I gripped his right thumb and pulled it back as far as it would go. He gasped and tried to speak, but no words came out.

"If I break your thumb, you'll never make a fist or write with a pen again. But I'm not gonna do that. You know why?"

His face was contorted from the pain in his hand. He didn't say anything, just grunted. It sounded like he was giving birth to triplets, maybe quadruplets.

"Because I want you to help my nephew. He's a good kid, don't deserve that shit. About them pills, I don't know. But I know you're gonna make sure none of them bullies give him a hard time no more. Nathan takes any more shit, it's on you. I'll find you and break both thumbs, rip your ears off too. You'll look like a fucking sideshow freak. So, we good? You gonna do the right thing?"

I wrenched his thumb over another inch, right to the breaking point. He wasn't grunting anymore. His face looked like a kachina doll that had been run over by a car.

"I said, we good?"

He moved his chin a few inches up and down. I let go of Ray's hand and stepped back in case he decided to come after me. But he just rubbed his hand and avoided looking at me.

"You have a nice night," I said. "Enjoy those beers."

I walked back in to the bar and signaled to Tommy that we needed to leave. He got up, shaking his head.

"Damn, again? Never do get to eat in peace when I'm around you."

23

About a week later, I came home around noon from a construction job in Rapid City to find Marie sitting on my couch. I knew right away that something was wrong. Her face was drawn, and her entire body looked tense.

"Hey, why aren't you at —"

"I got fired!" she said. "From my goddamn job! That bitch Delia terminated me. Can you believe it?"

I pulled out a chair. "On what grounds?"

"Insubordination. She said I went over her head on the bison grant, said she'd told me to stop working on it. She never said that! She's just jealous."

"Hold on," I said. "How'd you go over her head? Wasn't the grant thing your project?"

"Yeah, but she's claiming I neglected my duties, which is bullshit. She said the bison project won't work for us because we don't have the facilities to handle fresh meat, which is stupid. It's our job to make that happen, right?" She was pulling at her long black hair like there was something attached to it.

"I don't understand. Didn't you bring in a whole bunch of money? Seems like that's a good thing for the tribe."

"Yeah, of course! Two hundred thousand dollars. The money's just sitting in the bank. You'd think I'd be rewarded. But she said I wasn't focusing on my job, which is complete and utter crap. She's the one who barely does anything."

"Can't you fight this? If it's not true?"

"I don't know. She had all the paperwork filled out — I guess she'd been planning it for a while. She mentioned like five times that I'd been written up before. Yeah, twice. In three years! And those were bullshit too. I was out one day because of a scheduling mistake, and the other time I missed was because my mom was sick. Remember that?"

I didn't, but I let her go on.

"She just hates me and wants me gone so she can waste even more time."

I thought about comforting her, but she still looked wired to detonate.

"This doesn't make sense," I said. "It's

not that easy to fire someone. From an office job."

"I guess it is. We don't have employment contracts, so we can be let go any time. That's what she told me, anyway." She started twisting one of her rings, around and around.

"Yeah, but why would she fire a councilman's daughter? Especially when he's running for tribal president? Isn't she worried she'll get in trouble with your father?"

"I know, right? That's what I thought, too. I called my dad before you got here — he said I could meet with him later today. Like I'm some nobody off the street! I wonder if he knew about this."

"Don't think so," I said. "If he knew about it, why wouldn't he tell you?"

"I don't know. I'm going to his office later. You mind driving me? I'm so mad, I can't focus. This is the first time in my life I've been fired."

"Sure, happy to take you there. But take it easy."

She just shook her head, staring down at the floor.

Two hours later, I pulled into the parking lot for the tribal council offices, finding a spot next to an older-model American truck and a German sedan.

"You want me to wait out here?" I asked.

"No, come on in. I don't know if he's ready to talk yet."

We walked inside, past the vacant reception desk and all the flyers and posters tacked on the wall. Ben's office was at the far end of the building, the door slightly open.

"I'll see you in little while, okay?" she said, then rapped on the door and went inside. I pulled up a chair and sat down in the hallway. I could hear the two of them clearly from my seat, and wondered if I should wait in the car to give them some privacy. I got up and started to walk away, but then I changed my mind. No harm in hearing what Ben had to say. I might even learn something useful.

There was a sound like chairs being moved, and I heard Ben offering Marie some coffee.

"No thanks, I'm already too jittery," Marie said.

"All right, so let's talk," Ben said. "Wayne Janis told me a few days ago this was coming. I guess Delia Kills in Water cleared it with him."

"Wait, you knew about this? Why didn't you say anything?" More chair noises.

330

"Marie, I had to stay out of it — I didn't have a choice. I'm not on that committee, I don't have any influence over there."

"Bullshit! You've been on council for years — you know everyone. And you're running for president!"

"That's exactly why I can't interfere. If I protect you, Cecil LaPlante will destroy me in the election. He'll claim nepotism, corruption. Hey, I don't like what happened. But really, it doesn't make a difference. You're going off to medical school soon — who gives a damn about that job?"

"I care! You know the crappy food in the commodity boxes. My grant will change that. Fresh buffalo meat —"

"That's not going to happen. It was a nice idea, but the tribe doesn't have the capacity to process and store bison. The money's going to be used for education and promotion. That's what I heard."

"What? The grant is for bison meat. I know, I wrote it! How are they using it for other stuff?"

"That's how federal grants work. You apply in a certain area, but the government gives you leeway on spending the funds. Wayne doesn't think it's a good use of our resources to use the grant for buffalo meat. People won't eat it anyway — they like beef and pork."

"That's not true! Lack's been telling me that bison's better than beef; people just need to learn how to cook it, get —"

"Marie, this is out of my hands. Wayne and Delia have their own plans; I understand she already used most of the grant money for new programs. I hear she's going to Florida next month for training. They're very grateful to you for —"

"Grateful? She fired me, Dad!" I heard some loud banging, which sounded like a chair being knocked over.

"All right, we're done here," Ben said. "I know you're upset and you have a right to be, but this is over."

"It's not over!" Marie said, and the door swung open. She stormed off down the hall. I trailed after her, looking behind me to see if anyone was following.

I offered to stay with Marie at her place, but she wanted some time alone. Being fired was new territory for her. I'd been let go from plenty of jobs back in my drinking days, so it didn't bother me. But this was a big deal for Marie. She felt she'd been cast out by the reservation snobs again, that she wasn't good enough or accepted for who she was. And being fired by Delia was the final indignity. I gave her some space but told her to come to my shack if she wanted company.

Later that evening my phone rang. It was Marie.

"Hey, it's me. Can you come over? I've got something I want to talk about."

This didn't sound good. "Everything all right?"

"I'm fine. Just want to discuss something in private. You can leave Nathan alone for a while, right?"

"Yeah, of course. Be there soon."

I pulled up in front of Marie's little house. As I opened my door, I saw an animal run away. A stray dog, eating some of the food Marie had put out.

I always liked coming to Marie's place. It wasn't much larger than my space, but was much cleaner and had nicer furniture. Inside, she had a blue velvet couch, black end tables, leafy green plants, and a crate of vinyl albums in the corner. In the kitchen, there was one of those Kit-Cat clocks, the kind with the big eyes that move from side to side. Hanging on the walls in the living room were two abstract paintings, carica-tures of the images used in the media to depict Natives. I saw Chief Wahoo and other

Native sports mascots, their images defaced and mutilated by the artist. Another print portrayed three wolves running in an electric blue landscape.

Marie noticed me looking at it. "She's an Osage artist. Or was, I guess. She died a few years ago. My mom just gave it to me."

"I like it. Surreal. Looks like they're on the moon or something."

"You want something to drink?"

"Don't suppose you have any Shastas?"

"Matter of fact, I do." She poured a glass of cherry cola over ice and some water for herself, then sat down next to me on the couch. "Thanks for coming by so late."

"No problem," I said. "You feeling better about the job stuff?"

"Not really. Still super pissed off. It's just not right. I busted my hump over there for years, doing the work, making the program better. Don't know if I told you, but I fixed the inventory system last fall and got more choices on fruits and vegetables." She took a drink of water. "It doesn't make sense. To fire me. Yeah, I missed a few days, but there are people working for the tribe who barely show up."

"I hear you," I said. "It's not fair. Hell with them."

"I know I should move on, but I can't stop

thinking about it. That's why I asked you to stop by, got something I want to ask you."

"Yeah?"

I waited for her to say more, but she hesitated.

"Ask away," I said.

"Well, I don't want to sound paranoid, but something doesn't make sense. Delia could have canned me last year if she just wanted me out. You know, we don't like each other, but we figured out how to work together. Pretty much she ignores me and I ignore her, except when we have to talk about work stuff. So why fire me now?"

I took a gulp of my Shasta. "I don't know. Maybe she was waiting for the right time?"

"Maybe. But my dad said something today at his office. He said Delia's been using the bison grant money for some programs, that most of it's already gone. But that's not right. I get copies of all the financial reports and bank statements, and I haven't seen any funds being spent. Just four thousand for Lack's food truck; besides that, it's all still there. I just reviewed the last statement, so I know I'm right. I would have been notified of any accounts payable or pending liabilities. You see what I'm saying?" She looked at me with an expectant expression.

335

"You think there's something going on with the grant? Something shady?"

"I don't know," she said, and poured herself more water. "Either my dad's wrong about this, or she's spending the money somewhere, off the books. Sounds bizarre, I know, but my gut tells me there's no reason for Delia to fire me now unless she's hiding something."

I chewed on an ice cube, a habit my mother had always hated. "Okay," I said, "maybe she is hiding something. Wouldn't put it past her. But you don't work there anymore, so what can you do?"

She looked me straight in the eye. "I want you to help me break in to her office."

At first I thought Marie was mocking me. She'd never broken a law in her life, not even a speeding ticket, and now she was proposing to commit trespass and burglary.

"You're not serious? Why would you —"

"Hear me out. Maybe I'm wrong about this, but I don't think so. Something's not right with this whole grant thing."

"This is crazy. You can't break into someone's work because you got fired. What if we got arrested?"

"Oh, come on! You're the one who beats

people up when the police won't do anything."

She had a point. "All right, let's even say we could get in to her office. What makes you think you'll find anything there?"

"The budget and spreadsheets are on her computer, but I know the password. I can check out the department financials, see the expenditures. Maybe there's nothing, but at least I'd know."

I went to her refrigerator, got another Shasta, and sat down. "Look, I know you're mad about getting fired. But this isn't the way. If she's pulling some crooked shit, you should tell your father, let him handle it."

She shook her head. "I thought about that. Calling my dad, asking him to check it out. But he doesn't want any drama now, not with the election coming up. What if he accuses her, but it turns out she didn't do anything? I need to get the records first, then I can go to him."

I shook my head. "Marie, no. You need to step back. I don't know crap about medical school, but I bet they won't like it if you get popped with a felony charge."

"I know I'm right. If you're too chickenshit to help me, I'll do it myself."

Her eyes were blazing, and I didn't doubt that she'd follow through with her threat to go over there by herself. The woman who'd told me to stop taking the law into my own hands now wanted my help in committing a felony, all because of her enemy. Delia Kills in Water, the one who'd bullied Marie for years but never had to pay for her sins. Maybe it was time.

"Fine. I'll help you. But we do it my way."

Marie wanted to drive over there immediately and get inside Delia's computer, but I told her we needed to come up with a plan. I asked her about Delia's work schedule and any security procedures at the office. She said that Delia left promptly at five o'clock, and the last employee usually left around six, at the latest. A cleaning person came in once a week, but usually finished by nine. No alarm system or surveillance cameras. Marie still had her key to the outer doors, but I'd have to jimmy the lock on Delia's office door. This sounded pretty straightforward. We decided to go over there the next night.

"I still think you should let your dad handle this," I told her. "Sleep on it, see if you feel different tomorrow."

"I won't."

True to her word, she called me the next

morning and told me it was on. So I gathered the tools we'd need: a screwdriver, two flashlights, three pieces of wire, and an old grocery rewards card. And my Spyder knife. Just in case.

We left just after midnight, taking her car because it was quieter and more reliable. I parked a few blocks away so no one would see a vehicle in the parking lot. The area didn't have many houses, but there was no point in taking chances.

"Remember," I said, "if anyone's in there, just tell 'em that you're picking up some of your stuff and were too embarrassed to come by during the day."

"There won't be anybody, trust me."

"Just check first. Don't turn on any of the overhead lights, use the flashlight. Once we get in to her office, I'll stand guard by the back door."

"Okay, boss," she said, smiling.

She was a lot less nervous than I would have expected. She seemed happy, jaunty even, not like someone committing her first major crime.

"I feel like those burglars in that movie with the kid when his parents forgot him," Marie said.

"Home Alone?"

"That's the one."

"Hope it turns out better for us than it did for them."

We walked to the back door of the tribal office building. No lights were visible from the outside. Marie opened it with her key.

"Hello?" Marie's voice rang out down the hallway.

No answer.

"I think we're good," she whispered. I handed her a flashlight and turned mine on.

We walked down the hall, our beams lighting the way. It was eerie in there, like being in a dim underground tunnel. Marie was quiet now, her cheery mood gone as the reality of our actions became clear to her.

"There it is," Marie said, pointing her flashlight at a closed door. It had a lever handle lock, not the standard cylinder, which I knew I could open.

"Shit," I said, pulling out my screwdriver. "Never worked on one of these before. Keep your light on it."

I grabbed the lever to check the tension and twisted it. To my surprise, it turned all the way and the door swung open.

"I'll be damned," I said. Marie shone her flashlight, and I peered inside. Piles of papers, several coffee mugs, a few framed photos. It smelled like Delia'd left some food out to spoil, the odor sickly sweet like a rotten apple. I picked up my flashlight and waved it around the room. Delia's computer was an older desktop model, set off in the corner.

"That what you're looking for?" I asked.

"Yeah," she said in a low voice. "Should be no problem, unless the password's been changed."

"You do your thing. I'll be in the hall by the door." She sat down in Delia's chair as I moved out of the room. "Hurry."

She didn't respond, her attention focused on the computer.

I walked down the hall to the back door. The plan was for me to wait there and make sure no one came in. I sat down on an old plastic chair, the flashlight by my side. I could see through the window into the darkness beyond, pitch-black, no cars or lights visible from my vantage point. Then my eyes adjusted to the night, and I could see a stand of trees next to an empty lot, the weeds blowing slightly in the wind.

I tried to stay focused on the road, watching for cars, but my mind wandered, and I remembered playing with my friend Will as a child in a field not far from here, both of us no more than seven or eight, chasing each other in the grass. Then we'd seen the sky darken abruptly as thousands of butterflies flew by, landing on us, our entire bodies covered with them. I'd laughed and shrieked with delight, but Will was terrified. He ran away, screaming, convinced that he'd committed some terrible sin, and the butterflies had somehow punished him for his deeds. Will and I were never really friends after that; I sensed he'd associated me with his terror and fright from that day, but we never spoke of it, both of us taking our separate paths. Last I heard, he'd moved to California, getting as far away from the reservation as he could.

My memories were interrupted by a set of headlights off in the distance. Although faint, they were headed our way. I glanced over my shoulder — no sign of Marie. The headlights grew closer, and the vehicle started to slow down.

Shit, were they coming here? Could it be the cleaning crew or some worker, come to finish a project? I thought about running down the hall and getting Marie, but I waited. Better to stay in the hallway and let her finish. I instinctively felt for the knife in my back pocket as I rehearsed several cover stories.

Then the headlights came to a complete stop about a block away. My heart pounded as I readied myself. Why were they stopping there? There were no houses close by, just an empty field. The lights turned off, and I saw a faint glow inside the car. A match or a lighter, for a cigarette or maybe some peji. Probably just teenagers, or maybe someone from the bar, stopping to spark up before the long drive home.

I began to relax, and realized I could use a smoke myself. I watched the glimmering in the car with some envy. After a while, the headlights turned back on, and the car drove away. A few minutes later, I heard a noise from down the hall. The sound of a door closing, then footsteps. The beam of Marie's flashlight became visible, and she appeared in the darkness.

"You finished?" I asked, shining my light on her.

"Let's go," she said, and I saw her face was strained, a sour look playing across her features. We left as quickly as possible after checking to see that Delia's door was closed and the computer had been turned off.

"You find what you were looking for?" I asked once we were in the car and a few miles away.

"Yeah," she said. "It's not good."

"Tell me."

"Just like I thought, the grant money's

343

nearly gone. I found bank statements, check receipts, credit card payments. All the money was funneled to some company, none of it used for the bison program. It's embezzlement, fraud. No wonder she wanted me out of the office."

I looked over at her face. She looked despondent, not triumphant. "So what's wrong?"

"I found the company. The one she's been using for the illegal payments."

"Yeah?"

"It's called Indigi-Cultural Cuisine, LLC," she said. "Lack's business. He's been working with her. To steal from the tribe."

The next morning, she showed me the photos and copies she'd made of all the receipts and payments from the grant account.

"Are you sure this is Lack's company?" I asked.

"Positive. I authorized a payment for the food truck to the same account. Trust me, I've already gone over this in my head a thousand times. As the assistant director, I should have been notified of all disbursements. She kept the payments on a different account so I couldn't see them. As far as I can tell, about a hundred and fifty thousand dollars are gone." She poured herself some tea and brought me some coffee.

"My God," I said. "This is insane. Is it possible that Lack's not involved — that maybe it's someone else from his restaurant working with Delia?"

"Nope," she said. "His company's a sole-owner corporation. He's the only one who handles the accounts. There's no question she's been making payments to him for false expenses. I even pulled up the invoices she made up. Bogus receipts for catering weddings, baby showers, seafood purchases, you name it. I know none of that happened, I would have heard about it at the restaurant if Lack was doing any catering."

"You're sure?" I said. "Those sound legit."

"Not too many ten-thousand-dollar wedding receptions around here." Her face was drawn. "No wonder Lack stayed here longer than he'd planned. He's been getting all these phony payments. I'm guessing Delia probably split it with him."

"You find any evidence of that?"

She nodded. "Yeah, bank deposits to her personal account, a few other receipts. She's been cheating the tribe, no doubt. Probably find more scams, if I looked deeper."

"So what are you going to do? You finally got Delia, you can expose her as a thief and fraud. Just like you've been saying all these years."

"Yeah, she's the worst. Stealing money from the people — makes my blood boil."

"Well, she can rot in jail," I said. "Embezzling government funds — the feds won't ignore that. She'll probably get ten years or more."

She took a drink, then frowned. "You don't get it. If I report Delia, Lack goes down too. All the good work he's doing to help our people is over. So what do I do? Take out Delia and send Lack to jail? Then the oyate really suffer. Send two people to prison, hurt the entire tribe. No justice in that."

I couldn't believe what I was hearing. "Those assholes steal over a hundred thousand dollars from the tribe, they deserve prison time," I said. "Live in a cage, shit in a metal bowl — that'll be some justice."

"Right, and the indigenous food revolution stops. He'll be disgraced, which is fine, but so will the movement. Not to mention, the government will never award us another grant."

"It can't be just one guy with the healthy food?" I said. "There must be others talking about Native cooking and all that."

"Not really. He's the one getting the word

out there in the press. He gets arrested, the media would jump all over it."

"Can't you report Delia and leave Lack out of it?"

"I thought about that, but there's a paper trail leading to him. No way the prosecutors would miss it."

This seemed incredible to me. She was actually planning to let these thieves steal a huge sum of money from the tribe and walk away. This wasn't the Marie I knew.

"All right, I get that you don't want to involve Lack," I said. "I don't agree, but I see your reasons. But if you don't rat out Delia, she'll just keep stealing. From the people. You think about that?"

She sighed. "Yeah, I have. All night long. Best I can come up with is this: maybe after the election, I go to my dad and tell him to keep Delia away from accounts payable. But I know him. He'll start asking questions and figure it out." She looked over at me, and I saw the anguish on her face. "Probably the best thing is for me to stay out of it, go become a doctor. Then I can at least help a few people. Instead of just fucking everything up."

She put her head down on the table, only her black hair visible, her shoulders shuddering slightly.

347

I didn't know how to comfort her, not when she was in such pain. I settled for a hand on her arm, the scabs and calluses on my knuckles contrasting against her soft skin. After a while, she took my hand, and we stayed there, silent.

24

The next weeks were hard. Marie remained depressed about the fraud she'd uncovered and wounded by the discovery that Lack was just another swindler. She'd believed in his work to change Native diets, which made the discovery all the more painful. Despite my attempts to persuade her, she stood by her decision not to report the embezzlement, because she didn't want to derail the work Lack was doing nor create a scandal for the food program on our reservation. As for me, I would have happily sent both Delia and Lack to prison, but Marie had to work this out on her own, and she'd decided to focus on the greater good. She was convinced that Delia and Lack would receive the fate they deserved, that the universe would ensure it. I was skeptical, but kept my opinions on fate and justice to myself.

Not to mention, I had my own issues to

deal with. Although I tried not to think about it, Nathan still had to wear the wire in order to fulfill the terms of his agreement with the prosecutors. He'd been laying low at school as he'd been instructed, waiting to hear from the heroin dealers and not raising any suspicions. He didn't say anything more to me about kids bullying him at school, although I didn't know if this had anything to do with my intervention with Ray Sits Poor or if he was just keeping quiet about it.

One afternoon, Nathan said he had something to tell me.

"Leksi, I saw those guys. You know, with the drugs. They were hanging around after school, and they asked if I wanted to buy some. I said yes."

He looked at me like he'd done something wrong, but I think he was just scared. Scared of wearing the wire, scared of kids finding out what he'd done, scared that his life might change. Again.

"I'll call the lawyer."

I contacted Charley Leader Charge first. When I finally got in touch with him, he said he'd phone the investigators right away and I should wait to hear from them. It didn't take long. Dennis called me within the hour, said he'd start setting up the sting. Dennis spoke to Nathan on the phone, said that Nathan should talk to the dealers and find out when they could deliver the drugs. He told him to ask to buy more heroin, about ten times what he'd bought before. If they asked why he was getting so much, Nathan was to say that half of it was for a friend. He was to make sure that the deal would go down at the school, either inside or nearby. As soon as Nathan set up the day and time for the buy, he'd be fitted with the listening device. The wire.

The next morning Nathan went off to school, where he'd set up the purchase. He'd call me when it was confirmed, then he'd come home and meet with Dennis. They'd need about thirty minutes to get Nathan wired up. The reality began to sink in.

"Are you ready for this?" Marie asked while she brewed some tea, the Sparrow's Tears blend.

"Don't have a choice. Just hope Nathan can keep it together today. This shit is tough on me, must be a hundred times worse for him."

"One more thing," she said, pouring herself some black tea and adding a little sugar. "I don't know if this is the right time, though."

"Go ahead. Nathan's stuff won't get going until later today." I watched Marie stir the tea, little swirls of darkness in her cup.

"Okay. So, here's what's going on." She hesitated. "I guess you know I've been kind of down. The thing with Lack and Delia. Delia, she's always been terrible, but I thought Lack was a good man, my friend. To find this out, it's been . . ." She shook her head. "Now I don't have a job, and it doesn't feel right to work at the restaurant anymore. So I'm thinking maybe it's time for a fresh start."

She poured herself more tea, even though her cup was nearly full.

"Thing is, I have to give my answer to med school in two weeks. The one in Albuquerque. You know, I didn't want to say anything about this while Nathan was around. But I have to make a decision soon. Be sure I'm comfortable. With everything."

I'd been putting Marie's med-school issue out of my mind. But now it was here.

"What are you going to do?"

"It's what I've been working for, right?" she said. "Maybe I can do some good for the people this way. I mean, everything I did at the tribal office was for shit. And my folks are absolutely hysterical about it.

They'd have one daughter who's a banker and one doctor. That's their dream, to show how accomplished their children are — not rezzy at all. Mom says she'll disinherit me if I don't accept. She hates it here, wants me to leave and move to a city. But this is my home."

"Is this your dream, or your parents'?"

She looked away from me and began putting away the clean dishes in the drying rack. She'd come up with a new pattern of stacking bowls, cups, and dishes, a configuration she said made more sense than the haphazard scheme Nathan and I had been using.

"I don't know anymore. Maybe it never was my thing. The school's so damn far away. I mean, would you be able to visit me? I could come back for winter break and a few weeks in the summer. But that's probably it."

She stopped for a moment and looked closely at her teacup, like it had a minor flaw that no one but she could see. "I guess I'm wondering about you and me. What's going to happen? You know, we're good together. It's different — better — than it was before. You've changed. A lot. You're not trying to run away anymore — from what's been chasing you."

She put the cup down. "But what happens if I leave? Will you go back to being an enforcer? Do I get a phone call in a year telling me you've been killed, so I have to mourn the man I love?"

Love. A word we'd never used before. Did I love her? Of course. I always had. And if I loved her, then I had to do what was best for her. But I didn't know what that was.

She looked over, waiting for me to say something.

There is no word for goodbye in Lakota. That's what my mother used to tell me. Sure, there were words like *toksa,* which meant "later," that were used by people as a modern substitute. She'd told me that the Lakota people didn't use a term for farewell because of the idea that we are forever connected. To say goodbye would mean the circle was broken.

I pondered this. I sensed we needed to say goodbye to our old lives, whatever they were. Soon Nathan would cross a line he never knew existed, and Marie would be committing to a new life and career in New Mexico. Could I say goodbye to her?

And me? I didn't know what was in store for my world. Maybe it was time to stop taking vigilante jobs and get a new profession. I couldn't even remember the person I'd been before I started beating people up. All around me I saw Natives doing good work: Marie with medical school, Ben at the tribal council, even Tommy with his new passion for cooking. Perhaps it was time for me to take up something new, something that didn't involve using my fists. I remembered that before my father died, I'd helped him fix cars. He'd give me some little job and show me how to do it. Even though I must have been only seven or eight years old, I recalled the satisfaction I'd felt when I'd helped him with some minor repair. Taking out some part of an engine, putting it back in. The feeling of fixing something, not breaking or damaging things — or people. Maybe it was time for a long goodbye, farewell to what we'd known and lived, breaking the circle, severing our ties.

In the afternoon I put my thoughts aside while I waited for Nathan's phone call. Drug dealers were not known for their reliability, so the buy might not happen right away. I watched an old movie on TV, something about a con man and his mother. Then the door opened, and Nathan walked in.

"Everything all right? Thought you were

going to call," I said.

"Yeah, I'm fine. Got really hungry, didn't have any money for a snack."

"You talk to the guys?"

He opened the refrigerator and looked inside. Marie had cleared out most of the junk food he liked to eat. "Yeah, for like a second. They're coming after school tomorrow. With the stuff. When school ends, around four o'clock."

I wondered how he was so nonchalant. Maybe it was just an act, or the hubris of early adolescence. But perhaps it was for the best. I called Dennis and told him the buy was on. He said that Nathan should come home right after school tomorrow — early if he could — and meet with his team. They'd put the wire on him, give him some money for the purchase and a burner phone, and he'd go back to school to meet the dealers. After the buy, they'd be arrested and this whole mess would be over. Nathan would have satisfied his obligation to the prosecutors, and the charges against him would be dropped. We'd put our lives back together. If we could.

The next day passed by in a blur. Marie stayed at her house; I suspected she wanted to keep out of our way while things began to happen. I watched mindless TV shows, the first one about people who made bids at auction on abandoned storage lockers and the contents inside. It took me a while to understand; I didn't get why the people who'd rented the storage units would leave their belongings there. Why not just empty the unit if you didn't want to pay for it anymore? This made no sense to me, not to mention that storage lockers were a crazy wasicu concept in the first place. On the rez, people would toss extra stuff in their backyard rather than pay rent on some tiny garage-like storage space. Or give it away to someone who needed it.

Nathan came home after school, around three o'clock. Dennis was already at my house, waiting for him.

"Let's get you set up," Dennis said. "First things first, how much cash do you need?"

Nathan looked puzzled. "What do you mean?"

"To buy the drugs. How much did they say they'd sell you? Ten hits? Or did you ask for more?"

"Uh, yeah, they said they could do ten chunks."

"What's a hit go for here?"

"I guess ten or fifteen dollars."

Dennis handed Nathan some bills. "Here's

two hundred. If they offer you more, go ahead and buy it. I need you to sign this form; you're acknowledging I gave you the money. Government makes us keep track of every dime."

Nathan scrawled his name on a piece of paper. "What do I do with the change? You know, if any's left over?"

"Hang on to it and give it back to me later. Or not. Main thing is, buy as much drugs as you can. Okay, next thing: You still have the burner phone I gave you?"

Nathan nodded.

"Let's see it," said Dennis. "How's the battery doing?"

"Charged all the way."

"All right, call me; make sure it's working. There's only one number programmed on there."

Nathan punched some buttons on the cell phone, then we heard a buzzing sound from Dennis's pocket.

"Okay, it's operational. Remember, only use it if it's an emergency. We'll come in and assist if you call us. You remember the emergency code?"

Nathan shook his head.

"Say 'Going to a friend's house.' That's all you have to say: we hear those words, we'll be there in one minute. You got it?"

Nathan nodded and smirked. I could tell he thought Dennis didn't trust him to take care of himself.

"Last thing," said Dennis. "Let's get the listening device on you."

"You mean the wire?" I said.

"Yeah. We don't call it that anymore. It's all digital now." He took out a small black device that looked like a remote entry key for a car. "This is the transmitter. Just hook this on your key ring and keep it in your pocket."

"Where's the microphone?" I asked.

Dennis smiled. "The cell phone. The burner I gave him. There's an app on the phone called Envoy that automatically records and sends data in real time to our people." He turned his attention to Nathan. "But make sure you don't turn the phone off. When you're making the buy, just set the phone down like you normally would. The only thing you can't do is stick it in your pocket. We won't be able to hear you."

Now Nathan looked concerned. "Like, can you show me how to hold it? So I don't mess it up?"

"You don't have to hold it any special way. Just put it down on a chair or carry it in your hand. Like I said, don't jam it in your pants or turn it off."

Nathan looked dubious. "Uh, okay."

"There's one other thing I need you to do." He pulled his chair closer to Nathan. "Don't overdo it, but I need you to describe — out loud — what's going on at the buy while it's happening. Say something like, 'How many hits did you bring?' We only have audio, so we need a verbal record of what's happening. That make sense?"

Now I was concerned. "Won't he tip off the drug guys that he's recording the conversation? If he says something that sounds weird?"

"That's the whole point," Dennis said. "Be natural. Say things you'd normally say. Talk about what's happening, ask questions. You think you can do that?"

Nathan had an expression on his face that suggested we were the oldest and most ridiculous people in the world. "No worries. I can handle it."

"All right," said Dennis, "let's do a test, check the sound quality." He took the phone from Nathan and clicked on it. "I turned on the app, so you're in record mode now. You got the transmitter? Cool. Go in the other room and say some words. Virgil and I'll go out to my unit, see how it sounds."

Dennis and I walked out to his unmarked police car and got in. There was a small black console on the seat. He flipped on a switch and turned a knob, presumably the volume.

"All right, let's test her out."

He and I waited. All I heard was a faint electrical hum and the sound of the birds chattering to each other. We sat there for about thirty seconds. It felt like hours.

We waited some more. Still nothing.

"Shit," Dennis said, and started to open his door. Then some sound came from the device, surprisingly clear.

"Ah, testing, testing, test, test. Can you guys hear me? I don't know what to say, I feel kind of stupid, but I guess —"

Dennis clicked a knob on the console. "We're good."

We went back inside. Nathan came out of the bedroom with a curious look on his face. "Could you guys hear me?"

"Loud and clear," said Dennis. "When you meet with them, be sure to hold your phone that way."

Nathan nodded.

"Okay, we're locked and loaded. We'll be in the tech car, listening to your conversation and recording it. Your uncle will be there with us. There'll be another vehicle there — the follow car — watching you directly." Dennis looked at his phone, then turned back to Nathan. "Buy the drugs and come right back to the house, don't go anywhere else. I'll need to snap some pics of the dope and take your statement. We won't arrest them right away — that'd be a dead giveaway you set 'em up. We'll probably put the arm on them later today or tomorrow. Game-time decision. You ready? Kickoff in thirty minutes."

Nathan rolled his eyes at me when Dennis wasn't looking. The football references. Nathan hated football, thought it was stupid and violent.

"All right," Dennis said. "Head on out to the school. Any problems, call me and say the code. Like I said, the ghost car will have eyes on you."

Ten minutes after Nathan left, Dennis and I drove to the school and parked a few blocks away. "You sure we're not too far to hear him?" I asked.

Dennis was making some adjustments on the recording device. "Should be fine. Range is about a quarter mile. We don't get good sound, we'll move in closer."

We sat in silence, waiting for something to happen. After a while, the console began to make a scratchy sound. It sounded like a transmission from the moon landing. I realized I could hear the sounds from my car, the one Nathan was driving. I could tell he had the radio on, tuned to KOYA, the rez station, which was playing some powwow music. His phone was picking up the car's radio and sending the transmission to us. The song ended, and I could hear the DJ talking. *"Hey KOYA land, coming up by request is 'Somewhere Over the Rainbow,' the ukulele version, going out to little Robin Two Crow, who turns four today. Happy birthday, Robin, from your Unci Charlene!"*

"I think that's the radio in my car. Are we hearing that from his cell?" I asked.

"Yep," said Dennis. "He probably has the phone on the seat by the car's speaker. Or maybe not. Device is pretty sensitive."

The music continued for another few minutes, then stopped. We heard some rattling, the sound of a door slam, and then nothing.

"He put the phone in his pocket," said Dennis. "He needs to hold it in his hand when the guys show up. I hope he remembers."

"Don't worry, he'll do it."

"Hope so. Otherwise, we have to go through all this again. Let me call Mike. He's in the ghost over by the school."

Dennis made the call. "It's me. You got eyes on him?" He paused, listening to the cop. I listened in, trying to make out what he was saying.

"Uh-huh, uh-huh, right. Call if they move."

"What's going on?" I asked.

"He spotted Nathan and another male. They're walking to the back of the school near the picnic tables."

"Is he with one of the dealers?"

"No, they're waiting for them. Probably another friend looking to buy dope. Don't know which of the gang will bring the stuff — hope it's Rick Crow, but it could be one of the younger guys. I doubt Loco will come, he usually stays at the house, sends the younger dudes out for the deliveries."

We waited about twenty minutes. Occasionally we'd hear little bursts of sound from the console, but nothing I could make out. I tried to be calm, but my agitation felt like jolts of direct-current electricity coursing under my skin. Finally Dennis's cell phone rang.

"Yeah?" He stopped and listened, then gave a few more uh-huhs and okays.

"What's happening?" I said.

"The Denver guys are there. Three of them, one we think is called Manuel, the other we're not sure. And good news. Your buddy Rick Crow's there."

A jolt of pure adrenaline shot through my body.

"Mike says they're heading over to the tables now," Dennis went on. "Perfect. That's school property, right where we want 'em. Now we just need Nathan to take out the phone so we can hear the shitheads."

We waited some more — it seemed like an eternity — for the recording console to start transmitting their conversation.

Silence. *Goddamn it, Nathan, take your phone out of your pocket! Do it now!*

I decided to ask Dennis about the procedures in case we couldn't hear their voices. "What happens if we can't —"

All of a sudden the console erupted with voices.

. . . coming over later? I don't know, I gotta do some stuff Homes come over and chill we got the new — Look at that bitch Who? Walking over there You know you want some of that Fuck you No fuck you skin Damn she's fine You wish Go talk to her — Hell yeah You know her? Naw he don't know shit Hey I gotta go soon check out my uncle

Nathan's voice came through. It was hard to make out who was speaking from the chorus of voices, but I recognized his speech. I looked over at Dennis, but he was listening intently to the conversation, staring straight at the black console as if the guys were inside the unit itself.

It's all good Where you been Rick long time no time You know little of this little of that Y'all heading to the shack later? Might go to V-town to chow You wanna come N? Can't gotta do some stuff you know like keep it chill on the home front

Nathan again. It sounded like he knew these guys well, which worried me.

I do my shit and everyone leaves me alone you hear me? I hear We gonna be able to do this? I got some paypa Yeah it's cool We got to head over to the car do the thing All good Let's go What where you at

The conversation ended, and we heard a rustling sound from the console.

"Shit," Dennis said, "he stuck the phone in his pocket."

I started to say something, but Dennis held up his finger, then made a call.

"What are they doing?" he said into his phone. A short pause. "Okay, let me know."

He turned to me. "They're walking, possibly to their car. Probably do the deal in there so no one can see them. Pretty typical. Not a problem, as long as Nathan keeps his cool."

"Will your guy be able to see them?"

"Don't worry, he's a pro. One of my best

366

men. He'll move if he has to, just has to be sure he's not made. Should be able to hear more in a second on the device — still within range."

We could only hear a rustling sound from the console. I wondered if I should go to the school and monitor the situation myself. *Nathan, goddamn it! Take your phone out so we can hear what's going on!*

Dennis's phone rang. "Yeah?" A pause. "All right, do it, but be careful."

"What's happening?"

"They drove off. Nathan went with them. But don't worry, Mike's going to tail the vehicle."

I looked out into the field outside the car. It was early evening, when the snakes came out. Sure enough, I saw a small movement about a hundred yards away. A little rattlesnake, the brown-and-tan pattern barely visible, moving slowly between the rocks and the grass.

"What do we do now?"

"We wait," he said. "Find out where they're headed. Then we'll drive out there, get back in range for the wire."

"Any idea where they're going?"

"Don't know. Maybe they're heading out to their cabin to get more balloons. Not good — we wanted this to go down on school grounds. Don't worry, Mike is on them; he'll let us know where they're at." He put his phone down. "No reason to stay here. Let's go over to the gas station, wait for Mike's call."

We drove a few blocks to the convenience store.

"He'll call as soon as he has a bead on 'em. I'm gonna grab a soda, you want one?"

I shook my head. This was probably routine to Dennis, but I wanted him to be on full alert, not buying snacks. He went into the store, and I looked down at my old-fashioned phone, checking to see if Nathan had called me, even though I knew it was pointless. He'd call Dennis if there were any problems.

Dennis came out of the store with a can of Dr Pepper in one hand and his cell phone pressed to his ear, talking to someone. He stopped in front of the store and continued his conversation. From the look on his face, it didn't seem good. His expression was grim as he walked back to the car.

"Everything okay?" I asked.

"He lost them."

"What? Who lost who?"

"Mike. In the follow car. He lost track of the dealers. It was a loose tail, so he was staying back a little — turns out he was following the wrong vehicle. He thinks there might've been two cars at the site; he tracked the wrong one. He's looking for a red Dodge Charger now."

"So who was in the car? The one he followed?"

"Some high school kids. Both vehicles were headed southbound. Mike's headed back out to see if he can pick it up."

I tried to process all of this. "Does he know where they were going?"

"Don't know. Right now, it's wait-and-see mode."

Wait and see? That didn't make any sense to me. "They're not just driving around, right? Maybe they're going to their place — where they're staying."

Dennis thought for a second. "Possibly. Worth a shot to go out there. Worst-case scenario, we drive back here. Either way, this buy is shot to shit. Let me take you back to your house, and I'll head out to the gang's shack."

"Take me back? No fucking way. I'm in this, all the way."

"We don't know what's going on out there. I let you ride along today as a courtesy. But you're going back to your place. Nonnegotiable. I can drive you, or you can walk."

It had come to this. But there was no way I was abandoning Nathan after leading him into this clusterfuck.

"Then you better put the cuffs on me," I said. "If you think you can. Because I'm getting in that car." I squared off in my stance, facing him. "Nonnegotiable."

He stared at me, wondering if I was going to back up my challenge.

I looked right back at him.

"All right," he said. "Get in."

We took off for Valentine, where Loco and the others stayed and did their business. While we drove, Dennis started to tell me about the dealers' cabin.

"Yeah, I know about it," I said. "The one at the travel park, outside of town?"

"You know where it is? Did Nathan tell you?"

"No, I did some digging and figured it out. Drove out and took a look."

He shook his head in disgust. "Goddamn, we had to do a shit-ton of surveillance to locate the place. You go inside?"

"No, just watched it for a while. I saw Rick Crow there."

"Not surprising. Let me check with Mike, see where he's at with the Charger."

He made a call on his cell phone while we

sped down Highway 83 to Nebraska. I listened to his end of the call as best I could while I watched the road shimmer in front of us.

"Damn," he said. "Mike can't locate the vehicle."

"What? He can't find the car?"

"That's what he said. He's still looking."

I was close to boiling over, but I kept my temper in check. It took about thirty minutes to get to the campgrounds. We pulled into the entrance of the Pay-E-Zee and stopped. Same story as before, the place looked deserted, a ghost town. There was one beat-up camper parked off to the side but I couldn't see any vehicles parked by the cabin in the back. The gang's place. Dennis circled slowly around to the rear, a few hundred yards from the cabin behind some bushes.

"We'll monitor it. If we're lucky, they'll come by and we can pick up the wire again. Mike's driving back to the reservation to see if he can locate them."

We waited in silence for a while. The only movement came from the wind and the birds. Dennis checked his phone periodically for text messages.

"Fuck this, I'm going in," Dennis said. "Wait here, just stay put."

He slipped out of the car and walked over to the cabin. First, he peered inside the window, then he tried the front door, which was locked. Then he went around to the rear. I watched closely, waiting to see if he'd found anyone inside. I opened the car's window so I could hear any sounds of a struggle — or gunshots.

Nothing. Minutes passed with no sign of Dennis. Something must have happened. Maybe they'd been lying in wait and got him from behind. Maybe they'd shot him, and I didn't hear.

My only option was to go in. I looked around Dennis's car for weapons. Nothing under the seat. Nothing in the glove box, just a car manual and some tire wheel locks. That was fine, I had my Spyder knife with me. And my fists.

I stepped out of the car and pondered my strategy. I didn't know how many were inside or if they were strapped. My best weapon would be surprise, so I decided I'd kick the front door open and burst in, then improvise. I walked slowly over to the cabin and stood by the door, waiting for the right moment.

Just then the front door swung open, and Dennis appeared. He saw me by the door and looked at me with a puzzled expression. "What are you doing?"

"Ah, nothing. Checking things out," I said. "You were in there a long time."

"They're gone. Place is empty. No one left."

Before he could object, I went inside to see for myself. A little bit of trash on the floor in the living room, a dirty bathroom, and some food wrappers in the kitchen, but no sign that anyone was still living there. The only thing remaining was a faint odor of burned matches and some other scent I couldn't place. I was happy to get out and go back outside.

"Where do you think they went?" I asked.

"Tough to say. They're smart, they move around. Might have rented another place."

"What do we do now?"

"Not much we can do. We'll head back and wait to hear more."

Just then, Dennis's phone rang. He picked it up and listened, then said, "Where are you? Are you —" Then he put the phone down. I waited for him to say something.

"It was Nathan. He said he's going to a friend's house."

I paused for a second.

"The emergency code," I said. "He's in trouble."

25

Dennis walked away and immediately began making calls. I followed him, trying to listen in, but he held up his hand. My first thought was that Nathan was pranking us, using the code as a bad joke, but that was stupid. He was letting us know that things had gone wrong, but why had he hung up on Dennis? He hadn't said anything about his location, which meant that the dealers must be close to him and listening in. What sort of trouble was he in? Had they discovered the wire?

After a few minutes Dennis came back, a somber expression on his face. "I called Mike. He's heading back to the FBI field office. He'll put out a BOLO in a few minutes —"

"What's that? Like an APB?"

"Same thing, different word. Maybe send out an Amber alert, too. Every law enforcement agency in the state will be looking for a red Dodge Charger. Shouldn't be tough to locate. We'll trace his phone, too. That won't be a problem — we already have the cell ID, no need for Stingray, but the FBI can use it if they need to."

"Stingray?"

"It's a device that tricks a cell phone into sending location data. Won't be necessary. That's our phone I gave to Nathan, so we have the cell identifier. Point is, we should have a handle on these guys soon. I ordered an aggressive search. When we find 'em, we'll send multiple units, get Nathan back pronto."

He stuck his phone in his pocket. "All right, let's take off. I need to get to the field office; I'll drop you off at your place."

There was no point in arguing with him about going home. There was nothing I could do to help with this high-tech surveillance stuff. Dennis drove me back to my house, and I got out of the car. But I motioned to him to roll down the window. There was one last question I had to ask.

"Have you ever not found someone when you ordered a search like this?"

He looked me right in the eye.

"Never."

"That's good, because anything happens to him, it's on you. Understand?"

He drove off without saying anything, the dust from the road drifting in the air.

I called Marie as soon as I walked in the door. She came over within minutes, and brought some food she'd cooked. I was too distracted to eat, so I drank some coffee and filled her in on what had happened. I told her about the call from Nathan, and the search the feds were conducting.

"What are we supposed to do now?" she said, putting away the food she'd brought.

"He said to wait for his call."

"Are the Rosebud Police helping with the search? They know this area better than the state cops or the FBI," she said. "All the back roads and unmarked streets."

"Good point. I assume they're involved, don't know for sure."

"Maybe I should call Ty Bad Hand? He's tribal police — can't hurt to check with him, right?"

"Sure, call him. See what you can find out. If the feds left the Rosebud cops in the dark, I'll rip them new assholes."

She walked away to the other room with her cell phone. While she made her call, I considered the drug buy and what we knew. Rick Crow had been with them, along with two people from the Denver gang, but not their leader, the one called Loco. Their cabin was empty, but they may have gotten another one in the area. Finally, Nathan felt worried enough to make a call with the emergency code. So where were they going? Maybe they had a new spot where they kept the heroin, and Nathan was trying to alert us to the new location. On the darker side, maybe they suspected — or discovered — that Nathan was wearing a wire. But how? He wasn't wearing one of those old-fashioned microphones under his shirt. The wire was his phone and key fob.

I stared out the window and let my mind travel, trying to tease out the answer. Then I thought I saw something, far off in the fields beyond my house. It was just beyond my field of vision, but it looked like a pair of buffalo, slowly trotting in the grass. An older bull and a calf. But that was impossible. There were some bison over in Pine Ridge, but none around here.

Marie came back into our little living room, a somber expression on her face.

"I talked with Ty. He says they got the alert — whatever it's called."

"BOLO. Guess it means 'be on the lookout.' "

"Okay. He says they're helping with the search. That's the good news. The federal

377

cops included our people."

Marie sat down and started picking at a hole in her jeans. The hole was about the size of a quarter, but she began to really go after it. Before long, the hole was the size of a half dollar. At this rate, her entire pant leg would be gone by the time I finished my coffee.

"Did he say anything else?" I asked. "About how the search is going?"

"No, he didn't say anything about that. I'm sure they're getting close." Now she started to pull threads out of the hole and curl them into a little ball. It looked like a tiny globe in her hands, twisting and rotating as she fidgeted with it.

"Marie. Is there something else? I need to know."

"Well, Ty Bad Hand is just local police. He's not the best person for this sort of information."

"Marie." I moved over and sat closer to her. "Tell me."

She took her little thread globe and put it on the table between us, a tiny planet of her making.

"Well, he said the first few hours are, you know, critical if an informant is taken. He said that if they don't find the person in a day or so, he's probably been . . ."

378

"Killed," I said.

She didn't say anything, just picked up her thread world and crushed it between her fingers, the little sphere now in disarray.

After hearing that, there was no way I could just sit around and do nothing. I told Marie that I was going to drive around and look for Nathan. I took my old car and drove aimlessly around the streets of the rez. There were children playing, packs of stray dogs roaming, and random men and women sitting, walking, talking. I wanted to shout at them, tell them to help me look for my nephew, that he was missing and needed to be found. Instead I drove up and down the byways of the reservation, looking for a red Dodge. Then it hit me. Why not check out Rick Crow's trailer? I was sure the cops had already been there, but what could it hurt?

I pulled up to the gray metal trailer. No cars that I could see. The front door that I'd kicked in before was still broken, but it had been propped up to keep out the wind and the animals. I pushed it open, no longer caring about being quiet or stealthy. The same piles of trash that I'd seen so many weeks ago were still there, the same devastation. I poked around the place, looking for anything that might give me a clue. I looked in drawers, cabinets, closets. Nothing. I pulled up the mattress and looked under there. The box of ammo that had been stashed there was gone. So someone had been here, most likely Rick himself.

I tore apart the dirty bedroom and the living room, taking care not to fall through the rotted floor. Then I sorted through a mound of food wrappers and garbage in the tiny kitchen. Used rags, discarded matchbooks, old pizza boxes. A Runza wrapper. That couldn't have come from Rick. Midwest chain Runza, with their signature loose meat sandwiches, called "loose bowels" by locals. Then I spotted a scrap of paper on the counter, a receipt, with the words "Cropper Cabin" on it.

What was Cropper Cabin? A vague flash of recognition. I wasn't sure, but it might be one of the crappy motels down in Valentine, the kind that catered to the less wealthy in northern Nebraska. I called Marie and had her look it up on her phone.

Sure enough, it was listed as a "modest roadside motel" in her search results, located on the outskirts of town. Marie wanted to know more, but I cut her off, told her I'd call later. It was unlikely that Nathan was there, but it couldn't hurt to see for myself.

I started walking out to my car, but stopped. Should I call Dennis and tell him what I'd found? He'd said there was an aggressive search ongoing for Nathan and the dealers, so it made sense to contact him, let the professionals investigate.

Fuck that.

It was time for me to step up and do what I could to find Nathan. Not to mention, I wasn't bound by legal rules and procedures, like probable cause and search warrants. Time to take some action.

Cropper Cabin was a run-down, shoddy, piece-of-shit motel; that was clear at first glance. The kind of place that rented by the week — at inflated prices — to families down on their luck, itinerant workers, and gang members, six to a room. Peeling paint, and a large dilapidated sign that advertised FREE CABLE and WEEKLY RATES. Below that, VACANCY and AMERICAN OWNED & OPERATED. An assortment of older cars was parked in front of the rooms. I cruised around the parking lot slowly, looking for a red Dodge Charger or any car with Colorado plates.

No luck. There was a light on in the office, but I didn't see anyone inside.

I opened the door and did a double take.

It was like someone had vomited American flags all over the room. There was a framed flag, a flag made out of painted wooden panels, two smaller flags on miniature flagpoles on the front desk, some American-flag pillows, and red, white, and blue curtains. The lone non-flag item was a Nebraska football sign that read HUSKER POWER. Not surprising, as Nebraska football fandom approached religious fervor levels in the state, even this close to the border.

I rang the bell on the front desk and waited. After a minute a middle-aged white guy came out wearing a T-shirt that proclaimed GOD, GUNS, AND GLORY. He looked me over, up and down, and I could tell he didn't like what he saw. It wasn't hard to figure out that this guy probably hated Indians, thought we were all a bunch of welfare-cheating, food-stamp-loving drunks that had interfered with his God-given right to possess our land. That was okay with me; I didn't plan on having a long discussion about Native property rights with this dude.

"Help you?" There was no hint of a smile on his face, not even a facade of shopkeeper friendliness.

"Yeah. I'm looking for a few guys that might be staying here. One Indian, some Hispanics, maybe a teenager — Native boy.

Anybody like that here?"

"You a cop?" He had the flat Kansas-Nebraska accent, which told me he was a local shit-kicker.

"No, just looking. Important I find them."

"We don't give out information about our guests. Company policy."

"I understand. Not looking to cause any trouble, but the kid with them needs help. Just need to know if they're here, or if they've been here, and I'll be on my way."

The guy puffed out his chest. "Maybe you didn't hear me. We don't provide personal information on our residents. No exceptions. Now why don't you get the hell out?"

I took a step closer. "I don't need personal information. Just tell me if they're here. Otherwise, I'm gonna have to go open up every goddamn door in this shithole. Don't want to do that, so why don't you spare me the hassle?"

"You bother anyone here, you'll answer to me. And I'm a veteran. Of the armed forces. The Merchant Marine. Not that you'd know anything about serving your country — you people are too cowardly to fight." He turned his back to me, and I heard him say, "Fucking prairie nigger."

I reached over the counter and wrapped my arm around his throat, choking him. He gasped and coughed as he used his arms to try and free himself. I increased the pressure around his throat, cutting off his air almost completely. I held him tight as he flailed and flapped his arms.

All of a sudden I heard a sound. The front door opened, and an older man and woman dressed like bikers walked in. The woman screamed, and I lost my focus for a second. The shithole manager broke free, gasping for air. The couple, dressed in their Harley Davidson gear, quickly ran out of the building, and I saw the guy move to a drawer behind the counter. He was fumbling with it, trying to get it open.

Nope. He wasn't going to get his gun.

I leaped over the counter and pushed him away from the drawer. He stumbled, then straightened up and threw a roundhouse punch at my face, connecting solidly. He still had some power left, I was surprised to find out. I feinted with a left jab, then threw a right hook that hit him in the temple. He went down with a thud. I put my knee on his lower back and grabbed his right arm, twisting it behind him.

"You're lucky I don't have time to take out your goddamn kneecaps. You'd roll around in a wheelchair, then you could really pretend to be a soldier. Merchant

Marine, my ass. My grandpa stormed Normandy Beach, you heard of that?"

He didn't say anything, so I put more pressure on his arm until he shouted "Yes!"

"And let me tell you one more thing, shitbag. More Indians serve in the military than any other group. Defending the country that broke every promise. So keep your goddamn mouth shut, or I'll knock out any teeth you got left. Agreed?"

More pressure to the arm. He gave a muffled grunt.

"All right, answer me and you get to walk away. Is there a group staying here, bunch of Latino guys, maybe one Indian man with long hair, and an Indian boy? Tell me now."

He said something, but I couldn't make it out, so I twisted some more.

"They left! A few days ago! But no kid! Let me go!"

I let go of his arm and removed my knee from his back. He rolled over and started moving the arm back and forth, trying to determine if it still worked. I took a look out the window. No police yet. Likely the couple had run off, too scared to get involved. Still, it was smart for me to get out of there.

I looked down at the piece of shit, now laying on his side and softly whimpering. I thought about what he'd said — *prairie nigger* — and I reared back and kicked him full in the face with my boot.

"Thank you for your service," I said, and walked out.

I went out to the car, the adrenaline still flooding my body and making it difficult to stand still. My right hand hurt like a son of a bitch from the punch I'd landed. I drove off quickly, as fast as my shitty car could go, my hands trembling and my body shaking, looking for a spot to pull over and get myself together.

There was a dirt road off the main street, so I turned onto that and shut off the car, the engine ticking like a homemade explosive device. After I calmed down, I thought about what the clerk had said: the gang had been at the motel, but left. None of this made sense: Why had they switched from the Pay-E-Zee, and why did they leave Cropper Cabin? Perhaps it was like Dennis had said — the gang moved around a lot to avoid detection. But why now? And where had they gone?

My phone rang as I was thinking all this over. It was Dennis.

"Got some news," he said. "About the search."

386

"I'm listening."

"I think you know, we issued a multi-state BOLO for the vehicle. Well, we found it. The Dodge Charger."

"Is Nathan okay?"

"The car was abandoned. No one in it. Located it off I-90 near Murdo."

"Murdo! I thought they were heading south."

"So did we. Looks like they ditched the Charger and switched cars."

"But you're still tracking Nathan's cell phone, right? So you'll be able to find out where they are."

"Yeah, well, that's the bad news," he said.

There was good news?

"We found Nathan's phone. It was on the ground next to the vehicle. Crushed. Appears they left it there and took off. It's not good."

My brain was a mass of white noise, and I couldn't focus on anything except the road in front of me. I drove mindlessly, on autopilot, as I sorted through what Dennis had told me. The gang had abducted Nathan, switched cars, and smashed his cell phone. That could only mean they'd discovered he was an informant. I understood what this meant, but didn't even want to think it, because voicing it would give it form and shape. Everyone knew what happened to snitches.

Dennis had tried to put a hopeful spin on things, but I was no idiot. The feds didn't even know what type of car to look for, or where they might be going. They'd issued another BOLO for four male suspects, but without a vehicle description attached, the odds were shit they'd be found. I told him about Cropper Cabin and what I'd learned there, and he said that his people would look into it immediately. He tried to tell me that they knew everything about the gang and where they usually gathered, but I knew that time was critical. Marie's friend had said the first day was the most important, and that made sense. The longer they had Nathan, the greater chance I'd never see him again. I used evasive maneuvers in my head to avoid what Dennis had told me about Loco, the resident torturer of the cartel, and the tactics he used.

Before I realized it, I was back at the cemetery. I pulled over into the little lot off the dirt road and walked over to Sybil's grave. I tried to speak, explain to her what had gone wrong, what I'd tried to do, but no words would come. I knelt down with my head in my hands, the wind blowing, a cold scythe on my face and body.

I sat there, and the wind stopped. The sun set, but I remained. I didn't want to get up and face what I'd almost certainly lost. What I'd lost and still had yet to lose. The country of the living was gone to me, and I knew that I'd entered a different space, one that offered no solace but only the wind and the cold and the frost. Winter counts. This was the winter of my sorrow, one I had tried to elude but which had come for me with a terrible cruelty.

26

It was early in the morning when I went home, still dazed and numb. Marie met me at the door when I walked in, her hair askew and wearing one of my old Megadeth T-shirts, her eyebrows furrowed together in an angry line.

"I called you like thirty times. I thought something had happened."

"I was at my sister's grave. All night. Left my phone in the car, fell asleep at some point. There's some bad news. Turns out that —"

"I heard," she said. "My dad told me. I'm really sorry. But you should have left a message. I called everyone looking for you. Tommy, my dad, even Jerome. No one knew where you were. I thought maybe the drug guys had shot you."

"Needed some time," I said. "Sorry."

She softened. "You hungry? Let me make you some breakfast."

"We got any of those corn cakes left?"

I hadn't realized how carved out I was. I sat at the table as she brought food to me. I felt my mind begin to clear as I inhaled cornbread, berries, and strong dark coffee.

"So tell me what's going on," she said. "My dad said they found the car Nathan was riding in, but no one was in it."

I finished my coffee and poured another cup, then told her about the abandoned car and the smashed cell phone. The fact there was practically no chance of finding them without a description of the car they were now driving.

"What are they going to do?" she said. "The police."

"I don't know. He just said to trust him, that they'd call when there was news."

By the look on her face, I could tell she had the same degree of trust in the feds that I did. She poured herself a cup of coffee and put it in the microwave to warm it up.

"I have an idea," she said. "I don't know if you're going to like it. Here's the deal. I was trying to find you last night; like I said, I even called Jerome Iron Shell. Thought you might be over there, drinking sodas or something. Jerome usually knows what's going on around here."

I nodded. "He's a good guy."

"Anyway, I told him about Nathan, that he'd possibly been, you know, captured, and we didn't know where he was. Jerome said there's a way to find missing people."

"Yeah?" I didn't know where this was going.

"He said we need to have a yuwipi. Most people think it's for healing, but he said it's also used for other stuff, like finding missing objects — or people."

I started to say something, but she kept going. "He said if you pray hard enough at the ceremony, the spirits will grant your request, tell you what you need to know."

A yuwipi. I'd never been to one. If a person was badly ill, people gathered at a house with the windows completely blacked out, then the medicine man would be tied up with ropes and wrapped in a star quilt. Then a ceremony would supposedly call up the spirits, who would heal the sick person and release the yuwipi man from the ropes. I'd never heard it could be used to gain information or find missing people. But I knew one thing. It was a goddamn waste of time. And right now, time was critical if I had any chance of getting Nathan back alive.

"Hey, that's really cool of you," I said. "It's great you're thinking about Nathan. Appreciate it. But right now, I need to —"

"Don't patronize me," she said, stirring her coffee.

"What?" I saw that a little had spilled out of her cup.

"I know what you're doing. You're trying to shut me up. But you need to listen. I'm just going to say it — Nathan doesn't have much time, if he's still alive. That's a shitty thing to say, I know! But you've got to get past your own crap. About our traditions. Now's the time to use whatever you can. I don't know if it's the spirits or the placebo effect or whatever, but I've seen things at ceremony I can't explain."

She pointed with her lips to the corn cakes on the table, asking me to hand her one.

"Marie, I hear you. I'm not disagreeing with you about ceremony. But I can't see taking a whole day for some yuwipi right now, not when I can be out scouring the streets."

"It's not a whole day! Maybe two or three hours. And it's done at night. When you'd be finished looking. Why wouldn't you try this?"

"I don't know, let me think about it. Maybe in a few days, if Dennis can't find anything. We'll talk about it then."

She looked out the window toward the light. "Actually, I already told Jerome to start getting ready. The ceremony is tonight. When the sun goes down."

I drove around the streets of the reservation, looking for something out of the ordinary, something that would give me a clue as to where Nathan might be. I went down back roads and dirt paths, places that didn't appear on any GPS system. I covered the main streets quickly, then worked my way to the outskirts, driving to the small hamlets and communities of the rez, not really towns, just homesteads where people congregated to be near others and gain some comfort amid the vast spaces of the territory, the land that had been promised to us but whittled away by thousands of official seizures, done under cover of federal rules and regulations.

After a long time, I realized it was pointless. I felt foolish, thinking I might stumble onto the guys that had abducted Nathan. They could be anywhere from Rapid City to Denver or beyond. I called Dennis, hoping for some good news. He picked up right away and said there was no new information, but the search was ongoing. He'd contact me the minute anything turned up. His tone was abrupt, and I wondered if he felt guilty or was just busy. The last communication from Nathan had been exactly twenty-four hours ago. The critical time period.

I saw I was near Tommy's shack, so I decided to stop in and talk. I knocked on the door, and he answered right away.

"Hey Virg. How you doing? Come on in." He was wearing a flannel shirt, only half buttoned, and I could see the scars on his chest from the Sun Dance he'd taken part in.

I looked around his little trailer and noticed that he'd put up some posters: Honor the Treaties, Geronimo holding a rifle, and several *Billy Jack* movie stills, all depicting Tom Laughlin about to kick the crap out of the white townspeople.

"Ain't got no Shastas, but you want some Kool-Aid? I got tropical punch." He handed me a jelly jar filled with reddish liquid. "Any news about Nathan? Marie called last night, gave me the four-one-one."

I took a drink of the Kool-Aid and nearly spit it out, it was so overpoweringly sweet. I set the glass down on the table without drinking any more.

"No news," I said. "There's an alert out — all-points bulletin — so I'm hoping some cop spots them. But you know, there are only like ten tribal cops on the entire rez.

Half the time they're dealing with some family shit."

"Yeah, well, maybe somebody will see 'em. I'm sending out good thoughts to the Creator."

"Marie tell you she wants Jerome Iron Shell to hold a yuwipi to find Nathan?"

"She didn't tell me, but I heard. You know, word travels. That reminds me, I got something for you."

He went to the other room and came back, holding his hand out to me. "This is for you, bro. Belonged to my ciye, but now it's yours. You need to give it to Jerome tonight. He can't start unless you give him a pipe and ask the Creator for help. Don't worry, I already filled it for you."

It was a cannunpa, the sacred ceremonial pipe that had been passed down to him by his brother, who'd passed away years ago. Tommy had filled the bowl with tobacco, but the stem was disengaged, as was the custom.

"I can't take this," I said. "I know what it means to you. And I'm not going to have the yuwipi. That's Marie's idea, not mine."

Tommy held out the pipe to me. "Homeboy, take this. You fuckin' need it."

The pipe on my front seat, I traveled the

bruised streets of the rez, hoping to see something, anything. I knew these roads so well, my memories layered, dense, and compacted; nearly every corner triggered some recollection. Sybil, trying to breast-feed Nathan as a baby, her frustration mounting as he stubbornly refused to latch on and finally giving in and buying formula at the corner store. Nathan in diapers I'd bought at the market, dancing on a chair to some heavy metal tune I'd played. The time I dropped him off at the day-care center, his fear of being left with strangers, his little face a mask of surprise and panic. The nights he'd gotten up, sleepwalking, and how I'd quietly get him back in bed. The empty lot by Main Street, the sting in my hand when I caught a baseball he'd thrown with surprising heat. The sarcastic demeanor he'd assumed in junior high. The look on his face in the juvenile detention center.

Before I realized where I was going, I found myself at a familiar homestead south of town and got out of my car. Jerome Iron Shell greeted me.

"Been waiting for you."

I handed the pipe to him. He took it and nodded.

On his porch, he told me about preparations for the yuwipi. He'd already gathered friends and family, who were praying and making four hundred and five tobacco ties. He'd spoken to Marie, who was bringing food and drink. Rocky was getting the yuwipi house ready, blacking out the windows so no light could come in.

"But the most important piece is you," he said. "You can't have a negative attitude — the spirits won't enter. You need to have a good heart. Be best if you could sweat, really purify, but no time for that. Just try to keep any bad thoughts out of your mind. Maybe go out in the woods, sit for a bit. Clean your soul."

I wasn't sure if it was possible to keep negative thoughts out of my mind, but the suggestion to sit outside for a while sounded right. I drove out to a quiet spot in a patch of trees and angled my car seat back. The birds twittered and I heard an owl call, far off in the distance. In my half-conscious state, it seemed like a warning, a caution. Then I heard it again, very faintly, muffled, barely audible, and the world went dark.

Opening my eyes in the early twilight, I looked around and tried to determine how long I'd been asleep. A few hours. Then I remembered. The yuwipi. If I was going to go through with this, it was time to go. I drove out to the intersection, the one that led to the yuwipi house, but waited for a second. I could just drive away and let Jerome and the others figure out I wasn't coming. I didn't owe them anything. I could continue the search for Nathan by myself, alone, separated from the rez and all its people, problems, complications. But Jerome had told me that about forty people were coming to the ceremony, most of whom I didn't know, just people who'd heard about Nathan's disappearance and wanted to help. The community.

I turned toward the house, the car seemingly driving itself over the bumps and jolts of the unpaved road. A few dozen cars were parked out in front, but for once I didn't see any dogs or kids running around. It was strangely silent and still.

I opened the door and walked in. Someone had plugged in a few table lamps, but that was the only light. The windows had been covered with heavy paper and duct tape, and even the gaps between doors and frames had been sealed. Hundreds of colorful tobacco ties had been placed around the room and on the makeshift altar set up at the far end. Prayer flags, sweetgrass braids, a pitcher of water, and some food were placed around the altar. Two drummers and two singers sat off to the side, and dozens of others were sitting on the floor against the wall, looking at me silently. Some were smiling, but most looked serious. Marie was there, sitting right next to the altar — the place of honor — with a small smile on her face. Tommy was off to the side, next to Velma. He raised his hand and grinned at me.

Marie indicated I should sit next to her on a knockoff Pendleton blanket she'd laid on the floor. I sat down, the comforting smell of the sweetgrass thick in the air. About fifteen minutes later, Jerome's grandson Rocky and another guy I didn't know walked in, followed by Jerome himself. He slipped a leather bag off his shoulder, rested it against the altar, and carefully removed a few objects. He passed each one through the sweetgrass smoke before setting them on the altar. I saw eagle bone whistles, feathers, two large rattles, a porcupine quill medicine wheel, a Tupperware box full of soil and rocks.

When he nodded, the drummers started pounding, and the other two started singing in Lakota. The drums were so loud, they caused my teeth to vibrate as I followed the keening melodies of the song, the words rising and falling along with the rhythms. After the music ended, Jerome picked up the pipe I'd given him earlier, now fully assembled, waved it in each of the four directions, and put it, too, on the altar. Then he began speaking in Lakota. I couldn't understand most of what he was saying, but I understood that this was a prayer inviting the spirits to enter. Then he switched to English.

"I have seven children and four grandchildren. They've brought me the most joy in my life, even when they caused me grief. A lot of grief. To the Lakota, our children are sacred, wakan. It's our job to keep them safe and teach them our ways. But bad things can happen. Kids get sick. They wander away, get lost. That is the hard time, when we have to reach out to the community and to the spirits."

He paused, and the people said "Hau."

"I remember when my son — he was only two or three then — became sick with some illness. The doctors couldn't figure out what it was. He was in bad shape — couldn't get out of bed, wouldn't eat or drink anything. Coughing, sweating, moaning. I went up on the mountain and prayed for him nonstop. I asked the Creator to help my child. And the people prayed too. Family, friends, neighbors. The spirits heard me. They told me that I needed to believe in the pipe. Believe

401

in the pipe, and if I did, my son would recover. And he did get better."

"Hau."

"Tonight we pray for the return of Nathan Wounded Horse. Something bad has come to our community, and we ask the spirits to remove this evil and return the child to Virgil Wounded Horse and send the rattlesnakes away. These rattlers slither onto our land and tempt our children with lies. We ask the spirits to help Virgil, and also to heal our people, especially our young ones, and give them strength to resist this wickedness. Thank you, Tunkasila."

Turning to his helpers, Jerome said "Wana." They went over to him and tied his hands behind his back with a leather cord. Then a large star quilt was draped over him, and they bound him with ropes seven more times, from neck to ankles. In each knot, Rocky placed a small piece of sage. When Jerome was tied up completely, the helpers laid him down in front of the altar. The table lamps were turned off, and we were shrouded in total darkness.

The drummers began playing again, and the singers joined them. I could hear Jerome singing as well, his voice muffled underneath the blanket. Most of the people sang along, and I was embarrassed that I didn't know the words. The drums started off slowly, then began pounding out a more insistent tempo. The drums were like a heartbeat, pounding, pulsing, hammering, and then we were united by the sounds of the singers. In the blackness, it was difficult to tell how much time was passing. I focused on the rising and falling melodies of the songs, the voices of the singers, the words of prayer and lamentation.

Then a loud whistle sounded, and I heard rattles beginning to shake to the rhythm of the drums. It felt at least ten degrees warmer in the room, and the air seemed like it was charged with electricity. Negative and positive ions, transforming themselves, attraction and repulsion, gain and loss. The hair on my neck bristled as I noticed bluish sparks near the altar. Beginning to feel dizzy and disoriented from the heat and the sounds, I tilted my head back to breathe more deeply, and when I did that, something touched my head, something soft. It felt like a bird circling me, tapping the sides of my face and neck. Then it flew away.

The drumming became even louder, and the heat was nearly unbearable. Light-headed, dazed, I lowered my chin onto my chest to steady myself. I took deep breaths and concentrated on the sound of my own respiration.

Then I heard voices, screaming, and the sound of gunfire off in the distance, but coming closer. I opened my eyes and saw women and children running in terror, being chased by men in uniforms. Soldiers. They were firing on those fleeing, shooting them in the back. Hundreds of Indians were running in all directions, and I was surrounded by dead bodies in a grassy meadow. The sound of thunder split the sky, exploding in my head, the roar deafening. On a hillock above the field, the soldiers had a giant cannon firing directly on the panicked Indians while other soldiers ran out onto the field in pursuit. I saw one soldier shoot a woman carrying a baby. When she went down, the child wailed in terror, but then stopped crying for a moment and looked straight at me. I wanted to reach out and help her, but the soldier ran over and shot the child in the head.

I watched in horror as the soldiers kept firing on the unarmed people. Some people swerved suddenly to outwit the shooters, but it was useless with so many weapons trained on them. The screaming and howling grew louder as the bullets rained down. Then, almost on cue, the people started running in the same direction. There was a small hill at the other edge of the meadow with a building on its crest that looked familiar to me, but I couldn't place it. Then it came to me. The abandoned museum, the mass grave.

I was at Wounded Knee, the massacre unfolding before me.

The remaining Natives were running at top speed, racing up the hill and into the museum for shelter. I got knocked down in the rush and covered my head with my hands. Then I looked up and saw a rifleman in the distance drawing a bead on me. I tried to stand up and dash away, but something was wrong with my legs and I stayed, vulnerable, there on the hillside, helpless. I waited for the sound of the shot.

Then somebody grabbed me and pulled me up onto my feet. Still unsteady, I looked at who'd helped me.

It was Nathan.

"Come on!" he shouted, and he led me up the hill amid the crowd of people. Nathan ran inside the building, and I made my way to the door. I opened it and looked into the pitch-black darkness, then slammed the door shut behind me.

All of a sudden a dim light came on, and I could see people crouching around a fallen man, trying to help him. I peered over somebody's shoulder and saw that it was Jerome, flat on his back, freed from the ropes, but his face gray and ashen. His grandson Rocky was bent over him, saying something I couldn't hear.

"Did the soldiers shoot him?" I said to the woman next to me.

"What?" Marie said. "What soldiers?"

My mind whirled as I struggled to orient myself. I looked at the tobacco ties, the altar, and the darkened windows; I smelled the sweetgrass and the sage. Marie's face was an anchor, bringing me back to the yuwipi house.

"He collapsed during the ceremony," she told me. "I hope he just fainted, but I'm worried this could be a heart attack. It doesn't look good."

I was trying to focus on Jerome, but couldn't shake what I'd just experienced at Wounded Knee. The terror of the people, the unspeakable cruelty of the soldiers.

Then I knew what I needed to do.

"Come on," I said to Marie. "We have to leave right now. I know where Nathan is."

27

"What are you talking about?" she said, as we walked outside. "Did Dennis call you?"

"I'll explain later. But I have to go. Nathan's in danger." She stopped and turned to me. "No, you can't just leave me in the dark. I need to know what's happening. Where is he?"

"He's at Pine Ridge. The abandoned museum at Wounded Knee. The one on top of the hill."

Her mouth opened in amazement. "Are you sure?"

"Yes. But I need to get out there, right now. Tell you more later."

"Wait. I'll go with you. I know that place well."

There was no way I'd let Marie come along, given what I'd just experienced.

"You're staying here," I said. "Don't know what I'll be up against."

She planted her legs like a football lineman. "Not a chance in hell. I've been in this from the beginning, and I'm in it now. I'm coming along."

I knew better than to argue. "All right. But you stay in my car while I check it out. Bottom line."

She nodded grudgingly.

"Hold on," I said. "I need to get something first."

I opened the glove box in my car, grabbed the Glock, and pulled the clip. Loaded. But I didn't have any extra ammo, so I popped the trunk and got my backup, the little Smith & Wesson revolver that held only five rounds. I stuck it in the inside pocket of my denim jacket. It made a crunching noise, and I realized I still had the old items from my medicine bag in there — the sage, feather, and rocks. The items I'd carried with me as a kid.

Marie's eyes widened. "Why do you need two guns?"

"I might not need any, but I got to be ready."

"Maybe we should call Dennis?"

I considered this. "Okay, I'll call him. But I'm not waiting. I've got a feeling this is something I'm supposed to do by myself."

I phoned Dennis, but there was no answer. I left a message telling him to call and where to find me. While we drove, I told her about what I'd seen at the yuwipi. I was worried she might doubt my vision or tease me, but she just asked questions about what I'd witnessed. I told her it was no dream; it was real.

I gunned the accelerator all the way to Pine Ridge, and we got to Wounded Knee in record time. I hadn't been to the site for years. When I'd visited in the past, I always paid my respects to the Lakotas buried in the mass grave. Right after the massacre in 1890, the army simply dug a pit in the ground and just tossed in the corpses — men, women, children, and babies. It's a sad place, not only because of the innocent victims but also because it represents the end of the Indian era, when Natives lived freely on our traditional lands. After the so-called battle, soldiers rounded up the last few hostile bands and shipped them all off to reservations. The end of the dream, and, as Black Elk said, it was a beautiful dream.

But there was no time to pay my respects tonight. I pulled up to the makeshift museum next to the grave site. Not really a museum; the round building had only a couple rooms and a few crude paintings of Lakota leaders — Red Cloud, Sitting Bull — hanging on the walls and a little bit of

Native history scrawled underneath. There was no electricity and not much furniture inside; it was just a run-down structure that had been taken over by the locals. After complaints from tourists who'd wandered in and gotten scared by panhandlers, the building had been closed, and the doors were usually chained shut.

I parked at the bottom of the hill, about five hundred yards away. I stuck the Glock in my pocket and handed Marie the little Smith & Wesson.

"You know how to use this?" I asked.

"Of course. You want me to go in first?"

"Nope," I said. "I'll go check out the place, you keep watch down here in the car. You see anybody drive in, fire a warning shot so I know they're coming. But don't follow them! Just take off and get the hell out of here. You good with that?"

She nodded, unhappy, but seemed resigned. Before I left, I grabbed some plastic zip cuffs I kept in the car just in case I needed to shackle someone. Not really a long-term restraint, but they'd keep somebody's hands bound for a few hours.

I walked up the hill, checking for any activity. I had no idea what I'd find inside — the entire gang or maybe just Nathan, as I'd seen in my vision. The building had no windows; I couldn't look inside to scope out what I was up against. But the door wasn't locked when I tried it. Somebody was in there. But how many? There was only one thing to do: burst in, move to the side, and hope to get the drop on whoever was there.

I stood outside the door, waiting for a sign telling me when to go in. I heard the wind in the trees, and then an owl hooting. Good enough for me.

I lifted my gun up and slowly turned the knob. Then I kicked the door open and hurtled into the room, ducking to the side in case anyone took a shot at me. It was dark in there, but two small kerosene lanterns burned in the far corner. A man sat by the nearest lamp, but I couldn't see who it was.

"Don't move!" I shouted, pointing my gun. "Put your hands up!"

I think he raised his hands, though it was hard to see in the black space. I kept the Glock trained on him as I moved closer. When my eyes adjusted to the dim light, I saw who it was.

Rick Crow.

He had his hands up, and I pointed my gun at his chest, dead center, and moved closer to him.

"Where is he?" I said.

"Who?"

"Nathan, you asshole. My nephew. I know he's here, so don't fuck with me."

"He's not, so why don't you piss off and leave me alone?"

I looked around the large room to see if Rick was telling the truth. I didn't see anyone else. "You get one more chance. Where is he?"

"I told you. Not here, so clear the fuck out."

"You lose." I reared back and smashed his left cheek with the gun's muzzle. He grunted and held his head down, trying to unscramble his thoughts. While he was stunned, I walked behind him, moved his arms behind his back, and put the zip cuffs on him. Now I could relax a little. I looked up and noticed one of the crude paintings on the wall. It said THE INDIAN WARS ARE NOT OVER. I moved back in front of him.

"That's your freebie," I said.

He didn't respond, just stared outward, shaking his head, his eyes unfocused. I worried for a second that I'd hit him too hard and fried his brains. Then I saw him trying to speak and knew he was just dazed.

He struggled to speak for a few seconds, then he put some words together. "Eat shit," he mumbled.

Everybody had to be a tough guy. Christ, I just wanted to find out where Nathan was, but I could tell he was going to make this difficult. But on second thought, that was fine with me. Time for some payback. Payback for the years of bullying, the drug dealing, the fucking kidnapping. I wouldn't kill him. Well, not right away. I'd get some information, then decide what he deserved.

I took a good look at him. Long greasy hair, a dirty T-shirt that read SCARFACE, and the fading remnants of a black eye. It looked like he'd already been beaten down recently. And he'd take some more tonight.

"Here's what we'll do," I said. "You're going to tell me where Nathan is, and why your drug buddies took him. If you don't, I break your thumb. Then the other one. After that, I shoot your kneecaps. Last bullet goes through your head."

The kerosene lamp flickered, creating weird shadows on the painting of Chief Red Cloud, the only leader to defeat the US Army on the turf they'd stolen only a few years before. Red Cloud, who'd died forgotten and alone in his old age just miles from here. Rick would join him if he didn't cooperate.

"We in agreement? Because I don't got

413

time to waste. Now, where's Nathan?"

Rick stayed silent, a defiant look on his face.

"I'm not playing with you, scumbag. You know what I do for a living, right? I'll pound your ass right into the ground."

He sneered. "Yeah, I know what you do. Beat people up for money. Think that makes you a big man. But you're still just a half-breed punk."

I kicked him in the chin, but my boot glanced off his greasy face without doing any damage.

"Why don't you take these cuffs off, we'll go at it man to man," he said. "Unless you're the same pussy you were back in school."

"Nothing I'd like better. You tell me what I need to know, you get to leave here alive. I'll take you on another time, promise. Now, where's Nathan?"

"Fuck you."

The fun and games were over. I moved behind Rick and kept the Glock pointed at him. "You right-handed?"

No answer. I put my gun down on the floor, then took hold of his right thumb and started bending it back. The thumb is less flexible than other fingers, and it's the easiest to snap. I steadily increased the pressure

414

until it was at the breaking point. "All right, asshole, where's Nathan? Last chance to save this thumb."

He was making sounds, but no actual words came from his mouth.

"I warned you." I pulled the thumb all the way until it snapped, the ligament sounding like a chicken bone fracturing.

He screamed, his cries echoing off the walls of the museum. I stood back and let him endure the pain for a minute. He began to cry, the greasy rivulets running down his face.

"You'll never write with that hand again, but if you start talking, you can keep the other thumb. Maybe learn to be a lefty."

I walked behind him, took hold of his other thumb, and bent it back quickly, until it couldn't budge any farther. I could feel the tension in the hand as I worked it some more.

"Stop! Stop! They took him!"

I let go of his hand and stepped around in front of him. He was trembling and shaking with pain.

"Who took him?"

"Loco! And the others! He was here, but they took him. Jesus fucking Christ, this hurts!"

He was shivering like a wounded dog, but

415

that was nothing compared to the pain and misery he'd brought to the rez.

"Where'd they take him? You lie, I'll break it and cut it off."

"I can't say! They'll fuckin' kill me."

"I'll kill you if you don't."

"They're gonna torture him. Set an example."

"Example of what?"

"He's a snitch! They're gonna kill him so he can't testify in court."

"Who said he's a snitch?"

"How the hell would I know! They're not stupid, they figured he flipped after he was set up."

"What do you mean, set up?"

"Shit, how stupid are you? There's a war going on. The pill guys against the heroin guys. The pill guys set him up."

I didn't understand what this had to do with Nathan. I glared at him. "You better start explaining."

"They run pain pills on the rez. Oxys, vikes, dillies. They don't want to compete with heroin, right? No more sales. So they planted the pills in Nathan's locker. They knew he'd flip, rat out the heroin gang. They also hate your guts, wanted to get back at you. Set the kid up, he goes to jail or he flips. Win-win."

He moaned from the pain, his face contorted in a grimace.

"Who hates me?" I said.

"Jesus, who do you think? Guv Yellowhawk. He hates your guts after that beating you put on him. And he handles the lockers at the school."

I was trying to keep up with this crazy story, but it seemed like Rick was just trying to shift the blame and save his own sorry ass.

"You're telling me Guv controls pills on the rez? Bullshit, he's too dumb for that. And too lazy."

Rick sneered. "Of course he is. Don't you know who's in charge?"

I didn't say anything.

"Ben. Ben Short Bear. He's been bringing in pills for years, making bank and paying off dipshits like Guv. Got all kinds of scams going on. But it's the end of the gravy train once the heroin comes in. He's been playing you, using you and Nathan to run those Mexicans off the rez. But they figured it out and took your guy." He snorted a little. "Pretty goddamn funny, you're fucking his daughter and didn't even know."

Ben Short Bear, tribal councilman, dealing drugs? Yeah, Rick was feeding me crap so I wouldn't hurt him again. How could

417

he know all of this, assuming it wasn't a complete lie?

"You're full of shit," I told him. "You and the Aztec Kingz work together. I saw you at their cabin. How would you know anything about Ben? He thinks you're scum, he wouldn't tell you jack. Hell, he sent me to take you out. I think *you* set Nathan up." I moved toward him. "Had enough of your bullshit. Now I'm gonna break that thumb, then take it off."

I reached around him, trying to take hold of his arm.

"Guv told me!" he shrieked. "When he was drunk! He told me everything! Ben set up your nephew, not me!"

I grabbed his hand. "Sorry, not buying it, shithead. Here goes that thumb."

He started shouting, but I ignored him. He was flailing and thrashing, but I pinned him down, took hold of the left thumb and bent it back. When it snapped, Rick screamed again. But I wasn't finished. I started twisting it, trying to take it off with my bare hands, wrenching it back and forth, tearing through the skin and tendons.

"He's at the goddamn slaughterhouse! Now stop!"

I let go of his hand. "What slaughterhouse? Where?"

"The one in Porcupine! You fucking animal!"

I vaguely remembered hearing about some old slaughterhouse in Pine Ridge, but had never been there. There was no way of telling if this was the truth or more of his bullshit, but I had a hunch the pain was extracting something a little more factual out of him. "Who took him there?" I asked.

"Loco, Manuel, some other guy. I was supposed to meet 'em there after they're done."

"How long ago?"

"I don't know, three hours? Okay, I told you, so get me out of here. I need a goddamn hospital!"

Hospital? Did this asshole really think I was going to drive him to a doctor for some pain pills? The irony was pretty profound, though I didn't have time to savor it. This waste of human flesh helped snatch my nephew, after spreading misery and pain across the reservation for decades. He'd bullied me and countless others in school, then gone on to sell booze and drugs all over the rez. He'd had his hand in nearly every scam and hustle, every shitty scheme and conspiracy to make a buck, all at the expense of his cherished full-blood Indians.

That ended today. It was time, finally, that

Rick got his due.

I put the gun to his head. He started whimpering, sobbing, and I saw he'd pissed his pants. That was fine, he could die in his own urine. For years I'd been helping people get some justice on the rez, the only means they had left to them by a legal system that had sold them down the river. Rick Crow deserved to die for what he'd done to me, to Nathan, to all the people. There needed to be a reckoning, a balancing of the books. It was time.

I started to pull the trigger, then stopped, momentarily disoriented. I saw my sister, Sybil, standing behind Rick, and I wondered if I was still affected by the yuwipi and having some flashback. She looked sad, desolate, and it was like she was talking to me without speaking. I could understand what she was saying, even though her lips weren't moving. She said that, while I didn't like it, I was connected to Rick, that he was my relation. I needed to sacrifice, to take the tougher road by granting forgiveness to Rick, and to myself.

And what was justice? The wasicu version was to impose retribution — vengeance — for wrongs and injuries, but the Lakota principle was to repair whatever harm had been done. Kiciyuskapi, the untying-each-other ceremony, where the parents of a murdered child and the parents of the murderer would smoke the pipe, make amends, and release one another from retribution. But how could anyone heal and restore the countless evils Rick had wrought?

He kept looking at my gun, wondering what I was going to do, cowering, pathetic, a vision of wretchedness and desolation. Mitakuye oyasin, all my relations.

I lowered the Glock and walked back a few steps.

"It's your lucky day, loser. You get to live, for now anyway."

Relief passed over his face, and he started shaking. The stain on his pants had grown.

I heard a noise coming from the back door of the museum, and looked around.

"Put the gun down, Virgil."

I looked over and saw Ben Short Bear, pointing a Colt 1911 pistol at me. At this range, it'd blow a hole the size of a grapefruit out of my body. What was he doing here?

"Ben," I said, "I got it under control. This asshole is talking shit, but I got it covered."

"Virgil, put the gun on the ground and kick it over to me. Don't even think about trying anything. You do, and the first bullet goes in your chest. Do it now."

I studied Ben's face to see if he was serious. He didn't waver and kept his gun pointed at me. I did as he said and kicked mine over to him, the weapon rattling as it traveled across the pockmarked concrete floor. He picked it up and put it on an old chair to his right.

"Now, sit down next to Rick and put your hands behind your head. They come down, you get a bullet."

I sat down, Indian style, and held up my hands. Rick's odor filled my nostrils, the smell of piss and fear. *"I told you,"* he whispered.

"Ben, what's this about?" I said. "You hear this dirtbag's lies? He's trying to say you're selling drugs on the rez. I know he's full of shit, so let's —"

"Yes, he is a dirtbag. I've built a successful business, and this jackass and his Denver buddies are trying to take it away. I was hoping you'd finish him off, but it looks like you're not the tough guy everyone thinks you are. I suppose it's up to me."

He leaned over to Rick, put the gun on the center of his forehead and pulled the trigger, the sound like a bomb in the enclosed space. Rick fell back, most of his head gone.

28

"Why'd you do that?" I yelled at Ben.

He stepped back, pointing the gun at me again. "He knew too much. I was hoping your nephew's testimony could put them away, but he didn't get the chance once someone told them Nathan was working with the cops. Too bad." He motioned with the pistol. "The Mexicans have a code, you know. A crude type of justice. Anyone who cooperates with the police gets killed. But never a quick death. They make an example of snitches, usually hanging or burning them after cutting off some body parts."

I jumped up. "Let's go! I'll take those fuckers out!"

"Sit down, Virgil." He moved toward me, just feet away, the gun glinting in the dim kerosene light. "Now."

I sat down again next to Rick's corpse, the smell of shit and death beginning to fill the room. "Ben, you want those guys gone,

I'll do it. Just let me save Nathan. But I need to get out there now."

"You're not going anywhere," he said. "Both you and Nathan have outlived your usefulness. You and Rick were killed by the heroin cartel, sad to say, then those savage gangbangers burned this building down. And the FBI will soon learn that our Mexican friends tortured and murdered a teenager. The feds will really go nuts when that news breaks. And I can go back to my business, without any foreign interference. Sorry about your nephew — he seemed like a nice kid."

The thought of Nathan being tortured was enough to drive me insane. But I couldn't think about that. I needed to get past Ben and out of this stinking building. If I kept him talking, he might let down his guard. My only move was to make a play for his gun if and when he got distracted.

"One thing I don't understand," I said, eyeing the gun. "Why'd you tell the gang Nathan was an informant? Why not go through with the buy and let the feds arrest them? Then they're gone, and you're in the clear."

"I didn't tell them. Why would I? Not to mention the fact I have no contact with those thugs. I assume they discovered it on their own, or possibly this idiot said something to them." He waved the gun toward Rick's body.

"But you must've been working with Rick," I said. "How else did you know he was here?"

"You told me." He smiled, arrogantly. "I've had a GPS tracker on your car for months now. Needed to keep tabs on you, make sure you didn't get too close to anything you weren't supposed to know about."

A tracker, shit. No wonder Ben knew every time I'd visited the lawyer in Rapid City. "Ben, please. Nathan's innocent. I don't give a crap if you sell pills. I'll keep my mouth shut and won't say a word to Marie, I promise you."

"Too late for that," he said. "Time to clean up the reservation. It's for the best, I hope you see." He paused and looked down at the remains of Rick Crow. "This one is no loss. The fool was even trying to set up a marijuana grow out here with his buddies. But maybe we can save others from the poison he was selling."

He focused his attention on me and took a step closer. "And you didn't think I'd let my daughter be with you? She's been talking nonsense about staying here. Not going

425

to happen. I had Delia Kills in Water fire her. She'll go to medical school."

He moved even closer and pointed the gun at my head. "Goodbye, Virgil, I hope —"

"Stop, Dad!"

I looked over at the back door. Marie was standing there, pointing my Smith & Wesson directly at her father.

"Marie, what are you doing?" Ben said.

She held the gun steady. He lowered his Colt a bit, but it stayed in his hand, pointed at me. I saw her glance at Rick's dead body, but she kept the revolver aimed at her father.

"I saw you drive up and followed you in. I recognized your car."

"How much did you hear?" Ben said.

"Enough. Is it true?"

"Is what true?"

"That you've been selling drugs on the rez. To our people. And you had me fired!"

He frowned. I kept my eye on his gun.

"Not drugs," he said. "Pain medication. Medicine. Now put the gun down."

Her voice caught in her throat. "How could you? Sell that stuff."

"Marie, listen," he said. "Everything I did was for our family. How do you think we paid for Dartmouth for your sister? Not to mention your clothes, vacations, everything.

426

All I did was provide a service. These heroin dealers — they're bad guys, they sell to kids. My people never sold to children. Not once. Now, enough of this nonsense."

"No, Dad. This has to end. You're going to the police. Turn yourself in."

He laughed. "Police? I control those idiots. They won't do a thing to me." He changed his tone. "Honey, anything I did was so you and your sister could have a better life. That's how the world works. You have to take what you want, that's the wasicu way. Everyone skims from federal grants, that's how —"

"The buffalo money!" she cried. "You stole that, too?"

"Marie, it doesn't matter now. The money's for your medical school. That's a good cause, better than a freezer full of rotting meat. It was for you, don't you see?"

While Ben and Marie were engaged in their family drama, I studied the situation. Ben was about ten feet away, next to Marie. I could try for Ben's pistol, but that was far too risky at close quarters. The better move was to grab my Glock, which was on the chair. That looked to be my only play. I waited for the right moment.

"You aren't like the people here," Ben said. "We raised you to be different, do things —"

Seeing my chance, I jumped up and sprinted over to the chair, reaching for the Glock.

Too late! Ben saw what I was doing and kicked the chair, the Glock spinning away out of my reach. He raised his gun and pointed it at me.

BANG! A shot rang out, a deafening roar.

I looked up and watched Ben stumble and fall to the ground. Marie stood there with her arm still extended, the revolver in her hand.

I quickly pulled the Colt out of Ben's hand, but by then it didn't matter. She'd shot him right through the heart.

I could tell she was in shock. Her pupils were dilated and her skin ashen. I took the revolver from her hand and put it in my jacket. She didn't object. Instead of looking down at her father, she gazed out through the doorframe into the blackness of the night. Stars, space. I couldn't imagine what she was thinking at that moment.

I led her outside and sat her down on the ground, away from the bodies and the blood and the rank smell of death.

"Do you think my mother knew?" she said. "About the pills?"

"I don't know."

"I just — I can't believe he'd — I don't —" Then the tears came, quiet ones that looked like they hurt her skin. I touched her face. It was cold, like she'd traveled across an icy plain.

"You need to call Dennis, okay?" I said. "He doesn't answer, call the tribal police. Tell them what happened here and that Nathan's in the old slaughterhouse in Porcupine. That he's been kidnapped and they need to get there right away. Can you do that?"

She nodded, and I wondered if she'd come to blame me for all of this. I wondered if she'd ever see me again, or if I'd always be only a living reminder of the pain she'd suffered, and of the pain her father had wrought. The pain of our people. Perhaps I'd have to become a ghost myself, unseen but forever haunting her.

But now I had to save Nathan. I picked up the Glock and stuffed it in my pocket.

29

There was only one building in Porcupine that could've ever been a slaughterhouse. Most houses in town were prefab shacks, with satellite TV dishes screwed onto the frames and kids' toys scattered across the yards. But north of town I spotted a large building that looked like an old military structure, with foreboding gray walls, rusty ladders hanging on the sides, and giant circular ports with fans built into the walls. The exterior was unmarked except for some patches of bright pink graffiti that read KUKA and ZINTKALA NUNI in a cloudlike script. Though it looked deserted, a faint light was shining in one of the windows.

I kept the Glock in my hand — it was fully loaded, hadn't fired a single bullet — and put the Smith & Wesson in my back pocket. The front door was open, so I walked in, taking care to be as quiet as possible. I could barely make out faint voices coming from somewhere inside. It was dark, but there was enough moonlight so that I could see and step carefully around the piles of trash and old lumber on the floor.

The interior light was brighter on one side, and I followed the voices and the light down a central hallway, then I came to a stairway. I could tell they were downstairs, but I didn't have a clue about the layout of the area down there. The stairs themselves were wooden, rotted and rickety.

I walked down them as if barefoot, desperate to not make any creaking or scraping noises. Finally I got to the bottom, but stayed in the stairwell, listening. I could hear the men talking in the room around the corner. Their voices reverberated and echoed, so I knew it was a large space. They sounded cheerful, though they were speaking Spanish and I couldn't understand a word they were saying.

I didn't hear Nathan's voice.

I waited for the right moment to peer into the room. There was a sudden burst of conversation, and I crouched down so I'd stay out of their sightlines.

They'd put out some camping lanterns for lighting, which gave the space an eerie look. Even in the dim light, I could tell that this large, open room was the place where the cattle had been killed. There were big troughs, cables with hooks attached to the ceiling, and several concrete columns and pillars in the center, dotted with what looked like blood.

Nathan was tied up in a chair in the middle of the room, his shirt off and his head slumped down. His medicine bag was on the floor next to him. His hands were roped behind his back, and they'd also bound his torso to the chair. His legs weren't tied up, and they hadn't bothered to gag him. In the hazy light, it looked like he was sleeping. It tore my heart to see him like this.

I spotted the kidnappers off to the side. There were three of them, Loco and two others. Despite the bad light, I recognized the lightning-bolt scar on Loco's face. Rick had said one of the other guys was called Manuel, not that it mattered. They were sitting on a bench and smoking cigarettes. I didn't see any guns in their hands, but I knew their weapons had to be nearby. I scanned the room to see how heavily they might be armed.

Other objects were scattered on the floor around the lanterns — a hacksaw, some lumber, and a large butane torch, the kind used by jewelers or metalworkers. I also noticed a weird-looking device, a long yellow rod with a handle and a pointed tip. I realized I'd seen one of these years ago, at a ranch on the rez. It was a cattle prod, but the rancher had called it a hotshot.

A cattle prod.

There was a strange odor in the air, a smell like burned popcorn. I tried to get a better look at Nathan without exposing myself. My view wasn't perfect, but it looked like his face was swollen, and I saw some welts on his chest and arms. Burn marks. From the cattle prod? The torch? Or both?

The men quit talking, and the first guy stood up and threw his cigarette down. Then Loco and the other one joined him and walked across the room to Nathan. Loco said something to the men, then picked up and lit the butane torch, the flame burning a blue as bright as the sky on a beautiful summer day. He moved closer to Nathan, who stirred and started moving his head, muttering words I couldn't make out. Then Loco squatted down to adjust the torch, and the flame expanded, creating a longer, ominous flame that extended a foot or so, its base a white-hot supernova flickering near Nathan.

Oh, hell no.

Columbus and the Spanish conquistadors had burned Indians alive in their quest to subdue the continent, and I'd make damn sure these motherfuckers wouldn't do it to my nephew.

There was no time to make a plan. I leaped out from behind the wall with the Glock in my hand. The three men heard me and turned away from Nathan. I aimed the gun at Loco's chest and fired, but he was moving and the shot went wide, the sound booming in the cavernous room. He jumped behind Nathan, dropping the torch, and I took aim at the second man to his right, who was fumbling for his gun. I shot him straight in the chest, the casing flying off behind me, and he dropped down beside an old wooden table.

Where was the third asshole? I'd lost sight of him in the chaos and swiveled my head to see what he was doing.

A shot rang out, the bullet whizzing near my head and cratering into the wall behind me. I ducked behind a large concrete pillar for cover. In the dim light, I couldn't see where the third gunman was hiding.

"Nathan!" I shouted. "Get down if you can! Knock the fucking chair over!"

"Uncle?" he called. "Is that you?"

"Kick it over!" I yelled. "Get your body

down on the floor!"

I poked my head out and another bullet flew past me. Because of my limited ammo, I needed to wait for a clean shot. But when I saw Loco start moving from behind Nathan, I stood up and fired at him.

Another fucking miss. Loco ducked back down behind my nephew, still a sitting duck in that chair.

Three shots left in my Glock. I had the little revolver, but doubted it would do any good in here except at close range.

"Drop the gun, or I burn this rat's face off!" Loco yelled.

I looked around the pillar. Loco now had the torch burning full blast just inches from Nathan's face. In the light of the torch, I could see he was terrified. He'd moved his head back as far as he could go, still too damn close to the flame.

"You got one second, vato, or I burn him!"

What to do? I didn't have a clear shot at Loco, and the other jackoff would shoot me the second I exposed myself.

"Hey!" I shouted. "Let the boy go, and I'll toss you my gun. You guys can have me. Just let him go."

It was quiet for a second. "Throw the gun first, then we untie him," yelled Loco.

All of a sudden Nathan shouted, "Uncle,

435

run! Save yourself! Get out of here!" He was telling me to save my own skin, even with a blowtorch burning inches from his face.

Fuck that.

"All right," I shouted to Loco. "I'll give you my gun if you promise to let him go. Okay?"

No answer.

"I'm throwing my gun now! Here it comes!" I slid my Glock down the floor toward Loco, but the second shooter darted out to grab it. He'd been hiding near an exhaust vent in the corner. I quickly pulled the Smith & Wesson revolver from my pocket and stepped out into the room. The guy was reaching down for the Glock. If he got it, it was game over. Without even thinking, I shouted, "Look!"

It was enough. He stopped for a moment and glanced up, giving me time to move in closer. I shot him at close range, right in the head, then I fired again. His brains splattered against the wall and on Nathan, still tied up in the chair.

"You okay?" I yelled to Nathan.

"I'm all right!" His voice was high and shaky with fear.

Wait, where'd Loco go? No movement that I could see. He'd been right behind

Nathan when I shot his last backup, but now I didn't know his position, and that put me in a bad spot. I could hear the sound of the wind, blowing through some broken window high above me, and my own breathing, choppy and rough.

A shot rang out, and I ducked down. Damn! Loco must've gotten his own fucking gun. I had no idea what kind he had, much less where he was now.

How many rounds were still in the revolver? Marie had fired it once, and I'd fired twice, so there must be two rounds left. I heard a rustling noise coming from the far end of the room, and that gave me enough time to brace the gun with both hands. I wasn't sure if he'd come at me directly or try something else, but I had to be ready.

Loco jumped out and ran toward me, his gun already pointed in my direction. I got a clear look at him. He had a little goatee, and the hair on his face hadn't grown back from where he was scarred. He was wearing a polo shirt with blue stripes, kind of like the ones my mother had bought for me at Kmart when I was a kid. His eyes were ferocious, and I felt his hatred. It was either him or me — one of us was about to die. I hoped it was him, but I knew there was a good chance it would be me.

I steadied the little revolver and waited for my shot. I saw him aim his gun, his eyes squinting in the hazy light. I sighted mine on his chest and fired.

Missed! The shot went wide, and I pulled the trigger again. The gun clicked harmlessly, telling me I was out of ammunition and shit out of luck. There should have been one more round, and I realized it hadn't been fully loaded. Christ, how could I have made the fucking rookie mistake of not checking the cylinder?

Even before I heard the boom, I felt a stinging sensation in my shoulder. I'd been hit. I waited for the second shot, but it didn't come. I looked over and saw Loco hunched over his gun, which must be out of ammo, or maybe jammed.

Either way, I still had a chance. A slim one. I tossed the revolver on the floor and looked for something to use. The cattle prod was lying on the ground by Nathan, so I ran over to him. I was picking it up when he yelled, "Uncle! Watch out!"

Loco was coming at me again, gun in hand, having fixed his problem. I took a quick glance at the cattle prod, fumbling for the power button. There was usually a safety switch, and I had to hope it had already been turned off.

Loco stopped and put his sights at me, expecting that I'd run for cover. Instead, I went straight at him, much to his surprise. I thrust the prod onto his chest, right on his blue polo shirt, and hit the trigger. The voltage coursed through his body, and he fell down, shaking.

I stood over him and shifted the hotshot directly on his neck, hoping it was strong enough to disable him forever. I hit the power again, and watched as fifty thousand volts surged through his nervous system. I kept it there until he stopped moving.

The pain in my shoulder was getting worse, much worse. It felt as if somebody'd stuck a hot grandfather rock from the sweat lodge directly into my body. And if the bullet had hit an artery, I was in deep shit. I noticed that my shirt was drenched with blood, which wasn't good. I looked around for something to use as a bandage, anything I could stick on there to stop the bleeding.

Then the world rotated away as I was pulled backward onto the ground, my gaze fixed on the light fixtures up on the ceiling. It took me a second to realize that there was an arm around my neck, choking me. Loco was behind me, squeezing the breath from my lungs. He'd somehow shaken off enough electricity to put down a buffalo.

I struggled to pry his arm loose, but he had me in a sleeper hold. The move was highly effective; I'd used it many times when I needed to incapacitate someone. His right arm was looped around my throat, and his other pushed against my neck, cutting off the flow of both blood and air. He increased the pressure on my larynx, and I started choking, knowing that I had about ten seconds before I'd go unconscious.

I tried turning my head to open my airway, without success. My only chance of breaking a choke hold was to force his arms off my neck. I started clawing at them, but the loss of blood from the gunshot had weakened my strength, and I couldn't get any leverage. My vision started going gray around the edges.

I could hear Nathan yelling something at me. What was it? It seemed like he was saying he was proud of me. I didn't think there was a goddamn thing to be proud of — I'd had clean shots at Loco and flat out missed. Then I'd failed again with the hotshot. I thought about my life ending in this crappy building, how everything I'd experienced and lived had brought me to this place, this moment.

"The prod! The prod!"

Suddenly I understood that, while Nathan

was tied to the chair, he'd somehow managed to kick the cattle prod toward me with his foot. I grabbed it with my right hand and stabbed blindly at Loco with it. Startled, he lessened the pressure for a second, which gave me an opening. I finally broke his choke hold and breathed in deeply, the oxygen flooding my cells as I stood up.

Loco was kneeling on the ground and I kicked him hard, stunning him and knocking him on his back. "Fuck you!" he hissed.

"No, fuck you, wanagi." Ghost. Loco was an evil spirit, and it was time to banish him from this world and send him to the next.

I took the cattle prod and jammed it into his right eye socket. He screamed, and I leaned in with all of my weight, inserting the device as far as I could into his head. I pushed down until I felt resistance, the back of his skull. He started shaking, his body jerking and convulsing, then he began to babble and drool, trying to express some final thoughts.

I wouldn't take any chances this time. I hit the power switch on the hotshot, sending the voltage directly into his brain, frying whatever was left in there. His head shuddered and trembled, but I kept at it until he wasn't moving at all.

Though I knew he was dead this time, I

glanced down at his body to make sure. After a moment of staring at the corpse, I was convinced, then decided to sit down. I wanted to cut Nathan loose, but the pain from the gunshot was back in full force, and I felt tired. Exhausted, really. I stretched out on the floor and looked around for Nathan. The butane torch was still burning on the ground, blue sparks glimmering. I tried to tell Nathan to turn the damn thing off, but I couldn't spot him, and I don't think he heard me. I thought he was speaking, telling me something, but whatever he was saying, I couldn't understand. It didn't matter now anyway.

When I tried to stand, I couldn't make it up. Time seemed to expand and contract, and I could feel my thoughts pooling in my head. I wondered what sort of bullets Loco used, and if he'd used a hollow-point that had fragmented in my body. I reflected about what happens when a bullet explodes inside you, how dozens of little shards ricochet and bounce around, slicing open veins and arteries.

It started to hurt to lie on my back, so I curled up on my side. It felt good to rest after the day I'd had. I thought I saw an eagle fly above me in the room, which didn't make any sense. I heard sounds, but they were just like the ghostly voices in my dream, fleeting and evanescent.

Though Nathan was really yelling at me now, I still wasn't listening. I thought again about the vision I'd had in the yuwipi, and the little child — the lost bird — who had been shot by the soldier at Wounded Knee. The baby had looked at me in her last moments, and that's when I'd seen everything I would ever need to know. The expression on her face was compassionate, and I saw she'd accepted her fate and wanted me to understand that. She wanted me to know that I was forgiven, and that there was mercy for me and for all the wounded and the lost. I focused on the baby, her little face filled with love, and closed my eyes.

EPILOGUE:
NINE MONTHS LATER

I pulled into the parking lot for the pow-wow. Nathan got out of my truck, a used Ford F-150, and ran out to find his girlfriend, Shawna, who was already there. He'd been running cross-country at his new high school and had discovered he had a talent for it. He was talking about running cross-country and track at college, and he and Shawna spent every night discussing various combinations of universities they could attend together.

All charges against Nathan had been dropped once it became clear he'd been framed. But it had taken him some time to recover from the incident at the slaughterhouse. For a long while, he had trouble sleeping and suffered from a pretty deep depression. He wouldn't go to school — claimed there were too many bad memories there. But after a few months he started to open up, largely due to Shawna, who'd come by to visit him. He'd transferred to her high school, and it had made all the difference. He wasn't the same person he'd been a year ago, but maybe none of us were.

Guv Yellowhawk had confessed and was serving fifteen years for various charges. Ben's widow, Ann, had left the reservation in shame and anger, denying that Ben had ever sold drugs despite the overwhelming evidence otherwise. The feds arrested the remaining members of the Denver gang and were working to capture the leaders of the cartel. For now, there were no pain pills or heroin being sold on the rez, but I knew it would be impossible to keep that stuff away forever.

Delia Kills in Water was arrested for embezzlement after an investigation showed that she'd been working with Ben, not Lack, to defraud the government by diverting funds from the bison grant. Chef Lack had cooperated fully with the authorities and was cleared of any wrongdoing. Delia had been able to post a hefty bond to get out of jail while she awaited trial, and had retained Charley Leader Charge to represent her. Word on the street was that she planned to blame everything on Ben Short Bear at her trial. Nearly everyone thought that Delia would be convicted, but I wasn't so sure.

She'd never paid for her crimes in the past, and I wondered if she'd escape justice again.

As for me, I'd spent a few weeks in the IHS hospital recovering from my injuries, and don't remember much from that time. Nathan had been there as well, receiving treatment for the burns to his arms and chest. They told me I'd nearly died on the floor of the slaughterhouse, but they'd been able to bring me back. I guess it wasn't my time. They had to leave pieces of the bullet in my shoulder bone, and I'd never be able to raise my arm above my head again without pain, but I had no complaints. I just wished I'd been a better shot.

I gathered the two star quilts out of the back of my truck, along with the baskets for the giveaway. The small arena was already crowded, and the grand entry for the dancers would take place in two hours. An elderly man held the door open for me, smiling, as I walked inside with my items. As I set the baskets and star quilts at the front of the stage, I spotted the drum group off to the side. I went over to greet them and gave them a carton of cigarettes.

"You ready?" said Jerome, who'd walked up behind me. He'd recovered from his collapse at the yuwipi and wouldn't tell anyone what had happened to him at the ceremony.

He'd only said that he saw some "bad stuff." I think he'd had the same vision as me, but had somehow taken the full brunt of the pain into his own being, so that I could go out and save my nephew.

"Yeah," I said. "Nathan and I took a sweat last night. Felt good."

"All right. We'll get started in about twenty minutes."

I went over to my baskets, checking to see if we had enough gifts for the crowd. Nathan and I had gone to the dollar store in Rapid City and bought hundreds of little soaps, washcloths, kitchen utensils, kids' toys, and a big bag of rubber bands, then spent the night wrapping up the individual bundles, along with Nathan's friend Jimmy, who helped out for a few hours.

"Yo homes!"

I looked up and saw Tommy, still in his kitchen uniform. We hugged. I could smell the wild onions he'd apparently been chopping before he came to the powwow. He was working as a line cook at the new casino restaurant, Rations. Lack was starting a chain of these restaurants at Indian casinos across the country, and ours was the first. By all accounts, Tommy had been a model employee, and was talking about becoming a chef himself.

"Where's Nathan?" he said. "Don't tell me he ran off with that little girlfriend of his!"

"No, he's around. They're both here. He's excited. Is Velma coming?"

To everyone's surprise, Tommy and Velma were spending most of their time together, having drinks at the Depot, dinners at the restaurant, and arguing about music nearly constantly.

"Yeah, she's here! Having a smoke out back. Still need me to help with the gifts?"

"Yep. Should get started soon. I'll go find Nathan."

I scouted the arena and found Nathan with Shawna in a corner, engrossed in a deep discussion. "Nathan, it's time. Shawna, you want to help hand out the stuff?"

"Sure!" she said with a bright smile.

We walked back to the front of the stage, where Jerome was adjusting the microphone. I'd given him tobacco, as well as some to his grandson Rocky, who was helping out. There were five large baskets of gifts and two star quilts by the front of the stage. There was only one thing missing.

"Hope I'm not late." Marie kissed me, and I smelled her perfume as well as the aroma of the dishes she'd been preparing at the restaurant. "I'll be right back," she said, and left to help her assistants bring in large pots of bison stew and baskets of corn cakes for the crowd to eat after the ceremony was over.

Not long after the death of her father, she'd gone off — alone — to the Black Hills for a week to grieve for him and come to grips with what she'd done. When she got back, I tried to talk with her about it, but she said she wasn't ready. She did say she'd realized medical school wasn't for her, that she'd always known it, and that she'd honor her family by following her true path, which was working as a chef and changing the eating habits on the reservation. She loved cooking and creating new recipes, all based on the principles of indigenous cuisine, and Lack had put her in charge of the restaurant. It would be a long haul to replace frybread culture, but she and Lack were making a start. Lack had even flown in this week to help Marie with the preparations for the feast.

Jerome signaled to the drum group, and they played an honor song while everyone stood up. After they finished, Nathan, Shawna, Tommy, Velma, Marie, and I went into the crowd, handing out gifts to the people. We gave the soaps, shampoos, and kitchen stuff to the adults and the toys to the kids. After we were done, Nathan and I sat down in two chairs at the front of the stage, and Rocky draped the two star quilts around our shoulders. Jerome went back to the microphone, picked it up, and started speaking.

"Today we join in giving these two men their Lakota spirit names. Nathan Wounded Horse and Virgil Wounded Horse are important members of this community, and it's about time they were named. When they pass on to the spirit world, they'll call out these names, and the spirits will know who they are."

He brought an eagle feather over to Nathan and tied it in his hair. "Nathan Wounded Horse, your spirit name is Tatanka Ohitika; that means 'Brave Buffalo.' You earned this name through your courage — your bravery — in the face of harm and death. You stared at your enemy's face and stood strong. You are a true Lakota warrior, the Seventh Generation. Tatanka Ohitika, we greet you."

Nathan looked down, embarrassed by Jerome's words.

Now Jerome came over to me with an eagle feather in his hand. "Virgil Wounded Horse, your spirit name is Tatanka Ta Oyate, Buffalo Nation. This name means you are a

450

defender and guardian of the community. You are our inyan hoksila, our stone boy, the protector who is made of rock and can't be hurt. Our legend tells us that inyan hoksila once faced a great enemy, one much larger and more powerful than him. But inyan hoksila refused to surrender, and he looked the enemy straight in the eye and it shattered into a thousand pieces. You too gazed in the face of evil and did not turn away. Tatanka Ta Oyate, we greet you."

As he finished tying the feather in my hair, I saw that the people were cheering and shouting. I thought that maybe someone had walked in with the food, but I realized they were cheering for me. I saw Marie with tears in her eyes, Nathan clapping, Tommy standing next to Velma, both of them whooping and hollering, and even Lack standing and applauding.

Before I began the ritual of the handshakes, I reflected for a moment about my sister, my mother, and my father, what they'd lost and what they'd sacrificed. Nothing could make up for those losses, but perhaps tonight the circle could close. The passing of winter, the coming of spring. I adjusted my feather and turned to the people.

Nathan and I walked clockwise around

the arena, shaking everyone's hands, accepting their congratulations and thanks. I looked over and saw that he was smiling, happy to connect with our community, the young ones, the elders, even the kids from his school. I let him take the lead as we moved through the crowd.

Near the end of the circle, an older woman whispered in my ear and asked if she could speak to me when we were done. I motioned for her to meet me in the lobby.

"I'm Charlene. Charlene Two Crow. I know you're the guy who helps people when the police won't do nothing. I heard you're not doing that no more, but thought I'd talk to you anyway, ask you something."

I wanted to be with Marie and Nathan, but the pleading look on her face kept me there.

"Here's the thing. My daughter Crystal used to live with this guy, a real jerk, and she had a baby with him. Robin is her name, really cute girl, she's four now, almost five. Few months ago, the guy beat the hell out of Crystal and took Robin. We don't know where he took her, maybe out of state; we can't find her, no one knows where they are. Crystal called the tribal cops, they sent the case over to the feds, but they won't do nothing, say they don't have enough evidence. Crystal cries every night. We don't know what to do." She looked down at the ground, not meeting my eyes. "But see, I got a few hundred dollars saved up, it's right here."

She pointed at her bag, an old purple tote bag with a Native design. It reminded me of the one my sister had carried.

"Can you help us? Get our little girl back?"

I wondered what to say.

AUTHOR'S NOTE

This is a work of fiction, but it is informed by current and historical events. To serve the dramatic narrative, I've freely invented places, events, locales, and incidents, as well as fictional characters who bear no resemblance to any actual persons. I've tried to stay generally faithful to my sense of life on the Rosebud Reservation, but I encourage readers interested in these issues to explore some of the many scholarly and historical books on these topics.

I'm frequently asked two questions about this book: Do private enforcers actually exist on reservations, and are felony criminal cases occurring on Native lands often declined by federal authorities? The answer to both questions is yes. Private vigilantes (or "hired thugs," as Virgil is insultingly called by Ann Short Bear) are a part of Native life on many reservations, although there's been no empirical study of the profession, as far as I know.

However, the problem of federal authorities under-prosecuting certain felony offenses on reservations has been well documented. Because of the Major Crimes Act passed by the US Congress in 1885, federal investigators generally have exclusive jurisdiction over felony crimes on reservations, yet they often decline prosecution in these cases, even when the perpetrator has been apprehended. Although the percentages vary from year to year, federal authorities frequently refuse to prosecute murders, assaults, and sex crimes referred from tribal police departments. Recent figures from the government indicate that over thirty-five percent of all referred crimes are declined and over a quarter of those cases are sexual assaults against both children and adults. The reluctance of federal agencies to prosecute certain felony crimes on reservations is well known in Indian Country, and there's no shortage of academic and journalistic accounts on this topic. A good place to start is the book *American Apartheid: The Native American Struggle for Self-Determination and Inclusion,* by Stephanie Woodard. Other useful resources are *American Indians, American Justice,* by Vine Deloria Jr. and Clifford M. Lytle, and *Braid of Feathers: American Indian*

Law and Contemporary Tribal Life, by Frank Pommersheim. Regarding opioids and heroin distribution systems, I'm indebted to Sam Quinones and his wonderful book *Dreamland: The True Tale of America's Opiate Epidemic.*

The issue of writing about Native spirituality in a positive and respectful way presents a different set of challenges. I've taken part in a number of Lakota spiritual ceremonies, but there are certain aspects of those ceremonies that are private. My approach in this book was to use other Lakota writers as my guide and only write about those details that had been previously disclosed by them, and to write about these matters respectfully, in the manner of many authors I admire, such as Susan Power and Joseph Marshall III. I relied primarily upon the venerated Native intellectual Vine Deloria Jr. and his book *The World We Used to Live In.* I also used *Native American Healing: A Lakota Ritual,* by Howard P. Bad Hand, and *Sacred Fireplace: Life and Teachings of a Lakota Medicine Man,* by Pete Catches. These writers portray some Lakota spiritual ceremonies, and I went no further than those authors and their words. For readers interested in Lakota spirituality, I highly recommend *Life's Journey — Zuya: Oral Teachings from Rosebud,* by Albert White Hat Sr., the now-deceased Sicangu elder and educator.

This book was a joy to write, and I hope that it both entertains and inspires discussions about some of the issues faced by the Sicangu Lakota Nation. The Sicangu are some of the most resilient, joyful, and spirited people on the planet, and this book is dedicated to them.

ACKNOWLEDGMENTS

I've been fortunate to have a large number of people who assisted in the writing of this book, and it's my honor to thank them for their help. First, my amazing agent, Michelle Brower, deserves more gratitude than I can express here. Michelle believed in this project from the outset, and she's been a dream to work with, as has everyone at Aevitas Creative Management. I thank all of them.

At Ecco, my wonderful editor, Zachary Wagman, made this novel so much better on many levels with his insights and expertise. Thanks also to Dan Halpern and the entire Ecco team, including Sara Wood, Miriam Parker, Meghan Deans, Sonya Cheuse, and others who helped with the project. My gratitude as well to Miranda Ottewell, whose copyediting mastery improved my sentences immeasurably. I'm aware of my great fortune in landing with a house such as Ecco, and words can't do justice to their brilliant efforts in support of this book.

My writing journey began in the MFA program at Vermont College of Fine Arts, and Virgil Wounded Horse made his first appearance there in a short story back in the early 2010s. My time at VCFA was invaluable, and I give thanks to my instructors and classmates there for their feedback and support.

I transferred to the MFA program at the Institute of American Indian Arts, where I was privileged to work with a multitude of amazing students and teachers, and I thank all of them. Without a doubt, this book would never have seen the light of day without the unflagging support of Ramona Ausubel, whom I worked with for two consecutive semesters. Ramona provided the model for professionalism, teaching excellence, and generosity of spirit. Thank you again, Ramona.

I was truly fortunate to be able to attend a number of remarkable writing conferences, where wonderful workshop leaders and classmates helped me shape early versions of these chapters. My deepest thanks to the fiction workshop in 2017 at the VONA/Voices of Our Nations Arts Foundation conference. The feedback I received there gave me the confidence I needed to spend the next two years waking up at dawn to write this book.

At the 2018 Tin House Summer Workshop, I was lucky enough to work with the amazing Benjamin Percy, one of the best writers, best teachers, and best people in this business. Our workshop was filled with exceptionally talented writers, all of whom made this book better. Hope we can all meet in Oregon again soon. At Tin House, the esteemed Gary Fisketjon chose my manuscript for a mentorship, and he read the entire thing, providing his remarkably good line edits and general advice.

I'm grateful to acknowledge the support of the MacDowell Colony; I spent an amazing month at that magical place completing this book and communing with an astonishing array of talented artists. It was a gift to awake every morning in Garland Studio and write among the wildlife of New Hampshire. The equally wonderful Ragdale Foundation provided me with space to make final revisions to the book, and I thank them as well for their support.

So many other people have contributed to this project. Carter Meland provided a home for Virgil in the Spring 2014 issue of

Yellow Medicine Review, where I published the short story that provided the blueprint for this book. Benjamin Whitmer read early chapters and has been a source of support for many years. Thanks, man. The wonderful writer Danya Kukafka read a version of the manuscript and gave brilliantly perceptive advice. Thank you, Danya. Bill Henderson of the Lighthouse Writers Workshop helped me sharpen my thinking about the book in its early stages. I also thank all of my writing friends in Denver and across the country, who've been so helpful and kind as I pursued this project.

At Sinte Gleska University on the Rosebud Indian Reservation, Jim Green and Victor Douville provided invaluable Lakota language assistance, although I remain responsible for any errors, naturally. Also on the Rosebud Reservation, my cousin James Cordry answered every question with steadfast patience and grace. And I give my humble thanks to the elders and community members of the Sicangu Lakota Nation, to whom I've dedicated this novel.

I honor and acknowledge my ancestors, who endured unthinkable hardships, especially my grandmother, who spent most of her life on the Rosebud Reservation except for her time at the infamous Carlisle Indian

Industrial School in Pennsylvania. My mother and father have passed over to the spirit world, but I hope I've done justice to their memory with this book.

Finally, Erika Wurth read the entire novel and patiently listened as I worked out various plot twists and character changes. Thank you, Erika, for all the things.

And of course, I thank my two beloved sons, David and Sasha, who haven't read this book, but have been the joy of my life since the day they were born.

Thank you, everyone. Wopila.

ABOUT THE AUTHOR

David Heska Wanbli Weiden is an enrolled citizen of the Sicangu Lakota Nation and received his MFA from the Institute of American Indian Arts. He's a MacDowell Colony Fellow, a Tin House Scholar, and the recipient of the PEN/America's Writing for Justice Fellowship. He lives in Denver, Colorado.